KISSING LESSONS

"So what's your advice?"

"About what?" Holly stared at him blankly, trying to remember the subject matter.

"About kissing."

She curbed the urge to squirm, fully aware that she and she alone was responsible for this awkward moment. Interviewing male clients *could* get awkward, due to the personal nature of the questions she had to ask. And some, like Lance Wilder, couldn't resist teasing her.

Pasting a guileless smile on her lips, she said, "Well, I don't think kissing is something a person forgets. If I were you . . . I'd just do it when the moment was right. Don't think about it—"

The rest of her words lodged in her throat as he suddenly rose and came toward her. Before his intent could fully register, he placed a bracing hand on either side of her chair, leaned in, and captured her mouth.

It was a brief, but oh-so-memorable kiss, one that managed to make her forget any other kiss she'd ever received.

He was watching her with that unnerving intensity that set her teeth on edge.

"I believe you're right, Miss Wentworth. Spontaneity is the key . . ."

Jove titles by Adrienne Burns

THREE'S A CHARM
IT TAKES TWO
A HEART UNTAMED

Three's a Charm

ADRIENNE BURNS

JOVE BOOKS, NEW YORK

This is a work of fiction. Names, characters, places, and incidents are either the product of the author's imagination or are used fictitiously, and any resemblance to actual persons, living or dead, business establishments, events, or locales is entirely coincidental.

MAGICAL LOVE is a registered trademark of Penguin Putnam Inc.

THREE'S A CHARM

A Jove Book / published by arrangement with
the authors

PRINTING HISTORY
Jove edition / September 2000

All rights reserved.
Copyright © 2000 by Sherrie Eddington and Donna Smith.
Cover illustration by Leslie Peck.
This book may not be reproduced in whole or in part,
by mimeograph or any other means, without permission.
For information address: The Berkley Publishing Group,
a division of Penguin Putnam Inc.,
375 Hudson Street, New York, New York 10014.

The Penguin Putnam Inc. World Wide Web site address is
http://www.penguinputnam.com

ISBN: 0-515-12907-0

A JOVE BOOK®
Jove Books are published by The Berkley Publishing Group,
a division of Penguin Putnam Inc.,
375 Hudson Street, New York, New York 10014.
JOVE and the "J" design
are trademarks belonging to Penguin Putnam Inc.

PRINTED IN THE UNITED STATES OF AMERICA

10 9 8 7 6 5 4 3 2 1

For my younger brother, Jeff Nolen; his wife, Sandy; and their beautiful children, Dustin and Kendra; your dedication to God and each other shines like a beacon all around you and warms the hearts of others—especially mine. I love you all!

And for Chaos, the most lovable feline on the face of this earth—thanks for nine years of love and loyalty, and for keeping me company late into the night while I worked. If there's a cat heaven, I know you're there. We miss you.

Sherrie Eddington

They say that with age comes respect. I don't think it's the accumulation of years that prove this old adage to be true. Maybe it's the fact that we have had more time to do those things that are worthy of respect.

I'd like to dedicate this book to those men who have earned the love and respect that comes from loving and caring for those children who call them Grandpa, Pee-paw, Paw Paw, Papa, or whatever the title might be—although some are absolutely no relation to them. Harvey Eubanks, Sam Eller, and Herb Davidson are just three such men.

Donna Smith

Prologue

"Are you *certain* you know how to cook this thing?"

Mini Costello slanted a dark look at her husband as she rubbed crushed garlic into the skin of the chicken. "It's just a chicken, Reuben. And, yes, I'm certain that I know what I'm doing. We went through this step by step in cooking class. I even took notes." She indicated the index card on the counter with a nod of her head, her voice tinged with sarcasm. "Have a look—the instructions are so simple even a *spoiled* witch can follow them."

Ignoring the card *and* her smart comment, Reuben sidled closer, his silk pajamas whispering as he moved. He caught a whiff of butter, garlic, and lemon. His mouth watered. "Will it taste as good as something we could have conjured?" he persisted, swiping his finger against the chicken.

Mini caught his finger—a once powerful finger that could have flashed the chicken to perfection in seconds—before it reached his mouth. "It has to be cooked, darling. You'll get sick." Forcefully she brought his hand down and held his finger beneath the running faucet. "There's this bacteria called salmonella. It causes food poisoning in mortal bodies."

"Did you learn this in cooking class?"

"Yes." When she deemed his finger clean, she kissed the sensitive flesh before letting go, her appreciative gaze lingering over his fine, handsome features. He kept his shoulder-length hair, as raven black as her own, tied at the neck in a neat ponytail; it gleamed from his recent shower in the flourescent lighting overhead.

Yet beneath his outward air of bravado, Mini knew her arrogant ex-warlock was frightened of this mortal world. "We're doing fine, husband. We really are. We have an apartment—"

"More like a hovel."

"—food to eat," Mini continued stubbornly, "clothes, good health, and friends. We're luckier than a lot of mortals."

Reuben wasn't in the mood to be pacified. "If we don't find a job soon, we'll be without those things. The allowance the witches' council so *graciously* provided is nearly gone."

"We'll find a job," Mini assured him. She finished rubbing the chicken and placed it in the oven, checking the card for the required temperature setting. When she straightened she found Reuben watching her with an odd light in his coal-black eyes.

She knew that look. "Something on your mind?"

Slowly he nodded, crossing his ankles and leaning against the counter. "I'm wondering why you put up with me."

He was serious, Mini thought. They'd been married over two hundred years, and he could ask that question. "Because I love you," she said simply. "I couldn't let you go through this alone. Losing your magic was a hard enough blow."

His eyes darkened further. "You do realize that when you gave up your powers to join me, it might be forever?"

It was Mini's turned to nod, but she followed it with a shrug. "We've survived a month living as mortals; we can make it forever if we have to." She resisted the urge to offer comfort, sensing that her proud husband was struggling with his pride. Instead she reached for the plates above the sink. "If *I* had been the one with Jestark that night, would you have abandoned me when the witches' council took my powers?"

Reuben's dark brows lowered ominously. "I wasn't the one who revealed myself to that poor mortal woman. If I had known what Jestark was about, I would have stopped him."

"*I* know, but you have to see this from the council's point of view. You were with Jestark—"

"He's my friend!"

Mini closed her eyes and counted to ten. Anytime the subject arose, her husband became defensive. "Jestark is a warlock, and although you willingly forfeited your warlock status when you married a good witch, the council knows Jestark makes a hobby out of performing mean, spiteful tricks on mortals. So the fact that you were with him—"

"Makes me an accessory," Reuben finished. For a moment his jaw hardened. Finally he heaved a fatalistic sigh. Although he'd never admit it to *them*, he could understand how the council might have thought he was involved. Why, he asked himself for the thousandth time, did he let Jestark challenge him into going with him that night? Now, not only was he forced to live without the powers he'd always taken for granted, but so was his beautiful, loyal wife.

This bothered Reuben more than anything, and he was determined Mini wouldn't suffer because of his misjudgment.

Which meant he needed to find what the mortals called a job, and soon.

"Will you set the table?"

He snapped out of his reverie with a jolt. Obligingly he took the plates and utensils and turned in the direction of the table.

He froze.

Smack dab in the middle of the tiny dining table

crouched their protector, a homely looking cat with glittering gold eyes.

The witches' council had insisted on sending the familiar; they were angry but not insensitive. As mortals, Mini and Reuben were vulnerable in ways they'd never been as witches.

Reuben hesitated, clutching the plates against his chest and wondering again if the council had known how he felt about . . . animals, cats in particular. Was this another form of punishment? Would he never cease to pay for that one impulsive night cavorting with his old friend Jestark?

"What—" Mini caught sight of the orange cat. The feline leisurely groomed her whiskers. "Reuben, she's sitting on an open newspaper," Mini whispered, grabbing his arm in her urgency.

He failed to comprehend. "Still, it's unsanitary—"

"She's trying to tell us something!"

"Then why doesn't she just talk?"

"I'm sure she has her reasons," Mini muttered evasively. She knew the reason, but it wasn't something she cared to share with Reuben just yet. Let him get used to the idea of having a cat around before she revealed the familiar's identity. "Let's see what's in the paper."

She gently pushed him forward and they approached the table. The cat glanced up, let out a satisfied meow, and leaped onto the floor.

The paper lay open to the Help Wanted section.

Mini saw the claw marks circling a single announcement. Excited, she grabbed the paper and read aloud. *"Happily married couple needed to interview clients for dating service. No experience needed."*

With a squeal, she twirled with the paper. "Reuben! This is it! We're a happily married couple—and a *dating* service? Oh, it's too good to be true!"

"You're probably right," Reuben grumbled, still thinking about the cat. There was something familiar about those strange, yellow-gold eyes and the gaudy orange fur, but he couldn't put his useless finger upon it.

"We can help match mortal people with their soul mates, and perhaps gain approval from the council."

"I wouldn't wager—"

"Oh, don't be such a pessimist," Mini scolded, grinning happily. "Eventually they'll have to notice our good deeds, and when they do, we can plead for a lighter sentence."

Reuben crossed his arms over his chest in a familiar, stubborn stance. "I'll not plead with that bunch of narrow-minded, wrinkled, wart-nosed hags."

Mini dropped the paper and wound her arms around his stiff neck. Her lips nuzzled his throat until she found his pulse. It began to hammer wildly. "Oh, but you will, husband," she purred, "because I miss making love on a pillow of clouds right before a storm, or on dew-moistened heather in Scotland at sunrise."

Reuben groaned and admitted defeat.

One

"I believe that's game!" Lance Wilder shouted across the tennis court to his opponent. He jogged to the bench and scooped up a towel, then wiped the sweat from his eyes. With any luck, he'd get his breathing under control before Casey joined him. His physician friend never let Lance forget—as if he could—that Lance's father had died of a heart attack at the relatively young age of fifty.

Casey loped up and flung himself on the bench, eyeing Lance balefully as he mopped at the sweat running down his neck. "How in the hell do you stay in shape sitting behind that desk all day long?"

Lance chuckled at his obvious disappointment. "Your comment proves my theory that you never listen to what I say. I don't *sit* all day long. Sometimes we play pool, basketball, tennis, or swim. Might as well make use of that castle the old man left me."

He would have preferred his father's time, but that was something Alfred Wilder hadn't been able to give. It made Lance determined not to follow in his father's footsteps— *if* he ever became a father. When he died he wanted to leave memories, not a mansion and a 1979 Mercedes Roadster.

"Some guys have all the luck," Casey said with unabashed

envy, massaging his calf muscles. His mouth twisted in a grimace of pain. "If you hate the house, why don't you sell it?"

Lance shrugged. "It's where my office is." He hesitated before adding, "And because of the memories."

"Of you and Mona?"

"No," Lance drawled, "of me and Peppy."

Casey snorted. "I know that's a lie. That dog hated you."

Thinking about Mona's hyper little poodle, Lance smiled faintly. "I finally just gave up on trying to win him over."

"So why do you do it?"

As was so often the case when holding a conversation with his topic-hopping friend, Lance was lost. "I'm not following you."

"Spend all that time with those mixed-up kids."

"Because I'm a psychologist?" Lance suggested sarcastically.

"I'm just curious about why you go beyond the call of duty. I mean, how many of those kids are expecting you to go all out the way you do? I know their parents don't expect it and I'll bet they don't pay extra for the perks."

Lance watched the action on the court for a long moment. "Maybe they don't expect it, but it helps the kids relax." He hesitated, picking at a loose shoestring. "After two weeks of trying to get Sally to open up, I finally had a breakthrough yesterday. We were bowling—"

"Bowling? I didn't know you had a bowling lane!"

"I don't," Lance interrupted impatiently. "Sally doesn't like any of the sports I can provide at home, so we've been holding most of our sessions at the bowling center." To uphold patient confidentiality, Lance always referred to his female patients as Sally and his male patients as Junior.

Casey hooked his damp towel around his neck, his attention caught. "Is this Sally the Sally who refuses to go back to school?" He sounded smug that he remembered.

"Yes, and now I know why." Lance paused just to irritate his friend, pretending a sudden interest in the action on the court. Two women were playing a fast and furious game. Lance admired their strength and stamina.

Casey jabbed him in the ribs. "Well?" he demanded.

Lance gave in. "It happened at school. She forgot her backpack, and when she returned to the supposedly empty classroom to get it, she walked in on a scene between two adults. . . ." He let the rest of it hang, unwilling to voice the distasteful words out loud.

He should have known Casey would have to fill in the blanks.

"They were doing the wild thing? At *school*?" Casey squeaked. "She's what, nine years old? Poor kid! What did you tell her?"

"That it was something the adults never meant for her to see."

"Did you talk to her parents?"

"No, and I'm not going to. She doesn't want anyone to know that she saw them. She's suffering more from embarrassment than from shock."

"So you're not going to do anything?" Casey sounded censorious.

"I already have. I talked to the principal—without mentioning any names, of course. I don't think it will happen again."

"But if you didn't mention any names—"

"Think about it, Casey. If I didn't mention any names, then how *would* the principal know who I was talking about?"

For a moment there was nothing but puzzled silence. Finally Casey drew in a sharp breath. "Oh, I get it. The principal knew . . . because he was one of the adults!"

"Bingo."

Casey let out a sharp whistle. "I'm not so sure I would have let them off that easily. I mean, this girl could be scarred for life."

Lance shook his head. "She's a sharp kid, and like I

said, she was more embarrassed than shocked. She thought they'd seen her. Now that she knows they didn't, she's ready to go back to school."

"Case solved, kid cured, and the great Dr. Wilder becomes an instant hero. Again."

"Very funny."

"No, I'm serious, buddy. You're good at what you do. Damned good."

"If I wasn't, I wouldn't be able to pay the electric bill on that castle Dad stuck me with. So what's up with you these days? Any luck finding Ms. Right?"

Casey's love life was legendary. He wasn't heartless in his quest for the perfect mate, but he was relentless. Lance wouldn't have been surprised to discover there wasn't a woman left in Lovit, California, that Casey hadn't dated and ditched.

"That's right, I haven't told you, have I?" With his customary exuberance, Casey jumped to his feet. "Let's hit the showers and get a drink. Then I'll tell you all about Catherine, the new love of my life."

Lance lifted a questioning brow. "Catherine? This sounds serious." He ignored a pang of envy, reminding himself that compared with Casey's topsy-turvy life, his was peaceful and normal, and he preferred it that way.

"Yeah, Romance Connection got me hooked up with her."

"Tell me you're not talking about a dating service."

Casey glanced defiantly back at Lance as they circled the tennis players on the court to get to the showers. "This is no ordinary dating service, my friend. It's very elite. They're thorough, and I mean *thorough*. They can tell you everything about your date, right down to her pantyhose size."

"Something every man should know," Lance muttered, catching the door just before it smashed into his nose. He jerked it open and followed Casey inside the steamy locker room. It smelled of sweat, soap, and deodorant. As they stripped themselves of their damp clothing, Lance asked, "Just exactly how did you get involved with a dating service?" It wasn't as if Casey had difficulty finding dates. Quite the contrary. It wasn't unusual for Casey to have dates with two different women on the same weekend.

"Helping a friend out. He signed up, and they told him that if he could get someone else to come in for an interview, they'd knock fifty bucks off his bill *and* give him a free meal at his favorite restaurant."

"So you went in for an interview," Lance surmised. He turned on the shower and stepped under the stinging spray. Casey did the same, raising his voice to be heard.

"I not only went in for an interview, I let them match me up, and let me tell ya, Romance Connection knows how to connect people! Catherine's everything I've ever wanted in a woman. I think I'm really falling in love this time."

Lance dropped his soap, then cursed as he fumbled to retrieve it. He'd never heard his friend sound so enamored of a woman. Casey had usually compiled her faults by the second date and dropped the poor, unsuspecting woman before there was a chance for a third.

"I hope you don't mind, buddy!" Casey shouted over the spray of the water.

"Mind what?"

"I signed you up. Call it an early birthday present."

Lance dropped the soap again. Instead of retrieving it, he leaned over and twisted the shower faucet next to his own. Casey yelped at the sudden burst of cold water. He fumbled for the knob and managed to switch it off, glaring at Lance.

"What was that for?"

"For setting me up," Lance growled. "You know how I feel about dating."

"Yes, I do." Casey stood his ground. "But for Christ's sake, Lance, it's been over four years! Don't you think it's time you started *living* again? If I went that long without a woman, I'd go bonkers."

"You'd go bonkers in a week," Lance retorted. "I can find my own date. I don't need a dating service to do it for me."

"When?" Casey challenged. "You're around kids all day long, and you never get out at night unless it's with me." His tone turned wheedling. "Just do it for old times' sake, okay? What have you got to lose? You can't deny that you get lonely."

Lance started to deny it, just for the sake of arguing, but he clamped his lips shut. It would be a lie, and Casey would know it. His resignation must have shown in his expression, for Casey clapped him heartily on the back. Lance nearly slipped on the soap suds congealing around his feet. He braced himself against the wall in the nick of time.

"I knew you'd come around. And don't worry, Romance Connection guarantees satisfaction." He slapped his soapy chest. "They managed to please me, didn't they?"

"I'm not ready to get serious," Lance said, feeling disloyal already.

"That's the beauty of it—if you don't want serious, they match you with someone else who doesn't want serious!"

Perversely, the alternative didn't appeal to Lance either.

"Thank you again for choosing Romance Connection, Cindy. We'll see you on Thursday at two."

Holly Wentworth replaced the phone, giving in to a rush of euphoria that brought a giddy smile to her lips. According to her records, she had just scheduled her five hundredth client for an interview since opening the business in March of the new millennium.

It was the first week of October—six months later—and surely she could safely say her elite dating service was a success. Which meant that her skeptical father would just have to admit he was wrong.

Her glance strayed to the closed conference room door,

where her new employee, Mini Costello, was interviewing a client. Mini's husband, Reuben, had gone for Chinese take-out.

Each time she thought about the striking couple she'd hired two weeks ago, Holly had to physically resist the urge to pinch herself. From the first moment, she'd known there was something special about them, and it wasn't only that they seemed genuinely devoted to each other; they'd seemed almost . . . *otherworldly.*

The last two weeks working with them had convinced her she'd hit the jackpot, and unlike the last couple she'd hired, Holly felt secure that she wouldn't have to worry about either of them succumbing to the temptations of the job.

Each had unique, impressive qualities. From day one Mini had quickly revealed to Holly a natural perception that was proving invaluable, if not a little amazing; Reuben, Mini's wickedly handsome husband, had a knack for commanding honesty in the male clients he interviewed. These qualities, combined with Holly's instinctive talent for matching couples, had increased the company's success rate dramatically.

And success was the name of the game. Holly didn't want to just create compatible couples; she wanted to help people find their soul mates. Romance Connection's goal was to help develop lasting, special relationships. Holly was a shrewd businesswoman, and she knew that word of mouth was her biggest and best advertisement. A satisfied customer was a happy customer—and a *talkative* customer.

Of course, there were those individuals who sought companionship without strings attached, and Holly matched those without a hint of disapproval. But the results didn't provide nearly the satisfaction that the ever-lasting relationships did.

Holly twisted around to study the corkboard on the wall, literally hidden behind a confusion of colorful postcards, from exotic Hawaii to sultry New Orleans, sent by clients who couldn't resist boasting about their honeymoons. Reuben had laughingly referred to the board as her scalp collection. He'd sobered quickly when she and Mini had failed to share his joke.

The chimes over the entrance door interrupted her thoughts. Holly turned as Reuben shouldered his way through the door, balancing a stack of white cardboard boxes with his chin. The tantalizing aroma of sweet and sour pork reminded Holly of golden rule number one: an uninterrupted hour for lunch for herself and her staff.

No phones, no distractions. No exceptions.

"Lunch is served," Reuben said, carefully turning with the boxes as he attempted to twist the "Out to Lunch" sign hanging on the door.

Holly rushed around the desk to help him, mindful of the expensive new carpet and her employee's odd clumsiness. For such a graceful-looking man, he was prone to fumble over the simplest tasks. "Mini should be finishing up— Reuben, watch out behind you!"

Her warning came too late. The man coming in obviously didn't see Reuben—or the sign—and burdened as he was, Reuben didn't have time to move out of the way.

The edge of the metal-rimmed door caught his shoulder; the boxes came tumbling from his arms. Holly made a mad grab for them, but her fingers only grazed the edge of one box—just enough to open the flap.

Soup spilled onto her hand. She uttered a sharp cry, nearly drowning out the sound of Reuben's strange, desperate chanting. The soup was hot, but Holly didn't think it was hot enough to do any real damage. She clamped her fingers over her scalded hand, more concerned for her carpet.

Egg drop soup, chicken chow mein, and sweet and sour pork converged on the lovely forest-green carpet. Steam rose in lazy tendrils from the hot pile of Chinese cuisine.

"Clumsy mortals!"

Holly glanced sharply at Reuben. "Excuse me?"

Mini spoke from behind her. "He said 'Clumsy moron.' He was talking about himself, of course."

"Are you okay?"

It was the man who'd been watching his feet instead of where he was going. Before Holly could put a face to the low, sexy voice, gentle fingers closed around her wrist. A tingle shot from his fingers to her hand, startling her. Nothing more than static, she thought.

"Show me the rest room," he ordered, steering her away from the door.

"I beg your . . ." As Holly finally looked up, her mouth went dry.

The rest of her words lodged in her throat as her startled gaze locked with his. Framed by russet lashes that she quickly noted matched the glorious russet shade of his windblown hair, his violet blue eyes regarded her with obvious concern. A strong, square jaw framed his tanned face. Her gaze dropped to his mouth for a quick glimpse of firmly molded lips before she jerked her eyes back to his.

"Your rest room?" he repeated, still holding firmly to her hand. "We need to run some cold water over your hand." When she continued to hesitate, he added, "I've had some medical training, if that's what you're worried about."

"Oh." Holly tried to tug her hand free, but he refused to let go. She shook her head, bewildered at her reaction to this stranger. "That's all right. I'm fine, really." She tried to free her burning hand again, but he only tightened his hold.

"I insist."

And he insisted well, Holly thought, giving in and leading him to the small bathroom. She should be alarmed, she supposed, for Romance Connection certainly got its share of weirdos, and for all she knew, this hunk could be one of them.

The bathroom was too small. Why had she never noticed? Perhaps because she'd never tried to crowd inside the small cubicle with a broad-shouldered man wearing a killer face and butt-hugging jeans.

Had she really noticed his butt? She met hundreds of men each month, so why would she notice this one's butt? Or anything else, for that matter? Dazed, Holly barely felt the sting as cold water rushed over the reddened area of her hand. They stood hip to hip, shoulder to shoulder. Well, her shoulder came closer to his biceps, but they were touching all the same. She could feel the heat from his body and smell the clean, male scent of him as if she'd buried her nose in his chest.

Her heart did a triple somersault at the image her thought evoked.

His scent was fresh air and man, and just a touch of woodsy aftershave or cologne, a brand she didn't recognize. Whatever it was, it was making her light-headed. Perhaps she was allergic. That would certainly explain the surreal feeling she was experiencing—

"Better?"

Holly jerked her gaze to his again and swallowed dryly. He was staring at her, their faces only inches apart. The brilliant intensity of his eyes encouraged honesty. Tiny laugh lines fanned from his eyes; his nose was perfect, not too big and not too small. She searched in vain for something that might distract her from his perfection. A scar, a twitching eye—*horns*—anything that would shatter his perfect image and make him more human.

It was no use. The man was stunning, and that usually meant married or otherwise involved. Not that she would have been interested other than in a business sense, she told herself.

Keeping this important fact in mind, Holly said, "It's better. I don't think it's going to blister." She gently withdrew her hand and turned, intending to slide carefully by him to the door. He turned at the same time, his chest connecting with hers. To her mortification, her nipples sprang erect. She flushed and prayed he wouldn't notice. "Excuse me."

Instead of moving, his hands came around her waist, lightly and without a hint of force. She could have moved easily if she had wanted to. Not surprising to Holly, it was his gaze that held her in place.

"Lunch is on me," he said, as if they were standing on a busy sidewalk instead of in a small, cramped bathroom. "I'm early for my appointment, anyway."

"You're a client?" Holly squeaked in dismay. She immediately admonished herself. Of course he was! How foolish of her not to have realized it from the moment he walked in. And how clumsy of her to sound shocked.

But her dismay stemmed from remembering golden rule number two: Never get involved with a client.

The really sucky part was that *she* had invented the rules.

Two

"It was nice of you to buy lunch for everyone, but it wasn't necessary."

"I thought we established that it was my fault."

"Reuben shouldn't have been standing in front of the entrance door."

"Instead of watching my feet, I should have been looking."

"He's a little prone to clumsiness—"

"Is this one of those rules of business where the customer is always right?" Lance asked, exasperated by her tenacity. He liked her much better when she was breathless and confused, as she'd been in the close proximity of the bathroom.

The moment Holly Wentworth had stepped away from him, she had transformed into a distant, cool professional, as if what had nearly passed between them had never happened. Or maybe it hadn't. Maybe the instant chemistry had been all on his side. After four years of avoiding intimacy, Lance supposed his mistake was understandable.

"Mr. Wilder? Are you ready to start the interview? Would you like a refreshment before we get started?"

He liked her slightly husky voice. It had a smooth,

southern roll to it that reminded him of magnolias and iced tea—and shadowy cleavages. He gave his head a bemused shake, focusing on the slight tilt to her gray-green eyes. He discovered he wasn't ready to talk business.

"Do you conduct every interview personally?" he asked.

Her eyes flared in surprise at his unexpected question. "No, I don't. Reuben—Mr. Costello—normally screens the male applicants first, but he's on his lunch hour. I—I don't like to keep clients waiting."

The faint blush that followed her answer aroused not only Lance's hopes, but also his suspicions. "Afraid I'll change my mind?"

"It happens." She stared pointedly at her watch. "Now, if we could just start the interview . . . ? I'll need your full name."

"Lance Keely Wilder." As he spoke, he glanced approvingly around the interview room, which was decorated in soft, relaxing shades of gray and burgundy. The sofa he occupied was plush and comfy; Holly Wentworth sat across from him in an oversized, matching chair, her back straight, her legs crossed in that age-old fashion that attracted the male eye. Lance was no exception. Her legs were like the rest of her—nice, extremely nice, he noted. Slim, shapely, slightly tanned . . .

"Age?"

"Thirty-four." A dark curtain of hair had fallen against her cheek as she bent forward over the clipboard. Lance's fingers itched to hook it back in place. The urge to touch this woman both dismayed and delighted him. Perhaps he was finally getting over his loss.

"Date of birth?"

He answered automatically, then asked, "How's your hand?"

She glanced up, those big eyes wide and startled. "Fine, thanks. Your occupation?"

"Adolescent psychology."

This time when she glanced up, Lance smiled. "I take it you don't get many shrinks desperate for a date?"

"I'm not at liberty to say," she said primly. "Why are you seeking our services?"

"Is that one of the questions?" Lance countered.

"Yes."

Her expression never wavered, and Lance realized she was telling the truth. This was the part he had dreaded. Casey had praised the company's integrity, but Lance wasn't certain he trusted Casey's judgment when it came to women in any shape, form, or occupation. "Is this information confidential?"

Sounding defensive, she said, "The only people privy to this information will be my staff. When we find your match, she'll only know what she needs to know. The rest will be up to you."

Intrigued despite his reservations, Lance stretched his arm along the back of the sofa and settled in. "Very well. I'm here because a friend of mine decided it was time for me to start dating again."

"You're divorced?"

"Widowed."

She kept her eyes lowered to the paper. "How long since your last date?"

"What is your definition of a date? Have I slept with anyone, do you mean?"

Her gaze met his in challenge. "The question is, what is *your* definition?"

"Part of the interview, Mrs. Wentworth?"

"It's *Miss*. And yes, it is. Are you seeking someone for companionship or something more permanent?"

"Is this similar to rent with an option to buy?"

The lead in the pencil snapped. She opened a drawer beside her and withdrew another one. The drawer clicked shut with a little snap, revealing the agitation she was trying to hide.

"If you feel you're being pressured into this interview,

Mr. Wilder, then maybe you should give this some more thought before we proceed."

Her cheeks were flushed with barely concealed irritation. If it was possible, her back had become even straighter, and the sparkle in her eyes could only be described as flammable.

Feeling slightly ashamed for needling her, Lance realized with a jolt of surprise that he preferred her anger to indifference. But the fact that he cared about her reaction at all was a bigger surprise.

After a long slumber, his male ego was awakening, and if the stirring in his blood—and elsewhere—was any indication, so was his libido.

Heaven help Holly Wentworth.

In the small office they shared, Mini and Reuben huddled around their crystal ball, watching the exchange between Holly and Lance with unabashed curiosity. The magic ball, capable of viewing the past, present, and future, had been given to Mini by her grandmother on her thirteenth birthday. The witches' council had reluctantly allowed her to keep it, but had disabled its power to look into the future.

"I was right, Reuben. Look at the cosmic activity between them!" She tapped her fingernail against the surface of the ball.

Reuben bent closer. There were indeed visible sparks flying between the mortals seated in the interview room. He snorted, the accident still humiliatingly fresh in his mind. "Holly could do better, if you ask me. He's a clumsy mortal."

"And you're a clumsy witch, but I still love you." Before her husband could muster an indignant reply, Mini rushed on. "Holly would like us to believe she's perfectly happy going home every day to her dog, but I sense she's lonely. She's also jaded, disillusioned—"

"I get the picture." Reuben tried to sneak a fried wonton from the take-out plate they'd brought back for Holly, but he got his hand slapped for his efforts. "Tell me, if she doesn't believe in happily-ever-afters, then why does she get so excited when her clients tie the knot?"

"Good point." Mini frowned in thought. "I think maybe she believes it can happen to *other* couples, just not to her."

"Because of her parents' divorce," Reuben concluded, linking his hands behind his head. He needed a nap, but he was pretty certain it was out of the question. "Why do you suppose she volunteered to do the interview, then?"

"Because she didn't want you fainting from hunger, and she likes him."

"I can see that," Reuben muttered dryly, ignoring her comment about his insatiable appetite. "But so far she hasn't relented an inch. In fact, she seems to be going out of her way to ignore the flirtation." He let out a disgruntled sigh. "If I had my powers, I'd zap a little fire under her—"

"Reuben, didn't we agree not to harp on our lost powers?" Mini moved behind him and began kneading his tense shoulder muscles, her voice softening. She knew what was eating her husband, even if he wouldn't admit it. "What happened wasn't your fault."

"Of course it wasn't. Jestark is a jerk, just like you said."

"I wasn't talking about Jestark," she rebuked. "I'm referring to the incident earlier."

"You mean the accident."

"Yes."

"It wouldn't have happened if I had my powers."

"Of course it wouldn't," she said soothingly. Scolding him for chanting in front of the mortals seemed senseless; she just hoped Holly had forgotten. "Because we wouldn't be here if we had our powers." Mini hesitated, knowing she was about to step onto very thin ice. "But it did happen, and Holly could have been seriously hurt because of our . . . mortal clumsiness. I think we should try to persuade Holly to let us bring our protector to the office."

Beneath her expert fingertips, she felt him shudder. What made him so afraid of cats? she wondered. But it wasn't just cats—it was all creatures, great and small. "She could have prevented the accident, or at least moved Holly from harm."

"Ah, but if she had, then we might not be witnessing this little tête à tête in the crystal ball."

Mini felt his sudden tension seconds before he leaned forward to look in the crystal ball.

"Looks like things are heating up, too. . . ."

Holly felt her jaw drop. She quickly closed it, knowing even as she did that it was too late to gloss over her mistake. Clearing her throat, she said, "Would you mind repeating that statement?"

"The apology for being such an ass? Or the one about not remembering how to kiss . . .?"

There it was again—a flash of heat right in the pit of her stomach. *Low* in her stomach. If she'd had any doubts about the attraction she felt for her newest client, she didn't now. It was there—and it was real.

Determined to maintain her professional air—and to remember golden rule number two, never mind that she'd already broken golden rule number one—Holly tapped her pencil against the clipboard. "The one about not remembering . . . how to kiss."

"Oh, that one." His low, blood-heating chuckle sounded rueful. "I haven't kissed a woman since . . . my wife died. I'm not sure I remember how, or anything else that goes along with this dating ritual." His voice dipped along with his gaze. "I have to confess, the whole thing ties my stomach into knots."

Holly wet her dry lips, perversely wishing he'd go back to being an ass. He was making her feel sympathy she doubted he deserved. He was successful, handsome, young, and probably a dream in bed despite his obvious reservations. Her gaze fell to his mouth. Kissing? What more would he have to do but place that sensual line against a woman's lips to make her feel the world spin?

For the first time since entering the interview room with Lance Wilder, Holly wished she hadn't been so impulsive in volunteering to do this interview herself. This man was lethal, from his killer smile to his big lean hands with their neatly trimmed nails. Looking at him now as he lounged at ease against the sofa, it was hard to believe the man suffered an ounce of insecurity.

"So what's your advice?"

"About what?" Holly stared at him blankly, trying to remember the subject matter.

"About kissing."

Oh. That.

She curbed the urge to squirm, fully aware that she and she alone was responsible for this awkward moment. It reminded her of why she'd hired Reuben in the first place. Interviewing male clients *could* get awkward, due to the personal nature of the questions she had to ask. And some, like Lance Wilder, couldn't resist teasing her.

The only face-saving thing for her to do would be to go along with his game, to pretend she believed he was sincere. When he realized he couldn't ruffle her feathers, he'd give up, and then they could get down to finishing the interview.

Pasting a guileless smile on her lips, she said, "Well, I don't think kissing is something a person forgets. If I were you . . . I'd just do it when the moment was right. Don't think about it—"

The rest of her words lodged in her throat as he suddenly rose and came toward her. Before his intent could fully register, he placed a bracing hand on either side of her chair, leaned in, and captured her mouth.

The world didn't just spin—it rocked.

It was a brief, but oh-so-memorable kiss, one that managed to make her forget any other kiss she'd ever received. When it ended, Holly kept her eyes shut and concentrated on breathing. If any other client had dared touch her, she wouldn't have hesitated to scream. Verbal torment was one thing—touching was quite another.

Why didn't she? Why *hadn't* she the split second she realized what he was going to do? Holly slowly opened her eyes, prepared to face his smug smile and give him a blasting he richly deserved.

He was watching her with that unnerving intensity that set her teeth on edge.

"I believe you're right, Miss Wentworth. Spontaneity is the key."

A discreet knock at the door saved Lance from a scorching he wouldn't likely forget, and Holly from certain loss of dignity.

It was Reuben, looking apologetic and uncertain.

She had never been so glad to see someone in her life.

"Sorry to interrupt, but your lunch is getting cold. I thought you might want me to take over."

Face flaming, she stood and flashed Reuben a grateful, brittle smile. "Thanks, Reuben. I'm starving."

And without a backward glance, she walked stiffly from the room, conscious of Lance's heated, challenging gaze following her.

Three

"Is he gone?" came a raspy whisper from behind Mini.

Mini dropped the curtain and glanced down at the orange feline at her feet, who was in actuality her dearest friend, Xonia. "I think so. Hope he doesn't get lost."

"You drew him a map, Mini," Xonia reminded her scornfully. "And gave him a list. He's not helpless."

She bit her lip. "I know, but he's having a hard time adjusting. . . ." *And having you around isn't helping,* Mini wanted to add.

Xonia twitched her tail and sniffed. "If you'd stop babying him, maybe he'd adjust more quickly." Before Mini could once again defend her husband, Xonia gave her leg a friendly swat with her paw. "Come on, if you're going to do this, you'd better get started. Are you *sure* you don't want my help? I could zap—"

"No," Mini interrupted firmly. "We're mortals now. You're not supposed to help us unless it's necessary."

Xonia trotted ahead of Mini to the bedroom and leaped onto the dresser, nudging the scissors with her nose. "Suit yourself. I just hope you know what you're doing." She smiled to reveal sharp, overhanging molars. "Frankly I can't wait to see Reuben's face when he sees what you've done."

Mini shot her a dirty look. "I wish you would try a little bit harder to like Reuben, Xonia. He's my husband, and sooner or later we're going to have to tell him who you are. I don't like lying to him."

"It's not a lie exactly," Xonia argued. "Besides, *I've* been your friend longer than he's been your husband. I think *he* should try to be nicer to *me*." As she spoke she twitched her tail; the scissors rose and hovered in front of Mini's nose.

With an exasperated sigh, Mini snatched them out of thin air. "Stop wasting your spells, Xonia. If the witches' council sees you, you'll be eating cat food instead of those steaks you're so fond of."

Her comment made Xonia shudder. "Cat food? Not on your life. Well? Are you going to do it or just stand there all night?"

"Don't rush me." Mini gripped the scissors and took a deep breath. Would Reuben understand why? No, she decided. Not at first. Not until she detailed her reasons, at least those she wanted him to know about.

She closed her eyes and cut through the first swath of long black hair, starting just below her ear.

"Go on, you're doing good. And just keep in mind that if you don't like it, I'll reverse the damage."

"Damage?" Mini whispered faintly, not liking the sound of that. She opened one eye, then quickly shut it on a groan. "He's going to kill me."

"Over my dead body," Xonia muttered.

"Don't tempt him, my friend. He read somewhere that getting you fixed might improve your disposition." Taking another courage-inducing breath, Mini continued to clip a circle around her head. When she had clipped the last swath, she set the scissors aside as if they were scalding. "It's done."

Xonia tilted her head from side to side, studying the new style. "I like it," she announced enviously. "You look like one of those cool, chic models out of one of those magazines mortals seem so fond of gazing at."

"Speaking of cool . . . it *is* cooler, just as I suspected."

"And less of it to catch on fire," Xonia said dryly.

Mini winced at the reminder. "Luckily my cooking instructor keeps a fire extinguisher handy." The near disaster had been the catalyst in her decision to cut her hair, but not something she intended to share with Reuben. He would never again let her out of his sight if he knew that she had caught her hair on fire! It had taken an hour to calm Xonia, who had been watching helplessly in the crystal ball.

Before Xonia could twitch her tail and make it disappear, Mini gathered the orphaned hair and stuffed it into the trash can beside the dresser. She was already having second thoughts about what she'd done. Reuben would be crushed—he was constantly admiring her hair.

Deciding there was no use worrying herself sick, she retrieved her manicure set and brought it to the kitchen table. Xonia followed at a leisurely pace, leaping onto a chair to watch. Mini found the mortal task of painting her nails surprisingly fun.

Feeling Xonia's unblinking gaze on her, she glanced up. "Want me to do yours?" she offered.

Xonia snorted. "I'm not *that* bored, although you might ask me again in a few weeks. With nothing to do around here but sleep, I'm beginning to get a little stir crazy."

"Well, that's about to change," Mini informed her. "Reuben and I have decided we need you at the office."

"You have?" Xonia perked up, her yellow eyes rounding in anticipation. "Something up I should know about?"

Mini painstakingly stroked Seductive Mauve polish onto her nail. The brush slipped off the side and coated her skin, and she looked up just in time to freeze Xonia's tail in mid-twitch. "I'll get it, thank you." She swabbed the errant polish with a cotton ball dipped in polish remover, waving at the air to disperse the sharp, eye-watering odor; it made Reuben sneeze.

"Well? I'm bursting here!" Xonia complained.

"We've found the perfect match for . . . Holly." Mini

made the announcement with renewed excitement. "Actually, *she* found him, but we've got to get them together."

"If she found him, then what's the problem?"

"He's a client."

"Ah," Xonia murmured. "Holly's golden rule number two—she doesn't date the clients."

Mini nodded. " 'Fraid so. She's a stickler for the rules, too, which is why we need you. Holly is the only one who has access to the files on the computer. *She* decides who dates who, and she's working on matching her Mr. Right—Lance Wilder—with another client." Briefly she told Xonia what happened between Holly and Lance.

Xonia whistled, although it came out sounding more like a screeching yowl. "Hot dog! He's a bold one, isn't he?" Her yellow eyes began to glitter. "Sounds like *my* type of man."

"He's *Holly's*," Mini reminded her firmly. "We're here to help mortals, and *you're* here to help *us* help mortals."

"I know, I know. I just wish I could remember why I agreed to come along as your familiar in the first place."

"Because you couldn't resist being in a position to make Reuben beg for your help, even if he doesn't know who he's begging," Mini replied candidly, then added, "And because you're my best friend." Finished with her manicure, she tightened the lid on the polish and closed the case. "And, because you're my best friend, you're going to try to be nicer to Reuben. He's suffering enough without his powers."

"Ah, poor powerless warlock."

Mini had to bite her lip to keep from smiling at Xonia's outrageous mockery. "Please, Xonia? Give him another chance? Show him your good side—and I know you have one—before he finds out who you are. Then, when he *does* find out, he'll remember your kindness, and you two can be friends." Xonia and Reuben were old, old enemies, and Mini wanted desperately for them to get along. She loved them both, and felt their jealousy a ridiculous waste of time.

Xonia looked obstinate for a long moment. Finally she sighed. "All right. I'll *try,* but I can't make any promises. He doesn't like me as a cat any more than he liked me as a witch."

A key rattled in the back door. Mini gave a startled yelp and clamped her hands against her sheared hair.

"Speaking of the devil," Xonia murmured, but her voice gave her away; she was anticipating his reaction as much as Mini dreaded it.

"Ssh! He'll recognize your voice!"

Eyes riveted on the doorway, they waited in nervous silence as the door opened and Reuben shouldered his way in. Under one arm he carried a cylinder-shaped object about four feet long, wrapped in wax paper and tied with several strings.

He grinned at Mini and ignored Xonia. They stared at him in openmouthed amazement as he presented his prize. "I'm so clever, I surprise myself sometimes."

"What's . . . *that*?" Mini asked, staring at the object now lying across his outstretched hands.

With a flourish, Reuben bowed as if he were presenting the crown jewels to his queen. His expression was smug. "This, my darling wife, is what you asked for. The list said to buy bread, meat, tomatoes, lettuce, cheese, and salad dressing. On the way to the market, I passed a tiny little restaurant tucked between the dry cleaner and a jewelers and, being the curious witch that I am, I stepped inside to look around."

"You followed your nose," Mini translated.

Reuben grinned sheepishly. "Yes, I followed my nose. Anyway, I stepped inside and saw this displayed behind the glass case."

"This." Mini pointed a shiny nail at the object. "What is 'this'?"

"It's called a submarine sandwich. It has everything on the list in one neat package—and I didn't have to waste time searching through the grocery aisles. In fact, I didn't even *have* to go to the market at all." His smile faltered as Mini continued to stare at him, unsmiling. Slowly his gaze traveled over her, lingering on her freshly painted nails.

Like a boy who suddenly saw his way out of trouble, his smile returned, persuasive and charming. "Your nails look lovely, darling. The color suits you."

Mini rose from her chair, fighting unreasonable tears. Xonia's sympathetic gaze didn't help matters. Without a word to her baffled husband, Mini started to leave the kitchen.

"Mini? Darling? Did I do something wrong?"

Mini paused and glanced back, her short hair swinging against her cheek in a way that would have delighted her at any other time. Right now it only reminded her that Reuben hadn't noticed.

And it would be a cold day in hell before she'd point out the change.

"You forgot the milk," she said tremulously, and fled just as the tears spilled over.

With an outraged hiss, Xonia leaped down from the chair and followed her.

"She's no trouble at all." Mini lifted the pet carrier for Holly's inspection. "After her accident, we just hated to leave her at home all alone."

Holly didn't know what to say. A cat at the office? She'd never owned a cat, and had never considered bringing Nike, her golden retriever, to the office, for fear he'd frighten the clients. But a cat wasn't a dog . . . and it *did* look pitiful with its bandaged leg.

As if on cue, the cat let out a forlorn meow.

"The vet said we should watch her carefully . . . for signs of infection," Reuben said. "We could keep her in our office, and no one will ever know she's there."

Still, Holly hesitated. She didn't mean to be cruel, but having a cat in the office didn't sound professional.

"The alternative," Reuben added, "is for one of us to stay at home with her until she recovers. She's an old bat—er, cat, and we've had her since she was a kitten. Mini's very fond of her."

That settled it. Holly couldn't afford to lose either of her employees, not even for a day. They were booked for the next two weeks. "Okay, but what about a litter box?"

Their startled expressions following her question were identical. Holly looked from one to the other expectantly.

The cat broke the silence, clawing at the cage door with her uninjured paw and meowing plaintively.

Mini cocked her head as if listening, and after a moment, her expression cleared. Holly was left with the odd impression that the cat had communicated with Mini in some way. She shook her head ruefully at her fanciful thoughts.

"Reuben left the litter box by the back door," Mini explained. "She'll let us know when she needs to . . . go, and we can put her out."

"Does 'she' have a name?"

"Sheba" and "Haggetha," the couple answered simultaneously. Holly laughed. "Which one is it?"

"Both." It was Mini who spoke up, casting her husband a narrow-eyed look that promised retribution and completely mystified Holly. "Her full name is Sheba Haggetha Costello."

"Well, Sheba Haggetha Costello," Holly said to the cat, "I hope you don't expect a raise anytime soon."

Laughing at her joke, the couple thanked her for understanding and began to head in the direction of the office with the cat.

"Oh, and don't think that I didn't notice," Holly called after them, admiring Mini's stylish new haircut. At her comment, Mini and Reuben froze in stride but didn't turn around.

Mini sounded breathless. "Notice? Notice . . . what?"

"Your hair. I love it."

Sounding curiously relieved, Mini laughed. "Oh, that. Thanks. I'm glad *somebody* noticed."

Apparently Reuben *hadn't* noticed quickly enough to

suit Mini, Holly thought, catching sight of the scathing glance Mini shot her husband. She watched them disappear behind the closed door, smiling to herself and hoping she wouldn't regret her softhearted decision.

When the phone on her desk rang, she snatched it up, glancing at her watch at the same time. Eight o'clock on the dot. Someone was either very eager or very impatient.

"Romance Connection, Holly Wentworth speaking."

"Holly."

She slid into her chair before her knees buckled.

It was Lance Wilder, and his slightly husky, I-just-woke-up voice conjured instant erotic images of low-riding pajama bottoms, sexy, ruffled hair, and a shadowed jaw. How? Holly asked herself as the moisture in her mouth dried up quicker than a glass of water spilled on desert sand. How could the sound of his voice conjure an image she couldn't possibly know about? And why did this man—of the hundreds of men she'd met in the past half year—do this to her?

"Holly?"

"Yes, I'm here." She covered the mouthpiece and cleared her throat, wishing desperately for a drink of water. "What can I help you with, Mr. Wilder?"

"So you recognize my voice." He sounded not only pleased, but surprised as well.

Holly laughed silently, imagining his shock if she were to tell him that not only had she recognized his voice, but she'd also immediately pictured him in her mind . . . wearing nothing but a low-riding pair of cotton pajama bottoms and sporting a telltale wake-up call—

"I wanted to apologize."

Holly snapped to attention. The professional thing to do would be to pretend the kiss never happened. Instead, she heard herself saying, "No harm done."

Not exactly what she'd commanded her brain to say, but judging by the warmth uncoiling in her belly and the tingling in her breasts, her brain had taken a short vacation.

At least she *hoped* it was short. Water. She needed water. Or a new brain. He was a client, a widower, who for
the past four years had obviously been very content with
his memories. She'd seen *Message in a Bottle,* had felt
the heroine's pain and angst, and no way was she that
understanding or patient.

Besides, in her opinion the ending had sucked.

And Holly'd had her share of sucky endings.

"On the contrary," Lance argued. "You were a tremen-
dous help, and I'd like to thank you."

Holly tried to get her brain around his senseless comment. Thank her? For what? For melting in the chair when
he kissed her? For waking up each night since the kiss
soaked in sweat from a bout of dreamy lovemaking with
him?

She wet her dry lips, surprised to find that she had any
moisture left. Curiosity got the best of her; she *had* to
know. "How—how was I a help?"

"Fishing for compliments, Holly?" His low chuckle
thrummed through her body like a primitive drumroll.
"You helped by reminding me of what I've been missing."

"Missing?" She was still hopelessly lost. Her brain—
what there was of it—remained fogged.

"Kissing. I miss kissing a woman's soft lips. I miss
talking to a woman, sharing daily events and exchanging
neck rubs. I miss dinner by a crackling fire . . ."

Holly swallowed hard, swamped by images so erotic
she blushed.

". . . picnics in the park, drives in the country." His
voice deepened with a hint of sorrow. "I guess . . . after
my wife died, I didn't think I'd ever enjoy doing those
things with someone else."

For a split second, Holly's heart throbbed with sympathy. Then she remembered the movie that had caused
her to waste two boxes of tissues. In fact, she was certain
that if her brain weren't so fogged, she could recall *several* movies where the hero was still helplessly in love

with his dead wife. Oh, they always claimed to love the new woman as much, but in a different way. Never in the same all-consuming way they loved their memories, though.

Lance Wilder's nostalgic voice said it all.

The knowledge gave Holly the strength to say, "I'm glad to have helped you over your hurdle, Mr. Wilder."

"Lance. I think after what we shared, you should call me Lance."

She thought about arguing, but decided she didn't want to humiliate herself further by possibly revealing her disappointment. "Lance, then." Before he could form another innocent, yet wounding remark, she added quickly, "If there's nothing else I can help you with—"

"There is."

Holly closed her eyes and mentally braced herself.

"I want to take you out to dinner, show my appreciation."

"No." She was pleased to note there wasn't a single second of hesitation. "I'm afraid that's impossible, Mr.— Lance."

"Why?"

Why? Why? Holly bit her lip and mumbled a curse beneath her breath. She didn't want to sound condescending by explaining golden rule number two. "Because . . . because I've found a date for you."

She was very glad he couldn't see her flaming face, because if he could, he would know that she'd lied.

Four

Without prompting, Xonia had twitched her magic tail and
amplified the sound of Holly's voice through the door the
moment the phone rang. Nevertheless, the three of them
stood with their ears pressed shamelessly against the wood
until they heard the click of the phone landing in the cradle.

Quickly they dispersed. Mini scampered to the tall
metal filing cabinet and began to busily sort through the
files. Reuben returned to his desk and became seemingly
engrossed in checking over Friday's interviews before he
turned them in to Holly, and Xonia moved away from the
door, resuming her feline role with remarkable ease—she
began to groom her gaudy orange fur with her free paw.

After a few moments, Holly knocked on the door and
came in, casting Xonia an absent, sympathetic glance.
Mini had to bite her lip to keep from smiling at her dazed
expression.

Her boss looked positively shell-shocked.

"Another potential scalp?" Mini joked innocently, shut-
ting the filing cabinet drawer and returning to her desk.

Holly looked startled. "How did you know it was a
'he'?"

"Just a lucky guess, I suppose." Mini caught Reuben's

sharp glance and wrinkled her nose at his silent criticism, still miffed because it had taken him fifteen minutes to notice her haircut. She wasn't convinced he would have noticed *then,* if he hadn't been trying to console her.

Perversely she'd cried even harder when he'd declared that he liked it.

Holly wandered into the room and perched on the corner of Mini's desk. She idly lifted a pencil from Mini's pencil holder and twirled it between her fingers. As Mini waited, her boss glanced at Reuben, then leaned closer.

"I don't think this one's interested in marriage," Holly informed her in a low voice. "Or getting 'scalped,' as Reuben prefers to call it."

Mini sensed that Holly was in need of a little "girl talk," and she was just the girl to listen. She leaned to the left and said to her husband, "Darling, why don't you run down to the espresso shop and get us a cappuccino."

"I'd rather fly," he muttered crossly, but rose from the desk and strode to the door. "I get the picture. No need to get nasty about it."

As he passed Xonia, she twitched her tail.

Reuben stumbled and nearly fell through the doorway. He turned and glowered at the cat. She meowed sweetly, blinking her guileless yellow eyes. Then, with a toss of her head, she resumed her one-armed grooming.

"Reuben," Mini warned, catching the exchange. "You know *Sheba's* not feeling well."

Thankfully his mumbled response was inaudible. When he'd gone, Mini let out a sigh, pasting a rueful grin on her face for Holly's benefit. "Sometimes they rub each other the wrong way," she explained.

Holly nodded absently, clearly still befuddled from her conversation with Lance Wilder. Mini decided to get right down to business. She rubbed her hands together as if she couldn't wait to hear all about the new client, when in reality she probably knew more about Lance Wilder than Holly did. But without her powers, she couldn't read

Holly's mind, and Holly's opinion about Lance Wilder was what she was most interested in.

"So tell me about our new client. Is he the one you interviewed on Friday?"

"How did you know?"

Mini smiled at her alarmed expression. "You had that same dazed expression on your face when you emerged from the interview room last Friday, after interviewing . . . *him*."

Holly's alarm deepened. "Is it that obvious?"

"To me it is, though I doubt that Reuben noticed." They exchanged a woman-to-woman glance of understanding before Mini continued, "So, this new client isn't interested in anything long-term?"

"He's a widower, and my instincts tell me he's still in love with his memories."

"Can't you match him with a widow? Maybe he'd be more comfortable with someone who's gone through the same experience."

Holly tapped the pencil against her lip, mulling over Mini's suggestion. Finally she shook her head. "I don't think it would work, Mini. In my opinion, Lance—Mr. Wilder—needs to go on with his life, and being constantly around someone else who can't let go would only slow the process."

Mini hesitated before taking the plunge. She hoped it wasn't too soon. "Holly, since you're interested in Mr. Wilder yourself, couldn't you bend the rules—"

"No, no. I can't." Holly shook her head emphatically. She slid from the desk and began to pace. "It would be unethical, not to mention the fact that he still hasn't gotten over his wife. This may sound selfish, Mini, but when I finally fall for a man, I don't want a ghost hovering over my shoulder."

"And you don't think you can help Mr. Wilder banish this ghost?"

Holly pivoted sharply, becoming more agitated by the moment. "That's just it. I don't want to have to persuade him to love me. I want it to be something he can't control." She waved a passionate, agitated hand in the air. "I want—I want—"

When she sputtered to a stop, Mini supplied helpfully, "Romance?"

"Yes, romance! And passion."

"Trust? Faithfulness?"

"Yes, yes. And love—unconditional love. In other words—"

"You want the whole enchilada," Mini finished with a grin. "I don't blame you. You want what I have with . . . Reuben." She felt a chill sweep over her. Why had she faltered? She *did* still have the whole wonderful enchilada with Reuben, didn't she?

"Mini? Is something wrong? You look as if you just remembered something unpleasant." Holly walked to the desk, frowning. "Is . . . is everything okay between you and Reuben? I don't mean to pry, but I sensed a little discord this morning."

"What? Oh, no. We're fine." To cover the awkward moment, Mini hurriedly returned to their earlier subject. "About Mr. Wilder. Are you *positive* you won't change your mind?"

"Yes. I'm positive."

Mini was pleased to note that Holly's declaration sounded like a big fat lie. She pretended to believe her. "Do you have someone else in mind?"

Holly lowered her gaze and traced an imaginary circle on Mini's desk. Her confession came reluctantly. "As a matter of fact, that's what I wanted to talk to you about. You see, I told Mr. Wilder that I'd found someone." She looked at Mini, taking a deep breath. "The truth is I haven't even begun the search."

Behind Holly, beneath Reuben's desk, Mini met Xonia's amused gaze. Her friend had wisely limped for cover the moment Holly started pacing. Mini schooled her features into one of convincing puzzlement. "Why would you tell him you found someone when you haven't?"

"Honestly?"

When Mini nodded, Holly threw up her hands, allowing her total confusion to show.

"Honestly, I don't know!"

"Could it be," Mini suggested gently, "because you want him for yourself?" From the concealment of the shadows, Xonia nodded her head vigorously. Mini ignored her. "Maybe you're wrong about Mr. Wilder, Holly. Maybe he *is* ready to get on with his life, but he's being understandably cautious."

"Maybe." Holly pulled her bottom lip between her teeth, then let out an explosive sigh. "It doesn't matter. He's still a client, and it's my duty to find the perfect match for him." Her expression hardened with resolution. "And that's what I'm going to do."

"And if he falls in love with someone else?"

Holly looked stricken by the blunt suggestion. "Then I guess it wasn't meant to be me."

The door chimes effectively ended the enlightening conversation as Reuben returned with their steaming cappuccinos. He stopped just outside the doorway, darting a questioning glance at the two women.

"Am I interrupting something?"

Mini hoped she was the only one who detected his sarcasm. She knew he wasn't happy about being excluded, but hopefully he'd behave himself until she could explain. With a grateful smile, she waved him into the room. "Come on in, darling. We were just finishing up, weren't we, Holly?"

"Yes, we were." Holly took the proffered cup of cappuccino and lifted the lid. "Hmm, you remembered: Irish creme with a splash of cinnamon. Thank you."

Anticipating one of several flavors Reuben knew she preferred, Mini carefully pulled the lid from her cup and took a cautious sip. She barely refrained from choking on the hot liquid as she identified the underlying taste of chocolate and . . . *mint*.

She didn't like mint.

She'd *never* liked mint.

The tears that sprang to her eyes could easily have been blamed on the scalding brew, but when she met Holly's sympathetic gaze, she knew there was at least *one* person in the room who suspected the true cause.

A disgusted meow reminded her that there were two.

"That's three out of five," Casey bragged, scooping the basketball into his arms and flashing Lance a smug grin. "You may have me bested at tennis, but I beat you *down,* buddy, in basketball."

Lance started to remind Casey that he'd won the last two games, but decided it wasn't worth the argument. He was hot, tired, and in need of something tall, wet, and cold. His day hadn't gone well, starting with a bed-wetting five-year-old who refused to talk, and ending with a rebellious, spoiled teenager who had spent the entire forty-five-minute session complaining that his parents wouldn't let him have the sports car he wanted.

Maybe it was him. Maybe *he* was the problem, and not his patients. True, he'd slept little since his interview with Holly Wentworth, but normally he didn't require more than five hours of sleep anyway.

The interview had left him charged and ready, literally. He'd spent most of the weekend trying to figure out if Holly was the cause or merely the catalyst. Since he couldn't get *her* face and figure from his mind, he was pretty certain it wasn't the latter.

Inside his twenty-room house, Lance led Casey to the only room he truly felt comfortable in—the kitchen. He grabbed a gallon jug of orange juice from the enormous silver cooler and two glasses from a cabinet before joining Casey at the breakfast bar. The moment he sat on the stool, Casey began to bombard him with questions.

"How did the interview go?"

Lance drained his orange juice and poured himself another, keeping his expression deliberately blank. "Fine." He waited until Casey tilted his glass, anticipating his shock. "At least, it *was* going along fine until my brain slipped a gear and I kissed Holly."

Casey choked on his juice, spraying a disgusting amount onto the bar. He coughed and swiped his mouth. "Holly Wentworth? The owner? You *kissed* her? You're lying!" He laughed, shaking his head as if he couldn't believe that Lance expected him to fall for such a lame jest. "I know you're lying, because she doesn't *do* the interviews."

"She did mine." Lance told him about running into Reuben and how Holly had volunteered to do the interview while her helpers went out to lunch. "Very conscientious woman, Holly Wentworth." And beautiful, intelligent, sexy—

"She's a bombshell," Casey agreed enviously when he realized Lance wasn't pulling his leg. "So you really kissed her, huh?"

"Yes, I did." Lance felt a slow grin of remembrance tug at his lips. "She made me realize just what I've been missing."

"Well, thank God," Casey crowed, tapping his glass of juice against Lance's in a toast. "It's about damned time! So, are you going to ask her out?"

"Did. She refused." Lance's smile faded. "I think she *wanted* to, but I can't be sure. I'm a little rusty in that area."

Casey chuckled. "Buddy, you *are* rusty if you don't remember that women are—and shall remain—an enigma. They aren't predictable, and they can't be second-guessed." He clapped Lance on the back. "Why don't you ask her again. Maybe she just needs a little persuading."

Lance considered Casey's suggestion, but finally shook his head. "No. I may be coming out of the proverbial shell, but I'm not going to start at a dead run by chasing a woman who doesn't want to be chased."

"How do *you* know she doesn't want to be chased?"

It was a good question, and one Lance couldn't answer. Hedging around it, he said, "Get real, Casey. In her line of work, she not only can have any man she wants, but she gets a variety to choose from."

"You make her sound like a hooker," Casey joked. When Lance didn't join him, he quickly wiped the grin from his face.

But Lance wasn't listening to Casey. His own comment had sparked a realization. Not only could Holly have any man she wanted, but she *could* possibly be involved, despite Reuben Costello's hints to the contrary. But if she was involved with someone—why hadn't she used that excuse?

"So what are you going to do?"

Lance set his empty glass on the counter and studied the bits of pulp clinging to it. He injected a careless note into his voice to cover the bruise on his ego. "I'm going to get your money's worth, buddy boy. I'm going on a date." After all, there were other fish in the sea, fish that might be a bit less reluctant than Holly Wentworth.

And if his silent declaration echoed a little hollowly, Lance chose to ignore it.

The male figure in Holly's life preferred the right side of the bed, rarely brushed his teeth, and followed her footsteps with undying loyalty. He was the strong, silent type—unless his dog bowl was empty or he needed to find a bush. And for the past five minutes, the wet, cold nose nudging her elbow had become increasingly avid to do just that.

"Hang on, Nike." Hoping to stall him for another moment or two, Holly patted the golden retriever with her left hand as she skillfully maneuvered the computer mouse with her right. She frowned as the same name popped up for the third time.

Terri Prezly. Impossible! Holly shook her head. How could the sultry, rather flighty redhead be a match for Lance Wilder? The computer had to be wrong. She clearly remembered Terri Prezly, and the woman hadn't been shy about announcing she wanted to marry someone with a hefty bank account. Age, personal appearance, and common interests hadn't seemed important.

Yet right on the screen was her file, and unless there was a glitch in the computer, Holly had her all wrong. According to the file, Terri Prezly was a divorced second-grade schoolteacher with one teenage child—and matched up with the interests of Lance Wilder so perfectly it made Holly's stomach lurch in protest.

With a regretful sigh, she conceded that Terri Prezly and Lance Wilder would get together for a date. She forced herself to admit that there wasn't anything wrong with the program.

That only left one explanation: The glitch was in her heart.

Five

The Rodstead was the most expensive restaurant in Lovit, California. The lighting was tastefully subdued, the food prepared by several highly paid renowned chefs. Movie stars were rumored to dine in the more secluded corner tables, and dessert was optional.

Reservations were not.

"Why do you suppose she chose *this* restaurant?" Reuben whispered to Mini as they waited for the hostess. He stood regally in the doorway with his arm hooked beneath Mini's hand, in his element, dressed in a black tuxedo that enhanced his silky locks of blue-black hair. He'd had to do some fancy talking to keep the ivory cane, though. In the end he'd won, but only because he'd agreed to let their protector cast a spell that transformed his features.

He had adamantly drawn the line when the scruffy-looking feline had attempted to change his hair.

Mini's smile was secretive and satisfied as she checked her own fake platinum-blond coiffure. "Because she's after his money, and what better way to find out if he *has* any? My bet is that she'll order the most expensive item on the menu and a bottle of overpriced bubbly just to see if he protests."

Reuben narrowed his bushy eyebrows. "What if she

doesn't? What if she puts on an act just to lure him into her web?"

"Then our little friend will take care of it." Mini tapped her tiny silver purse with an elegant nail. Xonia crouched inside, waiting for the opportunity to wreak havoc with her magic. "That's why we brought her along."

The hostess wound her graceful way through the tables, her congenial smile widening at the sight of them.

Lowering his voice, Reuben bent closer to Mini. "Let's hope nothing goes awry with her shrinking spell. Can you imagine their horror if their clientele discovered her?"

Mini smiled, knowing her husband would like nothing better.

"Do you have a reservation?"

"No, we thought we'd just drop by and take our chances," Reuben drawled, wincing as Mini dug her long nails into his arm. Suppressing a sigh, he said, "Yes, we do. Under the name of Stephens." His grin, coupled with his ridiculously bushy eyebrows, gave him a devilish, maniacal look. "I'm Darrin, and this is my lovely wife, Samantha. We left Tabitha—"

"She doesn't want to know our life history, darling," Mini interrupted in a gushing voice before her prankster husband got them thrown out. "Let's go, I'm simply famished!" Fortunately she was the only one who seemed to hear the tiny snicker that came from her purse. "Traitor," Mini mumbled under her breath.

The hostess glanced curiously from Mini to Reuben, her gracious smile slipping a notch. "Right this way, please."

She led them to the table Mini had requested when she made the reservation. Their table was one of four clustered around a beautiful, gurgling indoor fountain; Mini had scoped the terrain out in her crystal ball.

When the hostess left them with their menus, Mini set her purse on a chair before glancing casually at the couple seated at the table next to their own. Her timing was perfect: Lance Wilder and Terri Prezly had yet to order.

Lance looked at ease in a gray suit, white shirt, and navy-blue tie. Mini's eyebrows rose as she inspected his date, who wore a tiny red dress with a neckline so low her ample breasts nearly spilled onto the table. Her chest sparkled and shimmered with some type of glitter-laced powder.

Mini shot Reuben a sharp glance, relieved to find him engrossed in the menu and *not* watching the redhead or her sparkling bosom. After a few moments, a waiter approached Lance's table and asked if they were ready to order.

"I'll have the Lobster Finesse," Ms. Prezly announced, "and a bottle of your best champagne." The redhead snapped the menu closed and handed it to the waiter, fastening her drooling gaze on Lance.

Sometimes Mini hated to be right, but this wasn't one of those times. After consulting the menu to see that Lobster Finesse was indeed the most expensive dish, she flashed Reuben a smug smile. He shrugged as if to say he'd never doubted her.

"Good choice," Lance was saying approvingly. "I think I'll have the same."

"Please do." Terri gave a husky, full-throated laugh. "I've got money to burn."

Mini's smug smile froze. *She* had money to burn? Terri Prezly was a gold digger who couldn't even afford to pay for dessert, much less a full-course meal at the Rodstead! Mini knew, because she'd read her file before Xonia had switched it with someone else's.

Her dismayed gaze collided with Reuben's, who sat across from her, looking disgustingly satisfied. With a muttered curse, Mini snatched her purse from the chair and opened the clasp. She brought it close, pretending to be searching for something. "Did you hear that?" she whispered to Xonia.

The golden glow of Xonia's eyes peered back at her, unblinking. "Yes, I heard."

"She's *talking* to you?" Reuben demanded, craning his neck in an attempt to peer into her purse.

"Ssh!" Mini glanced around quickly, relieved to see that nobody had noticed his outburst. Mini leaned as close to her husband as she could, holding the menu against her face to block Lance and Terri's view of her. "She does a little."

"How come *I've* never heard her speak?"

"Because she's . . . bashful. Yes, she's bashful." On the spur of the moment, it was the best fabrication Mini could rustle up. She wasn't ready to tell him the truth about Xonia.

Reuben's suspicion lingered, but he returned his gaze to the menu, muttering, "I've never heard of a bashful familiar."

The waiter returned to Lance's table and poured the champagne. When he moved away, Lance said to his dinner companion, "So, I guess it goes without saying that you love kids."

"Kids? I— Oh!" Terri jumped to her feet, grabbed a napkin, and began to brush furiously at the front of her dress, where a stain was spreading. "How could I be so clumsy? This dress cost—" The redhead gaped at Lance in horror, but quickly recovered. "I mean, this dress cost a fortune, but I've got a million others to take its place." Casting Lance a flirty smile, she resumed her seat. "Maybe we can swing by your place after dinner so that I can get this into some cold water."

Mini held her breath, watching Lance's expression. What would he say? Would he eagerly accept the blatant invitation? Or would he be disgusted by the easy way the redhead threw herself at him? On the first date, no less!

Lance neither accepted nor declined her not-so-subtle invitation, much to Mini's frustration. Then the waiter arrived, planting his body right between the tables and blocking her view. She quickly gave him her order, glaring at Reuben as he rattled off a list that would have fed half the present clientele. Mentally she tallied their budget for the week. The results deepened her frown. Reuben had apparently forgotten that in their mortal world, nothing was free. Xonia had been kind enough to conjure their disguises, but Mini knew Xonia couldn't pay for Reuben's outrageous meal without breaking the rules.

Mini kicked him beneath the table, interrupting his list of desserts—as if he could eat a slice of key lime pie, a hot fudge cake with ice cream, and two chocolate éclairs after ordering three entrées and four appetizers! "Now, darling, remember your ulcer." With a sweet, concerned smile, she turned to the waiter. "He'll have the filet mignon, medium rare, soup, and a small salad with low-fat Italian dressing." Before Reuben could protest, she added firmly, "And *one* slice of key lime pie."

The waiter moved away, and Mini pulled her warning glare from her husband just in time to catch Lance regarding her with amusement. Apparently he'd been listening to the exchange.

But he didn't recognize her, she was certain.

She gave him a polite, friendly smile and grabbed her water, wondering what Xonia was going to do next. They couldn't let Terri get her lusty claws into Lance. What she wouldn't give for five minutes of her powers—

"Don't worry, girlfriend. I've got it covered."

The tiny, whispered assurance came from the purse in her lap. Mini refrained from glancing down. She cupped her hand over her mouth and said, "We can't let them leave without making sure they don't go to his place!"

"I know. I said don't worry, didn't I?"

"What's she saying?" Reuben asked around a mouthful of crackers.

"Just that we shouldn't worry, she's got it covered."

"Well, she'd better hurry before *he* does the covering." He jabbed his head in Lance's direction.

While Mini and Xonia had been talking, the conversation between Lance and Terri had warmed considerably, Mini was not pleased to notice.

Her fingers tightened around her water glass. Whatever

Xonia had planned, she wished she would get to it. Lance belonged to Holly, whether he knew it or not.

Terri Prezly was not only a little too flashy for Lance's taste—she was a *lot* obvious about wanting to jump his bones.

But he'd be lying to himself, he knew, if he said he wasn't flattered. He was a man, after all. A man who'd gone too long without the pleasant company of a woman.

Still . . . he was glad when she cooled the come-on and began to ask serious questions, even if they were a little on the personal side.

"So . . . this house your father left you—what would you say it's worth?"

Lance laughed ruefully, thinking of the utility bill he'd paid last month. "I guess that depends on who's buying it. To someone with less than a six-digit salary, I'd say it would be a bad investment."

"But what's it *worth*?"

Arching a brow, Lance countered, "You thinking about buying it?" He knew she was loaded—she'd mentioned the fact at least three times during the course of their meal. She had also insisted on paying the bill, and had then proceeded to order the most expensive item on the menu without so much as lifting a carefully plucked eyebrow.

"I was wondering what real estate in that area costs these days."

"A lot. According to the last appraisal, the house is worth twice what my father paid for it when he bought it from Senator Rose twenty years ago."

"Your father must have been very rich."

Lance shrugged, uncomfortable with the gleam he detected in her eyes. His father *had* been rich at the time he purchased the house, but when he died, Lance had been able to keep the house only after depleting his savings to bring the taxes up-to-date. He could have sold the Mercedes, but had managed to talk himself out of it.

"I've always been interested in old houses," Terri explained with a husky little laugh.

That would account for the gleam in her eyes, Lance thought, relieved. Casey would call him paranoid for mistaking that gleam for greed.

"Oh, here's the waiter with our check." She opened her purse and began to rifle through the contents, a frown slowly settling on her pretty face. "Oh, darn. I must have left my credit card at home—*and* my checkbook."

"Likely story," Lance teased. "Don't worry, I'll get it." He hadn't been comfortable with her paying the bill anyway, no matter how loaded she claimed to be. As she continued to search through her purse, he pulled out his wallet and reached for one of his major credit cards, then handed it to the waiter.

"I can't believe I left them in my other purse!" Terri continued to berate herself, casting quick, covert glances at Lance.

Suspecting she was embarrassed, Lance tried to reassure her. "It's no big deal."

"But I *wanted* to pay for it."

"You can get it next time."

The waiter returned, handing him the credit card.

Lance stared at the card, then lifted his stunned gaze to the waiter. The young man looked sympathetic.

"I'm sorry, sir. This card's been canceled."

"Impossible," Lance grated, striving to keep his temper under control. He fished out another one and stuffed it into the waiter's hand. "Try that one."

How could this have happened? He knew he wasn't maxed out—he kept a careful accounting of his purchases! As for the card's being canceled, he'd been using the same one for years. No, the waiter must have punched in the wrong number.

When the waiter returned, Lance knew from his expression that he had bad news. This time he added a chilly smile to the rejected credit card.

"The manager says he'll take cash."

Through gritted teeth, Lance growled, "I don't carry that much cash around. Just credit cards." He yanked a Platinum Visa out of his wallet, but the waiter backed away, shaking his head.

"Sir, the manager said—"

They were both distracted by the screech of a chair being shoved back. Lance turned to find Terri red-faced and glowering. She snatched her purse from the table and clutched it to her magnificent bosom.

"You're scum, you know that?" she announced shrilly, drawing several curious eyes with her accusation. With a contemptuous toss of her red mane, she stomped past the startled waiter on the way to the door.

Lance gawked after her, floored by her reaction. It was a simple mistake—

"Sir, I'm going to have to call the police."

In one smooth move, Lance was on his feet and in the waiter's face. Violence wasn't his scene, but the last few incredulous moments had pushed him closer to it than he ever remembered being.

He'd never been so embarrassed in his life.

"You will not call the police, do you understand? You will lead me to a phone so that I can call someone to bring the cash for the damned bill."

The waiter backed away, effectively persuaded. "Yes, sir. Right this way, sir."

Lance was led to the manager's office to use the phone. The manager, a short, barrel-chested man with protruding eyes, insisted on dialing Casey's number himself. His mistrust brought a hot flush to Lance's face.

As luck would have it, Casey didn't appear to be home.

The manager folded his arms and blocked the doorway.

Lance replaced the receiver and was debating his next move when the waiter rushed into the office, knocking the manager aside in his excitement. Lance scowled at him, wondering what god-awful news he was bringing this time.

"The couple at the table next to you paid your bill, sir,"

he burst out, sounding as amazed as Lance felt. "They said they knew you and for you not to worry, they'd send you a bill. They even added a nice tip."

"Did you get a name?" Lance croaked.

"I believe it was Stephens, sir. Darrin and Samantha Stephens."

The names sounded familiar, but their faces hadn't been. "Where are they? I'd like to thank—"

"They're gone, sir."

"Great. That's just great." Lance squeezed the bridge of his nose between his thumb and forefinger, wondering if his face would melt from the heat. People he didn't even know had not only witnessed his humiliation, but had also pitied him to the point of paying his bill.

His first date had turned into a nightmare.

Six

It was wicked of her to be glad that Lance's date had turned out to be a disaster.

Wicked, childish, and unprofessional.

A naughty grin tugged at Holly's lips as she searched for a parking place near her apartment, but she stopped the shameful action by biting down—hard. Besides, Lance's failure to have a good time had to be a result of a computer glitch after all.

Holly should have trusted her instincts.

A tiny, shameful part of her was glad that she hadn't.

She parked the car and reached for the small plastic shopping bag on the passenger seat. On the way home, she'd stopped at the butcher and picked out a huge T-bone steak to share with Nike.

She wasn't celebrating. She absolutely was not. There was nothing to celebrate. Although Lance remained un-attached, she would have to find another match. It was her job. But this time. . . . *this* time she would trust her instincts if the computer popped up with someone she remembered as being totally unsuitable.

"Need help?"

Holly swallowed a shriek and whirled around, instinctively lifting the shopping bag to use as a potential weapon. The steak was a hefty one, and the uncooked baking potato—

It was Lance Wilder, looking ruggedly handsome in casual khakis and a short-sleeved cotton shirt the color of dark chocolate. The shirt was open at the throat. Holly caught a glimpse of russet chest hair peeping above the opening, and the bright flash of a gold chain around his neck. She'd always thought neck chains on a man sexy, especially nestled in a bed of curly chest hair.

He glanced at the bag clutched threateningly in her hand and presented his palms. "I come in peace."

She tried not to stare. "How did you know where I live?" she demanded, determined to ignore the fact that her heart was slam-dunking her ribs. She knew it wasn't just that he'd scared the daylights out of her. It was the sight and smell of him that sent her heart crashing out of control.

His broad shoulders rippled in a shrug. "I was pulling up to the curb in front of Romance Connection just as you were pulling out."

"So you followed me?"

He nodded. "I need to talk to you. Alone."

Gathering her willpower, Holly stepped around him onto the sidewalk. "You should have waited until tomorrow, Mr. Wilder, when I was in the office."

"Lance."

She pretended not to hear his correction.

"This can't wait." His rough, silk-and-leather voice deepened irresistibly as he added, "Please."

She'd never heard the word "please" sound so erotic. The man certainly had a way with words.

"Okay. Talk." Holly shouldered her purse and slipped the handles of the plastic bag over her wrist. She crossed her arms and waited.

"This is private." He glanced behind her in the vicinity of the remodeled Tudor-style house occupying the corner of Mistletoe and Anthony streets. Holly rented the second floor of the graceful-looking, two-story house; Mrs.

Teasedale, the owner, an elderly widow, lived down-stairs.

Holly suspected he was hinting for an invitation, but he was out of luck. She looked around them to make sure they were alone. "This is as private as it gets."

"You're not going to invite me in?"

"I don't conduct business at home."

The blue of his eyes darkened a shade at her curt tone. "I need your help," he announced.

"I think you've gotten all of the help you're going to get from me." Holly tried to sound flippant and did her best to push the memory of his soul-shaking kiss from her mind. Help him? Oh, no. Not again. Once was enough for her. Just as she hadn't forgotten the kiss, she hadn't forgotten his humiliating thank-you afterward.

He took a step closer, close enough for her to catch his heated scent. In response, her pulse began to race. And he expected her to let him into her *apartment*? The man was a walking sin!

"My date didn't go very well."

"So I heard."

He looked startled. "She called?"

Holly nodded, knowing she should confess that it was her mistake, that she had accidentally picked the wrong person for him. But she couldn't resist torturing him a moment longer. Her ego was still smarting over the kiss he'd had the gall to thank her for.

Lifting a finger to her lips, she pretended to ponder. "Let me see . . . Oh, yeah. She called you a 'cheap, in-considerate, lying bum.' "

His mouth twisted in a rueful smile. "Is that it? I figured a woman of Terri's . . . talents would be more imagina-tive."

She tried biting her lip, but it didn't work this time. Her answering grin was quick and spontaneous. "She is rather colorful," she agreed, chuckling. Now would be the perfect opportunity to tell him that the computer had picked the wrong woman. Just blurt it out, she lectured to herself, and assure him that it wasn't his fault that it didn't work out. It was becoming obvious that he blamed himself.

"I want you to go out with me."

Every rational thought in Holly's mind fled at his words. She stuttered, "Excuse me?"

"I want you to go out with me, show me what I'm doing wrong."

"Show." That one loaded word loomed large in her mind. Not *tell* him what he was doing wrong, but *show* him. The possibilities made her break out in a cold sweat. Of course, she couldn't agree with such a wild, hare-brained suggestion. She owned the company. It was unethical—

"It wouldn't be like a real date. Sort of a practice run."

Outrageous. Impossible. No way.

"Think about how good it will be for the business."

Business? What did this have to do with business? This was about the dangerous attraction Lance Wilder held for her. He was a client, and a widower to boot. A widower still grieving for his dead wife.

Holly remained tongue-tied. A simple, flat, unhesitating "no" was all she had to say. And she *would* say it, too, the moment she found her voice.

"Just think of it as a tutorial in dating. In fact, I'm surprised you don't have a class or something for people like me who are out of practice." His self-deprecating smile and the agitated hand he ran through his hair did not seem contrived, although the cautious side of her brain assured her that it was.

But . . . what if it wasn't?

Holly felt herself weakening, and she knew—*knew*— that it was because she wanted to go out with Lance Wilder. Wanted it in the worst way. She wanted to find out what made him smile, what made him laugh, or what made him frown. Oh, she knew the basics from his file . . . but a person could not know the *real* man behind those details until she spent quality time with him.

And he was offering her the chance to have one wonderful night alone with him . . . in the guise of business.

It was the business part that left a nasty taste in her mouth. "I don't think—"

"Don't think," he said, catching her free wrist in his big hand. Whether he did it consciously or without thought, his thumb moved in slow, persuasive circles across the sensitive skin of her wrist. "Just do it. I believe those were *your* words."

It was like before when he'd touched her—a jolt she felt all the way to her toes. Holly managed to jerk her wrist free, although she would have much preferred to leave it smoldering beneath his fingers. Her father had once accused her of obeying her brain and ignoring her heart, and right now she hoped fervently that she could live up to his characterization. Yes, right now, she decided, she needed all of the sane brain waves she could muster. A date with Lance would leave a lasting impression she didn't want and didn't need.

"Lance . . . *Mr. Wilder*," she corrected firmly, "I really don't think it's a good idea for you and me to go out."

"Why?"

Those blue eyes probed deep, she thought, swallowing. She'd just bet he was a pro at unveiling secrets and prompting confessions. "Because it's a ridiculous idea."

He shook his head, jamming his hands in his pockets and stretching the material of his pants taut across his hips. The posture reminded Holly of the visual she'd seen of him in her mind the day he'd called.

She jerked her gaze to his face, her own face warm.

"What's so ridiculous about it? All I'm asking is for you to go with me on a date." He held up his hands. "You'll be the teacher, and I'll be the student. By the end of the date, you can tell me what I'm doing wrong."

"You didn't—" Holly's confession died in her throat. To her horror, she found she couldn't tell him the truth. *And* this *isn't unethical?* her conscience sneered.

Something in her face must have convinced him she was weakening, for he said, "I'll pick you up at eight o'clock."

Frozen in place, Holly watched him as he loped to his car and climbed inside. With a cheery wave, he started the engine and checked his mirrors.

She was still standing there, bemused, confused, and more than a little terrified, when he drove away.

She hadn't told him about the computer glitch.

Why hadn't she told him?

"He convinced her."

Sitting on the lumpy sofa in their apartment, Mini looked up from the book she was pretending to read and focused on Xonia, who was perched on the coffee table in front of Mini's crystal ball, watching the scene between Lance and Holly unfold. "What did you say?"

Xonia sighed, rolling her golden eyes at Mini's unfocused expression. "I said he convinced her. Lance is picking Holly up at eight o'clock tonight for a date. This could be the night!"

Reluctantly Mini lowered the book, forcing herself to concentrate; Reuben had gone out over an hour ago, supposedly to meet some friends for a drink. Where could he be? What was he doing? Was he hurt? In an accident? He'd told her not to worry, and she was trying her best . . . but she couldn't help it.

"Want me to check on him?" Xonia asked shrewdly.

Mini blinked innocently. "Who?"

Xonia arched a brow. "Your dear husband, that's who. That *is* who you're thinking about?"

With a brisk shake of her head, Mini said, "No. I won't stoop to using the crystal ball to spy on Reuben. I promised him I would never do that."

"What if he's in trouble?"

"He isn't." Mini wished she felt as confident as she sounded. "Besides, what do you care? You don't even like him."

Xonia padded over and leaped onto the arm of the sofa. She swished her bushy tail over the book in Mini's hands. "What are you reading?"

"A romance novel—and you're changing the subject."

"So I am," Xonia admitted with a cackling laugh. "Nothing gets past you, does it, my dearest friend? I mean, if Reuben *were* doing something he knew you wouldn't like, you'd know it, wouldn't you?"

Mini snapped the book closed and laid it aside. After that sly, catty comment her concentration was broken anyway. Green eyes met golden ones. "Xonia, if you have something to say, just say it."

Xonia's gaze brightened. "Well, if you insist. I did happen to take a quick peep in the crystal ball. He's—"

The rest was muffled as Mini clamped a hand over Xonia's mouth. "You were spying on him," Mini informed her in an aggravated tone. "As my friend, you should respect my wishes." Slowly she removed her hand.

"But, he's—"

Again Mini stopped her with a hand to her mouth. Xonia's whiskers tickled Mini's palm as Xonia tried to talk. "No buts. Promise?" Only when Xonia nodded did she let go. "I trust Reuben explicitly. Now tell me more about the conversation between Holly and Lance."

With a disappointed sigh, Xonia stretched her fuzzy body along the arm of the sofa. "Well, Lance has convinced Holly that he's out of practice and needs tutoring. Strictly business, you understand."

Mini smiled. "And you think Holly is gullible enough to believe him?"

Xonia shrugged. "If she does, it's because she wants to."

"I doubt Lance can pull the wool over Holly's eyes."

"I doubt it, too—*if* that's what he's trying to do."

Xonia's tail swished quietly back and forth as she contemplated the scene she'd witnessed. Finally she said, "I'm not so sure he's conning her."

"Really?"

"Just an instinct." Xonia narrowed her golden eyes at Mini. "Are you sure you don't want to know where Reuben is?"

"I'm sure."

Resolutely Mini resumed her reading.

"You're nervous," Casey observed, lounging in the doorway of Lance's bedroom.

"I'm not nervous." Frowning absently, Lance glanced around the clothes-strewn bedroom. "What did I do with that damned tie?"

With a smirk, Casey pointed to Lance's chest. "You're wearing it, you goof. I can't believe she agreed to go out with you."

"I can. She believes I need tutoring."

"Ah, so that's how you convinced her."

"It wasn't a lie," Lance said, smoothing an imaginary wrinkle in his shirt. He lifted his socks from the bed and inspected them for holes. "I *am* out of practice. Look what happened on my date with Terri. It turned out to be a disaster."

"That wasn't your fault, Lance. The credit card companies admitted to having a glitch in their computers. They straightened it all out, didn't they?"

"Yeah, but *both* companies had glitches on the same night. What are the odds of that happening?" Lance still found it hard to believe. His gaze strayed to the photo of Mona he kept on his nightstand. "Maybe it was an omen," he mumbled, staring at the smiling blonde in the picture. His throat tightened, and an old familiar grief threatened to swamp him.

For the first time in four years, he fought against the tide.

Casey straightened and walked into the room. "I can't believe I heard that. You forget I knew Mona, too, and she would have wanted you to go on with your life, find someone else. The *last* thing she would have wanted you to do is mope around for four rotten years."

"I didn't mope," Lance denied, adjusting the brown-and-white-striped tie. He frowned at his reflection. What had he been thinking when he bought this tie? It was boring, and definitely not his colors. With a muffled curse, he quickly unraveled the knot and ripped it off, striding to the closet in search of something brighter.

"Okay, so you didn't mope. You nearly worked yourself to death with those kids."

"It's my job, Casey. I *like* my job." Most days, anyway.

"Whatever. And don't try to change the subject. You are not being unfaithful to Mona." He paused a beat before adding, "She's gone, Lance."

Lance flinched at Casey's raw statement. He knew his friend meant no harm, but sometimes he could be damned insensitive. "I think we're getting ahead of ourselves here. I'm going on a date—not getting married. As a matter of fact, marriage is the furthest thing from my mind." Okay, so that wasn't *quite* the truth. Since meeting Holly, it had crossed his mind a time or two.

"I wonder if Holly Wentworth knows that."

Casting him an exasperated look, Lance said, "Of course she knows it. She also knows my blood type . . . and what size pantyhose I wear."

"Very funny."

Lance finished arranging the tie around his neck and gave it one final tug. This tie had tiny blue diamonds scattered across a deep red background. Definitely brighter, he decided. He turned around to face Casey. "How do I look?"

"Nervous as hell," Casey said without hesitation.

"It shows that much?"

Casey's lips twitched; his gaze dropped, and his eyebrows rose. "Nice boxers. I always preferred cotton to silk, myself."

"Nice—" Lance followed his gaze, dismayed as he caught Casey's meaning.

He'd forgotten his pants.

Seven

She must have gotten the wrong size pantyhose, Holly decided, blowing out a hot, frustrated breath as she struggled to work the irritating material over her calves. Finally she admitted defeat and snatched up the empty package lying on the bed beside her, glaring at it. She found the word "petite" in tiny block letters in the far left-hand corner.

With a snort, she tossed the package across the room. Nike made a mad dash for it, skidding across the slick surface of the hardwood floor and nearly smacking into the far wall.

Holly watched the retriever's comical antics for a moment, trying to find humor in her situation. Petite she wasn't. She was of average height and weight, with curvy calves and rounded hips—a little *too* rounded, in her mind. The pantyhose she'd bought would come closer to fitting Nike.

She grinned, imagining the golden retriever slipping around in her pantyhose.

Just as she was contemplating her dilemma, the doorbell pealed. She gave a start and darted a swift glance at the clock on her nightstand. Fifteen till eight. Not yet time for Lance.

Mrs. Teasedale, popping up for her nightly chat? Probably. Sighing, she slipped the pantyhose from her legs and bunched them in her hand, trying to remember if Mrs. Teasedale wore pantyhose. She and the widow were close to the same size. Maybe she could borrow a pair.

Nike raced ahead of her, his tail wagging furiously. Obviously she wasn't the only one expecting Mrs. Teasedale; the widow often brought him a treat.

But it wasn't Mrs. Teasedale, Holly discovered when she opened the door. It was her date. All six feet plus of him, filling her doorway with his breathtaking physique. He looked anxious. Or was it eager? Yeah, right. Who was she trying to fool? Lance wanted to get back in the groove so that he could spread his considerable charms around to the ladies. He'd as much as confessed this to Reuben at the end of the interview.

She was nothing but a stepping-stone, something she'd be wise to keep in mind.

Nike halted his forward leap in the nick of time when he realized it wasn't Mrs. Teasedale. He sat on his haunches and regarded the stranger with slight suspicion.

Lance looked from Nike to Holly, then back to Nike. He held out a cautious hand for the retriever to sniff. "Your roommate, I presume?"

"Yes, this is Nike. Nike, meet Lance Wilder."

Nike promptly held up his paw. Laughing, Lance shook hands and ruffled Nike's golden fur. "Hey, a dog who likes me. Maybe I've improved with age." He straightened and focused on Holly. "I know I'm early but I was hoping I'd get lucky and you'd be ready." His gaze dropped to the bunched pantyhose in her hand, then did a double take on her flushed, reddened face. "Having trouble?"

His all-too-accurate guess surprised her. The struggle with pantyhose must be a universal complaint, she thought, reminding herself that he'd been married. *Not* something she needed to forget.

Holly shoved her hand behind her back, along with the embarrassing wad of pantyhose. "Ah, no, I was just about to put . . . them on," she lied. How had they gotten into such an intimate conversation so soon? She hadn't even invited him in!

"Need help?"

A sharp retort hovered on the tip of her tongue before she caught the gleam of amusement in his eyes. With a rueful smile she relaxed and waved him into the room. He was teasing her, and she'd been ready to bite his head off. It wasn't *his* fault she hadn't been paying attention when she bought those damned pantyhose. Shaking her finger at him, she said in a mock-warning tone, "Lesson number one: Don't interfere with a woman and her pantyhose."

He stepped over the threshold into her small living room, his gaze lingering on her lightly tanned legs. "You don't need pantyhose."

"Yeah, and I suppose the next thing you're going to say is that I don't need makeup, either?"

"Fishing for compliments?" he countered with a lazy lift of his brow.

Obviously he'd gotten over his anxiety attack, Holly thought dryly. "No, it's just that a lot of men feel as if they have to tell that lie just to make a woman feel better."

"I take it you're not one of those women?"

She shook her head, struggling not to laugh. "No, I'm not. I wouldn't believe you anyway." He dipped his hands in his pockets and sauntered closer, lowering his gaze to her mouth. Holly caught herself as her body started to sway toward him as if she were a magnet and his chest was made of steel. Staring at the hard outline of his pectoral muscles beneath his shirt at close range, she could almost believe it *was* made of something more solid than flesh and bone.

"I'm not one of those men, Holly. And I can *honestly* say that your lips are a sexy, natural red without lipstick."

His gaze continued to focus on her mouth, and Holly's breathing became shallow with anticipation. He was staring at her mouth as if he was thinking about kissing her. Would she let him? Did she want him to?

Yes!

When he spoke again he'd dropped his voice to a low, seductive whisper. Her eyelids drooped of their own accord.

"You have very kissable lips."

Did that mean what she thought it meant? Did he want to—

"How am I doing so far?"

She snapped her eyes open wide at the sudden, jarring buoyancy of his voice. Thank God her cheeks were already red from her exertions with the pantyhose! She cleared her throat. "I think maybe you're moving too fast."

At her husky comment, he moved away, looking so disappointed she felt a stab of guilt.

"Am I? You think that's what happened with Terri?"

"Did . . . did you tell Terri she didn't need lipstick?"

He frowned and shook his head.

"Did you stare at her mouth as if—as if you intended to kiss her?" God, had she really said those words out loud? And with such obvious disappointment? The man didn't seem to have a clue about how he affected her! Or . . . did he?

Again he shook his head. "I didn't think about kissing her."

Holly let out a slow breath of relief, her face burning. And to think she had the rest of the evening to get through without revealing her increasing attraction to this man. "Well, maybe you should take it a little slower," she suggested. Before her makeup melted from her face.

"You're probably right." He hunkered down and began to stroke Nike, who promptly rolled onto his back and offered his belly. "I'll wait here while you finish getting ready," he said. "Nike will keep me company."

Watching his big hands stroke the dog, Holly swallowed an unreasonable knot of jealousy. Neither dog nor man seemed to notice when she left them.

Mini and Xonia sat around the small dining table observing the scene between Holly and Lance. Reuben was still missing in action, and Mini's wifely concern had progressed to the dangerous, seething boil of an angry witch.

Lucky for her husband that she was powerless in her anger. She'd once lost her temper and turned him into a lovebird. The peacemaker for the witches' council hadn't been happy with their petty squabbling and had sentenced them both to live as lovebirds for several weeks in a gilded cage.

Although the adventure had turned out to be a lesson in love for all involved—including the mortals they'd helped reunite—Reuben had never let her forget that *she* had been responsible for their predicament.

This time her temper hadn't been responsible. But unlike Reuben, Mini didn't rub it in at every opportunity that it was *his* poor judgment that had gotten them into this latest scrape. Now she was tempted to remind her husband that she could have kept her powers and left him to serve his sentence alone.

Mini ground her teeth in frustration—over her loss of powers and her errant husband.

How dare he worry her this way? Then again, she knew that if Reuben was in trouble, Xonia, as his protector, would not only tell Mini, but would race to his rescue.

Which meant her worry was in vain—and that he was an inconsiderate, insensitive oaf.

Xonia broke into her murderous thoughts. "Do you think we should go along and keep an eye on the lovebirds?" Before a startled Mini could answer, Xonia added slyly, "But then, you probably don't want to be gone when Reuben returns. We wouldn't want the poor, powerless warlock to worry."

Mini narrowed her cat-green eyes at Xonia. "I never knew you possessed such a mean streak, Xonia."

Affronted, Xonia leaped onto the table and began circling the crystal ball, her tail flicking back and forth. "I don't know what you mean. I merely suggested—"

"*Challenged,* Xonia. You challenged me. And don't think that I don't realize you'd like nothing better than for Reuben to come home to an empty house, wondering where I'd gone." She secretly agreed that it would serve Reuben right, but she knew that Xonia needed no further encouragement in antagonizing her husband.

"We could leave him a note," Xonia suggested. "After all, you can't be expected to miss an opportunity like this just because he's—"

The rest of her words were muffled by Mini's firmly clamped hand. After a warning glare, she removed it. "If you tell me where he is, that's as good as *me* spying. So don't. And for your information, I had already decided to follow Holly and Lance, so don't get it into your feline head that I'm doing this because you dared me to, or because I'm giving Reuben a taste of his own medicine." It wasn't the total truth, but Mini didn't think her nerves could stand a gloating Xonia.

Xonia sat on her haunches, curling her tail around the crystal ball and emitting a low, satisfied purr. "So, we're going to go?"

"We'll have to have a disguise."

"Do you still have that gold charm bracelet Reuben gave you for your birthday last year?"

"Yes."

"Then it's as good as done."

"Let me write a note, then."

Xonia lifted her tail, ever helpful. "Let me—"

"*I'll* do it," Mini interrupted, disappearing into the bedroom for pen and paper. She was already thinking about what she would say in her note. Something lighthearted and casual, she mused, as if she hadn't had a care in the world since he'd left the apartment over three hours ago.

Angrily she wiped a misguided tear from her cheek. *Insufferable warlock!*

• • •

She was stunning and didn't know it, Lance mused as he stared at Holly across the flickering candle flame. She wore her thick brown hair straight and parted on the side so that when she bent her head, it shadowed her face in an uncalculated yet coy way that made his gut clench with longing. He suspected the dress she wore beneath her short jacket would reveal soft, rounded shoulders and just a hint of cleavage, but to his disappointment, she'd opted not to remove her jacket when they were seated.

He wanted to reach across the table and cup her chin, look into her gorgeous gray eyes and tell her just how sexy she looked to him, but in the end he decided to heed her advice about moving too fast. He'd finally convinced her to go out with him; he didn't want to risk alarming her before the evening started. For reasons he had yet to uncover, Holly Wentworth was determined to keep her distance.

Lance let a contented sigh slip between his lips. He felt as if he was awakening after a deep sleep, and his suspicions that Holly was the cause grew stronger each time he was near her. Now, if only *she* would admit there was something going on between them. . . .

After an agonizing debate while getting dressed, Lance had decided to throw caution to the wind and take her to the relaxed atmosphere of a local sports bar and grill that served draft beer in frosted mugs and a wide variety of foods. With her consent, he'd ordered the house specialty: in-the-shell jumbo shrimp simmered in a spicy barbecue sauce.

A football game was in progress on the huge projection screen suspended from the ceiling, and occasional shouts and curses could be heard from a group of avid sports fans. There were perhaps two dozen or so people scattered around the room; the majority of them were male.

"Will you excuse me for a moment?" Holly asked, rising, "I need to find the powder room."

Lance directed her to the ladies' room with a nod,

shamelessly watching the interesting sway of her hips as she walked. She was built like Marilyn Monroe, he decided, smiling. Not fashionably thin, thank God. Curvy hips, nice bust line, great legs . . .

As she disappeared around a doorway, Lance's gaze skimmed briefly over a lone woman seated in the next booth.

The woman's odd green eyes triggered a vague memory. He frowned, trying to remember where he'd seen those eyes before. She was dressed in a pinstriped gray and black suit, and looked young, possibly in her late twenties. A chic black hat perched at a jaunty angle on top of her short cap of spun-gold hair. She wore a heavy gold charm bracelet around her wrist, and as she lifted her arm to take a sip of her beverage, Lance saw that one of the dangling charms was in the distinct shape of a cat.

He didn't know her, yet he couldn't get the niggling idea out of his head that he *should* know her. He looked at her again. It was the eyes, those odd-colored eyes. Of course, the woman probably wore tinted contacts, because eyes that shade of green had to be manufactured, he decided. He'd once counseled a teenager with startling purple eyes.

Holly slid into the booth and immediately followed his gaze. She lifted an inquiring brow when she sighted the chic blonde. "Homework already?" she asked.

He smiled and shook his head, wishing it were jealousy that had prompted her question, and knowing that it wasn't. "I thought I recognized the face, but I was wrong. So, what do you think of the place?"

She took a dainty sip of her foamy beer as she considered his question. When she set the mug down, there was a faint line of moisture clinging to her upper lip. Lance bit the inside of his jaw, wondering just how hard she'd slap him if he slipped into the booth beside her and licked the foam clean with his tongue.

"You made a good choice," she said, looking around approvingly. "Not too fancy, not too obvious, and if the gleam in your eye is any indication, the food will be excellent."

"Food has nothing to do with the gleam in my eye." He wiggled his eyebrows suggestively, enjoying her husky, spontaneous laugh. When her pink tongue made a quick sweep over her upper lip, Lance stifled a groan. *He'd* wanted to do that for her!

As if they'd conjured the food by talking about it, the waitress appeared at their table carrying a steaming casserole dish and two warm, wet towels folded across her arm. Balanced on her elbow was a plate of crusty rolls and a small crock of honey butter.

"What are the towels for?" Holly asked suspiciously.

The waitress left, and Lance wasted no time sliding into the booth next to Holly. Their thighs touched, and he was pleased to note she didn't jerk away. "Don't worry about the towels. You won't be needing them."

"I won't?" She cast a dubious look into the casserole dish.

"Nope." Innocent-faced, Lance carefully fished out a large, sauce-drenched shrimp and began to peel the shell away as he announced casually, "Because I'm going to feed you."

In the booth behind Holly and Lance, Mini pulled a cell phone from her purse, flipped it open, and pretended to dial a number. She then pressed the phone to her ear, bringing the charm bracelet almost even with her mouth so that Xonia, who was dangling from the bracelet in the shape of a cat, could hear her.

Keeping her voice low, she said, "That was close. For a moment I thought he recognized me."

Xonia's voice came through loud and clear—surprising, considering the fact that she was less than an inch long at the moment. "My fault. I should have changed the color of your eyes."

"It's too late now. Anyway, I think we should leave them alone." The couple had their backs to Mini, but she could almost *feel* the sexual tension sizzling between them. She smiled. "Looks like you-know-who has things well in hand."

"Ooh, turn your wrist so that *I* can see!" Xonia demanded. "The damned phone is in the way!"

Mini laughed. "I didn't mean that literally, my friend. It's a figure of speech. Right now you-know-who has *shrimp* in his hand."

"Oh." Xonia sounded disappointed. "I thought we were going to see some action."

"Are you becoming a voyeur on me, Xonia?"

"No, I am not!" There was an indignant sniff, then Xonia said, "Do you think they'll do it tonight?"

Shaking her head at Xonia's crude question, Mini said, "I don't know, and if they do, it's none of our business. We're not here to watch mortals do . . . have . . ."

"Hot lusty sex?" Xonia supplied helpfully. Her screeching laughter nearly split Mini's eardrum. "You're turning into a prude, dear."

Her comment touched a sensitive cord in Mini, and sparked a worry. She bit her lip, forgetting to keep her voice low. "Xonia, do you really think I'm a prude?" When her friend remained silent for a moment too long, Mini asked sharply, "Xonia? Are you there?"

"Yes, I'm here."

Mini gripped the phone. "Why aren't you answering?"

"Well," Xonia began, sounding reluctant, "it's just that since we've been in Lovit, I haven't noticed much action between you and the warlock. You know—*hot* action."

The way she said "hot" brought a quick flush to Mini's cheeks. "We don't have any *privacy,* Xonia." She hadn't wanted to come right out and say it, but it was true. With Xonia living with them in the small apartment, Mini didn't feel comfortable making love. She suspected Reuben felt the same way. At least she *hoped* that was the reason he hadn't been amorous.

"Why didn't you say so?" Xonia cried, jingling the bracelet on Mini's hand for emphasis. "I could have been taking an evening stroll, watering a few bushes—"

"You're a cat, Xonia. Dogs water bushes. Cats prowl."

"Well, I can prowl, then. While I'm gone, you and the warlock can do—"

"I get the picture," Mini cut in hastily. "You won't get into trouble?"

"Me?" Xonia squeaked, as if she were amazed at the possibility.

"Yes, you. What if you run into a big mean tomcat in an alley somewhere?"

Xonia purred throatily into the phone. "Hmm. What an interesting scenario. Maybe we'll *all* get lucky tonight."

"Oh, you're impossible!" With an exasperated sigh, Mini snapped the phone together and grabbed her purse from the table, casting the couple one last satisfied glance before leaving.

As she passed by their table, she heard the faint sound of Xonia giggling. She shook her wrist in warning. Tonight, while the mortals were occupied with each other, she and Reuben would recapture the whole enchilada.

Her steps quickened with anticipation as she neared the exit.

Eight

Lance Wilder was going to hand-feed her the shrimp.

In her college days, Holly had once parachuted from a plane at ten thousand feet. She'd believed the paralyzing shock, the raw, almost giddy fear, and the wonderful anticipation she'd felt before and during the jump were a combination of emotions she'd never experience again.

She was wrong.

He was going to feed her the shrimp.

He couldn't have known how dry her mouth was, or that her hands were trembling where they lay in her lap, or that her teeth were on the verge of chattering.

He could also not have known that shortly after opening Romance Connection she had given in to temptation and filled out the interview forms on her idea of the perfect date. The results were safely locked in a file on her hard drive, and *she* was the only one who could open it.

The information was useless anyway, because she had known her fantasy man didn't exist.

Correction. She had *believed* he didn't exist. Now she wasn't so certain.

Somehow Lance Wilder knew what she wanted, how she wanted it, and when to deliver. He wore a sexy gold chain around his neck. He was handsome, and his butt was cute. He said all the right, mushy things she'd always wanted to hear, like how kissable her mouth looked. He'd kissed her without asking, without warning, and without a hint of hesitation.

And now he was about to hand-feed her—as if he knew about her silly little fantasy in which a gorgeous man with a cute, tight butt fed her juicy morsels as if she were a queen. *His* queen.

But of course he couldn't know. Impossible.

"Open those beautiful lips, Holly," Lance instructed in that knee-knocking voice of his as he twisted in the booth until their thighs were pressed tightly together.

Holly felt her lips part, although she was fairly certain she hadn't ordered them to. She watched through lowered lids and constricted lungs as he slowly slipped the warm, spicy shrimp between her lips.

"Now chew." He smiled crookedly as he watched her mouth, his expression one of boyish expectancy. "What do you think? Is it good?"

Is it good? Holly wanted to laugh helplessly as she nodded, but managed to hold herself together. It *was* good, but the shrimp wasn't the best part. Oh, no. In fact, she hardly tasted the food. The texture of his fingers as they touched her lips and the simple, erotic act of his feeding her were the best parts. He could have been feeding her snails, and she would gladly have eaten them, as long as he did the feeding.

A small, wistful sigh escaped her lips as she thought about the rest of her fantasy. In her impossible fantasy, he'd slowly kiss her mouth after each—

He leaned forward and placed his mouth gently on hers, sending her thoughts to a crashing, incredulous halt. She felt his tongue as it made a slow, leisurely sweep across her lips. Holly was on the verge of lifting her arms and saying to hell with their audience, his late wife, *and* her ethics, when he broke the contact.

"Now you know why you don't need the towels."

"Yes, I do." Holly cleared the huskiness from her throat, reminding herself that she was the teacher, and he was the student. A very talented student, at that. "Do— do you come here often?" Did he used to bring his wife? Had he fed her shrimp until her bones melted like butter in the sun? Had he kissed her mouth clean afterward? These questions and more whirled inside her head, but Holly knew she had no business asking them. They were not only personal, but probably painful as well. For both of them.

A very *good* reason she shouldn't be thinking the thoughts she was thinking!

"I come here when I get a hankering for shrimp," he said as he peeled another and popped it into his mouth. Then he fished around in the bowl and withdrew a particularly plump specimen.

This one, she knew, would be for her. Holly swallowed hard and sternly tamped down the anticipation. It didn't work. She watched him with the eagerness of a child waiting for an ice cream cone, and when his fingers touched her lips, her tongue turned traitor, seeking to lick the sauce from his fingers as her teeth latched onto the shrimp.

Holly froze at the contact, her gaze darting up to lock with his. The blue of his eyes had darkened to a deep violet; his lids had dropped to half-mast.

"I'm beginning to think this was a bad idea," he said, the low timbre of his voice sending sparks shooting through her veins.

Her heart began to pound fiercely. She licked her lips and averted her gaze, wondering how one simple dinner with Lance Wilder could turn her into a panting, sex-starved she-cat. Praying he wouldn't notice her shaking hands, she reached for her beer. "What—what do you mean?"

"Feeding you brings out the beast in me. It makes me want to grab you and carry you out of here."

Sipping desperately on her beer, Holly slanted him an

innocent look. "Really?" His faint grin told her that she wasn't a very good actress.

"Am I moving too fast?"

"Depends on the woman, I suppose." Holly mentally cursed her wicked tongue. She should have just told him that, yes, he was moving too fast. He would have gotten the hint and saved his seductive talents for the next woman.

Which is precisely why she didn't tell him.

"Am I moving too fast for *you*?"

Well, what had she expected after her provocative comment? Holly pretended a great interest in the frost sliding down the side of her mug as she considered her answer. Finally, and with great reluctance, she said, "I'm not the issue, am I?" Before he could answer yet another provocative question she hadn't meant to ask, she hurried on, "I mean, it wouldn't be fair of me to set an example, when the next woman might—" Might what? Holly bit her lip. What woman *wouldn't* want to be hand-fed by a man as if he thought she was something special? *Especially* if that man was someone like Lance Wilder?

She shook her head and started over, determined to keep this date in the proper perspective. It wouldn't be fair to Lance if she didn't answer honestly. "Scratch that. I can only answer for myself." She took a deep breath as he began to peel another shrimp. "So far I like the way you move just fine," she blurted out, bold as brass.

Gulp.

"Ah."

Leaving her in suspense after that single syllable, he took his time eating the shrimp, wiping his hands on the wet towel when he was finished before beginning the peeling process all over again.

Her turn. And, yes, there it was. That fluttering, excited feeling all over again. The man was lethal. How many more of those damned shrimp were left? She was beginning to sweat.

Fifteen torturous minutes later, Lance finished the last shrimp and moved to his own seat so that he was facing her once again. Only then did Holly's breathing return to normal and her heart rate decrease. She reached for one of the towels and carefully wiped her mouth. He hadn't kissed her after the first time. She didn't know which she felt more keenly—disappointment or relief.

Lance draped his arms along the top of the booth and regarded her with an enigmatic expression that made her want to squirm. What was he planning next? A romantic walk in the park under a full moon? Dessert in front of a seductive, crackling fire? Could her rattled system handle the overload? Holly stifled a nervous laugh at her analogy.

"Holly . . ."

She tensed, wishing she had insisted on using an alias for this date. Hearing her name from his lips made it very hard to remember this wasn't a *real* date.

"Do you swim?"

"Yes, but I don't have a suit." Holly grabbed the excuse like a lifeline. Swimming with Lance was definitely out of the question. It was difficult enough to resist him with his clothes *on*.

"Don't worry, I'm sure I have something you can wear."

Before she could form a protest, he was out of the booth, reaching for her hand. He pulled her up with little effort.

"Come on." He smiled into her startled face. "The night is young, and so are we."

Damn, even his clichés turned her on. She finally found her voice. "But I—"

He silenced her protest with a kiss. When he pulled away he explained, "You had sauce on your mouth."

But Holly knew that wasn't true, because she'd just wiped her mouth with the wet towel. She was grateful to note that at least *part* of her brain was still functioning. "I did not," she argued faintly.

"Okay. I confess, I kissed you because I couldn't help myself."

Holly stifled an exasperated chuckle and allowed him to tug her along the aisles between the booths. When they reached the register, Holly couldn't resist muttering in an undertone only Lance could hear, "I hope you brought cash."

His startled expression made her laugh out loud, and the look that followed promised retribution for her wise comment. Considering the impressive . . . talents he'd displayed so far, Holly didn't dare dwell on just what form this retribution would take.

The apartment was eerily quiet when Reuben let himself in through the door leading into the kitchen. Scanning the shadowy room, lit only by a low-watt bulb over the range, he let out a sigh of relief to find it empty. Good. If he could manage to get out of his clothes and get them into the washing machine before Mini could see them, his secret would be safe. Otherwise, he'd have to explain where he'd been and what he'd been doing.

Leaving his shoes by the back door, Reuben crept across the tiled floor to the small utility room that housed the compact washer and dryer. He eased the door open and slipped inside, closing it behind him before turning on the overhead light. Frowning, he studied the appliances, wishing he'd listened more closely to Mini's instructions. How hard could it be? With a shrug, he lifted the lid on the washer and began to remove his shirt and pants. The pants were probably okay, but he didn't want to take any chances.

He stuffed the clothes around the agitator and grabbed the box of soap from the shelf above the washer. One cup, or two? To be on the safe side, he added two, then another for good measure. It surely couldn't hurt, he decided with another careless shrug.

Reuben closed the lid, then turned the knob and made a rough guess before stopping. He pushed down, and was relieved when he heard the sound of running water. He dusted his hands, turned out the light, and left the utility room, clad in a pair of cotton briefs.

As a witch he'd worn nothing but the finest silk or satin against his skin. His mouth tightened at the memory. No sense whining about it, as Mini often reminded him.

He found his wife fast asleep in their bed, a paperback book resting against her chest. Reuben hovered over her, his throat constricting at the sight of her short, tousled hair and flushed, beautiful face. The black fan of her lashes lay against her cheek, casting mysterious shadows against her skin. His eyes moved down her body in a familiar, loving perusal, going wide when he realized that Mini was naked beneath the sheet. His brows rose in a silent question, then swooped down as realization dawned.

Mini had tried to wait up for him because she'd wanted to make love.

Guilt swamped him. Mentally flaying himself with curses, he lifted the book and set it on the nightstand, then turned off the light. Silently he tiptoed from the room. He'd make himself a quick snack, then join Mini. With soft, well-placed kisses, he'd awaken his sleeping—

He stopped in the doorway to the kitchen, staring in horror at the white foam creeping from beneath the utility door. Scratching his bewildered head, Reuben slowly approached the door and pulled it open.

A mountain of white foam rushed over his legs and into the kitchen. Startled, he let out a yelp and stumbled back. His bare feet slipped out from beneath him on the slick floor. He felt himself falling backward, flailing his arms in a vain attempt to recapture his balance.

An invisible hand planted itself in the middle of his back and propelled him upward with amazing strength. Reuben nearly toppled forward from the force, but managed to grab the doorway in the nick of time.

He glanced quickly around, searching the shadowy in-

terior of the kitchen for his savior. The only one capable
of magic was that damned ugly cat, and he knew she had
to be close. It was humiliating for someone of his stature
to be forced to rely on a familiar.

Beneath the small dining table, he found her, as he had
known he would. The cat crouched on the tile, her golden
eyes glowing in the dim light. He saw her tail twitch, and
when he looked down again, the foam was gone.

Reuben came from a long, infamous line of arrogant
warlocks, and although he'd pledged to put his warlock
ways behind him and become a good witch when he married Mini, words of gratitude did not emerge easily from
his mouth. He forced them out anyway, not wishing to be
beholden to this creature who flaunted powers that he no
longer possessed.

"Thank you," he growled, albeit grudgingly. It was difficult to hide his jealousy.

The cat blinked, and for a moment she simply stared
at him with those strange gold eyes as if assessing his
sincerity. Finally she nodded. Her tail rose and twitched.
A sandwich appeared in Reuben's right hand, a glass of
cold milk in the left. He nearly dropped the milk in his
surprise.

It was the first kind gesture the familiar had demon-
strated. Hastily covering his surprise, Reuben took a ten-
tative bite of the sandwich, half expecting to find it
empty. It wasn't. Chewing and swallowing, Reuben continued to stare at the cat. Finally he asked, "Is she very
angry?"

The cat nodded, hesitated, then shook her head.

Puzzled by her contradictory answer, Reuben sipped his
milk. It was fresh and cold, just the way he liked it. "She's
mad . . . but she's not mad?"

Again the cat nodded, then shook her head.

In a burst of exasperation, Reuben asked, "Why won't
you talk to me? I know that you speak to Mini."

A note appeared in front of him. Reuben scrambled
to snatch it before it fell to the floor, nearly dropping

both the sandwich and the milk. He finally caught it with his little finger. He moved to the table and pulled out a chair.

The cat leaped into the opposite chair, regarding him across the table. Setting the milk aside, Reuben read the note while continuing to eat his sandwich. When he'd finished, he looked at the cat. "She's not only mad, but hurt, and you won't talk to me because you're not allowed. Who says? The witches' counsel?" He frowned, honestly bewildered when she confirmed his guess with a slight nod. "But why would they make such a stipulation? What harm could be done by talking?"

Shrugging, she jumped to the floor and onto the windowsill above the sink. For the first time, Reuben noticed that the window was open. She gave him one last, mysterious glance before disappearing through the window into the night.

The window lowered slowly; the lock clicked into place.

Left alone, Reuben let out a bewildered sigh and reached for his milk. He caught sight of the note he'd placed on the table and realized the words had changed. *"You've got two hours alone with Mini before I return. If I were you, I'd make the most of it."*

"Bossy feline," Reuben muttered, draining the last of his milk. He rinsed the glass and put it in the dishwasher before making his way to the bedroom. Along the way, he began to perk up as the familiar's meaning began to sink in.

That "bossy feline" had just given him two hours alone with his *naked* wife. Maybe the familiar wasn't such a bad sort after all. She *had* saved him from a nasty fall and eliminated a mess that might have taken him hours to clean up the mortal way.

And she had made him a sandwich.

Reuben forced himself to consider that he might have to rethink his opinion about familiars in the form of cats.

After all, she wasn't *truly* a cat. Somewhere beneath her furry chest beat the heart of a witch.

Which reminded him: Those golden eyes still seemed *awfully* familiar. . . .

Nine

⌣

"It's beautiful." Holly's voice held a touch of awe. She stood in the foyer of Lance's home and made a slow circle, her appreciative gaze noting the overall elegance of the decor. Chandeliers, gleaming marble floors, curving staircases, and dark mahogany wood combined to create a rich, hushed atmosphere.

Lance barely glanced around before shrugging. "It's stuffy, and too big, but I haven't had time to place it on the market."

"You're going to sell it?"

"It's too big for one person," Lance repeated as if to convince himself. "Come on, let's go see what I have in the way of swimsuits."

Holly followed him along a well-lighted hall, then through what she determined must be a music room, and finally into another room. She caught her breath. One entire wall was glass, from ceiling to floor. Through a set of patio doors, she could see the outdoor pool. It was also well lighted, surrounded by foliage and waterfalls instead of concrete and vinyl. Water tumbled from the falls and into the glimmering blue depths of the pool, creating ripples along the surface. Holly felt an odd disorientation as she looked at the pool, as if she had stumbled upon a hidden paradise in the middle of an asphalt jungle.

"This is the sunroom, which also serves as a bathing house," Lance explained, opening another door into a huge closet. He began to sift through a small rack of garments. "The bar is right behind you, if you'd like to make us a drink."

More than a little overwhelmed, Holly pivoted to face the east wall, where there was a well-stocked bar backlit by gleaming mirrors. Her throat *was* dry, but she doubted it had to do with thirst. How foolish she was to think Lance Wilder would do anything as mundane as take a romantic walk in the moonlight.

He had much bigger ammunition!

Curbing the impulse to run like a coward, Holly approached the bar and carefully looked through the selection. Anything alcoholic was out of the question. She wasn't a big drinker, and the beer she'd had at the sports bar was just about her limit for one night.

Besides, she suspected she would need her wits about her.

"What would you like?" she asked without turning around. Maybe he wouldn't find anything in her size; she didn't relish wearing a swimsuit that another woman had worn, especially if that woman was his dearly departed.

"Orange juice over ice, please."

Relieved at his choice, Holly prepared two glasses of orange juice. Finding the ice bucket filled with sparkling cubes gave her a moment's pause. Lance either had a very conscientious maid, or he'd planned ahead.

The latter possibility made her stomach quiver with shameful anticipation; she quickly squashed it with brutal logic. Of course he'd planned ahead—just as he would have been wise to have had this been a real date.

She turned around with the drinks and found him holding up two swimsuits for her inspection. Both were one-piece, she noted with relief. She hesitated, reluctant to voice her dismay at wearing either one.

"They didn't belong to her," Lance informed her quietly, guessing her thoughts. "She kept them on hand for extra guests."

"Her" and "she." Holly searched his bland expression, wondering why he didn't mention his wife by name. Too painful? Too personal?

"I can look again if you'd like."

Holly shook her head, feeling foolish for constantly questioning his motives. He had given her no reason for her suspicions. In fact, it was the first time he'd mentioned the former Mrs. Wilder at all. He'd laughed and played, had even kissed her in a public place—not the actions of a man still grieving for his deceased wife. She forced herself to admit that she was picking, looking for an excuse to run. Why not just forget and have fun? Wasn't that why she accepted the date in the first place? Because she wanted to spend time with Lance?

Taking a deep breath, she chose the black suit, ever conscious of her curvy hips. The other suit was bright yellow, cut high on the thigh, a style she avoided like the plague.

He exchanged the orange juice for the suit and showed her into a small changing closet/bathroom. When she emerged a few moments later, he had already changed into a pair of aqua-blue nylon swimming trunks.

He was firm everywhere, Holly observed, swallowing hard. At least he'd removed the gold chain from around his neck. A half-naked Lance *with* the sexy gold chain around his neck might have done her in. She almost giggled at her silly thought.

His heated gaze made a leisurely sweep over her body, and by the time he had finished, Holly felt herself blushing.

"Turn around," he ordered softly.

Holly fought the urge to dart back into the changing room. "Why?" she asked, forcing herself to look him in the eye. She wasn't ashamed of her body, but she wasn't *that* confident! Besides, she'd discovered that the suit revealed much more of her back than she felt comfortable with. She suspected now that he had known it would.

"Just turn around."

With an exasperated sigh, Holly did as he asked and presented her back. A shiver trailed down her exposed spine, as if she could feel the heated stroke of his gaze. That damnable quivering started again in her belly, spreading to her legs and leaving them weak.

"Just as I suspected," he announced in a husky, satisfied tone that made her jump. "Dimples."

Swinging back around, Holly stared at him in confusion. "Dimples?" Was he talking about her *butt*? Sure, she'd gained a few pounds in the last few years, but she hadn't been aware of any—

"In your back," Lance explained. "You've got dimples in the small of your back. I have a thing for dimpled backs."

"Oh, you do, do you?" Holly arched a playful brow, relaxing at the sight of his crooked smile. "You're a fabulous flirt, you know." "Fabulous" was an understatement, but Holly didn't think it would be wise to overdo it.

He seemed surprised by her comment. "I am?"

Holly wasn't convinced by his innocent tone—or by the faint blush that seemed to be darkening his cheeks. Surely it was her imagination? "Stop fishing for compliments," she said, snatching her orange juice from the edge of the bar where he'd put it. No way was this man unaware of his charisma. Impossible . . . or was it? He'd professed to have been practically celibate for the last four years. Perhaps he *didn't* know?

Moving soundlessly, Lance appeared at her side and removed her drink from her hand. He cupped her waist and turned her around to face him. Holly's mouth went dry as she gazed at his tanned, handsome face.

"Did you mean what you said?" he persisted, sounding earnest. "Or are you just feeding a client's starving ego?"

Holly licked her lips, oh-so-conscious of his warm hands at her waist and his beautiful, bare chest just inches away. "I meant it." His hands shifted slightly upward;

weakness flooded her knees just thinking about how little space separated his hands from the underside of her breasts.

Slowly he pulled her against him until they were hip to hip. Holly caught her breath, then bit down on her bottom lip to keep it inside her. She could feel his semi-arousal against her as if they were naked—which they nearly were. Lance seemed to be asking a silent question by showing her the state he was in.

Holly knew the answer, although it pained her to voice it. "This . . . this is just a dry run, Lance. I don't think we should carry this farce too far." A reminder they both needed, apparently. At least *one* part of him needed reminding!

He arched a brow, his gaze intense and unwavering on her face. "Point taken. So . . . hypothetically speaking, if you were my *real* date, how would you respond right now?"

Wildly, Holly nearly blurted out. Her breath came quickly—revealingly. He would know if she lied, unless he was deaf, blind, and dumb. Which he wasn't. She settled for a half-truth and a casual laugh she hoped would help dispel a little of the sexual tension between them. "If I were your real date, I'd probably be tempted to . . . put my arms around your neck and relax against you." Before the spark in his eyes could fully ignite, Holly rushed on. "*But* I wouldn't do it."

"Why not?"

"Because I don't know you." At least that much was the truth, Holly thought. "So I would probably pull away." Which she did, despite the slight resistance of his hands and her brain. His arms fell slowly to his sides. "And then I would suggest we go for that swim."

The lusty, regretful sigh that exploded through his lips was purely male. It made her smile.

Threading his fingers between hers, he tugged her through the patio doors and in the direction of the pool. "You're the teacher. Let's go swimming."

• • •

Casey was right, Lance conceded after a half hour of pool play with Holly: He'd waited too long to come out of mourning. And Holly was just what the doctor ordered. She was like a blast of cool air on a sunburn. Welcoming, refreshing, soothing, and healing.

Lance pushed wet hair from his eyes and searched for Holly beneath the water. He spotted her, swimming desperately for the other side. With a mighty lunge, he dove beneath the water and caught her ankle. She broke the surface, sputtering and laughing.

He caught her close, reveling in the feel of her skin against his. They were both breathing hard from their exertion, and the close contact didn't help matters. He sensed that the attraction went both ways. Why did she fight it? Unless there was someone else? On the day of the interview, Reuben had hinted strongly that Holly was as free as a bird. Only he'd said "duck," not "bird." Lance grinned at the memory. Mini and Reuben were certainly . . . different.

"Getting tired?" Lance asked, his gaze shifting to the swell of her heaving breasts. When she nodded, he pulled her on top of him and backpedaled to the ladder, ignoring her laughing protests. He helped her up and handed her a towel, then grabbed one for himself.

"I haven't been swimming in ages," she confessed, squeezing water from her hair. Water sluiced from her slick skin and ran in rivulets between her breasts.

Lance decided he liked the suit she'd chosen. Liked it *very* much. He liked what was in it, too. In fact, there wasn't anything about Holly Wentworth that he *didn't* like so far. Well, she could have been a little less stubborn, he decided on second thought. And a little more honest with him. He didn't believe for a moment that outrageous flattery earlier about his being a fabulous flirt. He was woefully out of practice, and he knew it.

That was possibly why he kept striking out with Holly. She was just too kind to tell it to him straight. Maybe he *did* need to practice on other women before he asked her out again. Then maybe he wouldn't keep making the same blunders over and over again. It had been so long since he'd kept company with an attractive woman that just being near Holly made him a bundle of nerves, and when he was nervous, he sometimes acted impulsively.

In the bathing house, Holly disappeared into the changing room while he quickly shucked his swimming trunks and pulled on his pants and shirt. He smiled at her muffled and very pleased "Yes!" just seconds before he heard the hum of a hair dryer.

His smile faded as he slipped his gold chain around his neck. When they'd changed into swimsuits earlier, he'd discovered to his horror that he'd forgotten to remove the wedding ring from the chain. He'd then put the ring in his shirt pocket and hoped to God she hadn't noticed it earlier. Now, shaking his head again at the near miss, Lance checked that the ring was still safe in his pocket and tucked the chain into his shirt collar. He was pulling on his shoes as she emerged, looking happy, flushed, and truly gorgeous.

His smile returned. "You lied."

"Excuse me?"

"You *do* look great without makeup."

She lifted a self-conscious hand to her face. "Oh, I forgot. I probably look a wreck, and *you* are probably as blind as a bat."

"I can see just fine," he argued softly, itching to run his hands through her newly dried hair. "Ready for a walk in the garden?"

"You have a *garden*?"

He nodded, slightly embarrassed by her astonishment. People assumed he was wealthy because he owned a twenty-room mansion. What they didn't know was that it took a big chunk of his income every month to keep it running. He was far from wealthy, which didn't particularly bother him. He wasn't interested in becoming a billionaire like most of his colleagues. Though new tires would be nice, he thought ruefully, remembering the appointment he'd missed last week as a result of a flat.

"Ready?" He held out his hand, anticipating the warmth of her skin against his own. It was as warm as he'd expected, and soft. "It's this way." He led her back through the patio doors, around the pool, and down a cobblestone path. The ethereal glow of cleverly hidden torches lit the way.

Hand in hand, they walked in silence for a moment. The air was warm and fragrant, and overhead the moon hung heavy and full against a poster-perfect starlit night. Holly tilted her head and stared at the sky. Lance saw her mouth curve in a faint, mysterious smile.

"A penny for your thoughts," he murmured, his mouth watering at the sight of her creamy neck. He felt like a vampire on his first date.

She cast him a startled look. Her smile widened with a hint of mischief. "I was just thinking of how your date will react to this moonlit walk."

"And?"

"I think maybe this will be the best part for her."

Up ahead on the path was the gazebo. Lance spotted the dark shape and steered her in that direction before asking, "What about you?"

"I like it just fine."

He loved the way she said "just fine," with that slight southern accent. "Good, because there's more."

"More?"

"Yes, more. Watch your step," he instructed, leading her into the gazebo. Once inside, he opened a hidden panel in one of the posts and pushed a button. Soft music began to play. Above them, the ceiling of the gazebo parted in the middle, the panels sliding slowly open to reveal the sky.

Holly's startled, breathless little laugh heated his blood.

"Are you this thorough in *everything* you do?"

Lance closed the panel and turned, then captured her in his arms. He pulled her close, and they began to sway to the music in a slow, tender dance. With his lips hovering near her ear, he answered honestly, suspecting she'd be amused. "You wouldn't believe how fast I can move when I have only two hours to prepare for a date with a beautiful woman." She rewarded him with a husky chuckle in *his* ear, which had a devastating effect on his determination to behave.

"Seriously, Lance. If you're looking for a casual relationship, I think you would have had me—I mean your date—hooked when you fed her the shrimp. Maybe *too* hooked."

When she snuggled her head into his shoulder, Lance stifled a moan. She didn't seem to notice. Somewhere in the night—somewhere close—he heard the startled yelp of a dog, followed by the frightened yowl of a cat. The sounds stopped abruptly.

"So you might want to consider dinner and a movie the first time around," she mumbled. "Some women might be a bit overwhelmed by the house." Tilting her head, she stared at the moon. "And this."

"Are you overwhelmed, Holly?"

She hesitated. "I might be if this were real, which we both know it isn't."

Lance lifted her chin, gently coaxing her to look at him. Their faces were mere inches apart. Soft moonlight made her eyes appear to glisten, and her full, red lips tempted him to taste and touch. Lance could feel her heart thundering where her breasts pressed softly against his chest.

His voice came out husky and low as he said, "It *could* be real, Holly."

Just as softly, she replied, "But it isn't, Lance."

"Afraid?"

She lifted a brow at his taunt. "I prefer to think of it as being realistic."

"Are you always realistic?"

"Most of the time." She smiled, and his gaze dropped hungrily to her lips. "My father says it's one of my worst faults. But then, he's a dreamer."

"Nothing wrong with being a dreamer," Lance murmured, aching to find out what made this woman tick. "Since meeting you, I've had some very good dreams." He wasn't talking about the dreams associated with ambition, and judging by the slight flaring of her eyes, she knew it.

They swayed to the music, hip to hip. He had linked his arms around her waist, and her hands rested lightly on his shoulders. The snug fit of their bodies was almost too good to be true.

"When you originally became interested in girls," she asked, "did your parents ever warn you not to fall for the first girl who came along?"

Lance trailed his fingers along her spine, and felt satisfaction when she shivered and pressed closer. The lady was dynamite. "I vaguely remember my mother quoting something like that after my first heartbreak."

"It's good advice."

"I'm not a teenager," he countered.

"No, but correct me if I'm wrong: Am I the first woman you've brought here since . . . your wife died?"

He tensed. He knew it was a mistake the moment he did—because *she* tensed along with him—but it was a reaction he couldn't control. "Yes, you are, but I don't see the connection."

She hesitated, curling her fingers around the lapels of his shirt as if to anchor herself. "Four years is a long time to be alone. I'm the first woman you've brought here. Your judgment could be clouded; it's sort of like the rebound theory—"

He shut her up by kissing her. When he finally lifted his head, they were both breathing fast and hard. He leaned his forehead against hers as they struggled to breathe. "Still believe in your theory?" he whispered.

She answered him by throwing her head back, giving his hungry lips access to her throat. Lance eagerly obliged. He was hot and hard by the time his lips reached the creamy tops of her breasts. Hell, that was a lie—he'd been hard since the day he met her.

Funneling his hands through her hair, he brought her head forward to drink from her luscious mouth again. She kissed him back with the same hunger, pushing the opening of his shirt aside and sliding her palms against his chest.

There was a bench behind them.

Locking on to her mouth, Lance slowly walked her backward until they reached it before turning with her in his arms. He sat down and pulled her onto his lap. His hand went to the zipper on her dress, his need to see and feel her flesh overriding caution and common sense.

Her fingers grasped the first button on his shirt at the same instant he found the start of her zipper. They both hesitated, but only for an instant before they began to work feverishly, as if some silent agreement had passed between them.

It was madness, he knew. He suspected she knew it, too, but he was equally sure they couldn't stop. When she finished unfastening his buttons and impatiently tugged at the material, Lance reluctantly stopped working on her zipper long enough to shrug out of his shirt. He was just as eager to feel her bare flesh against his. . . .

Vaguely he heard something fall to the concrete gazebo floor and bounce with a pinging noise. A button from his shirt was his first thought. Or one of Holly's earrings. Who cared?

Apparently Holly did, for she broke the kiss and looked down at the floor, searching for the source of the noise. Stifling a groan at the unwelcome interruption, Lance began looking too.

And really, really wished he hadn't.

Standing on end and twirling like a zealous ballerina in the moonlight was the wedding ring he'd hastily slipped into his shirt pocket.

With a bad feeling in his gut, Lance watched as it

slowly spun to a halt, tottered for a second, then fell to the concrete with a metallic little *ping*. There it lay for God and everyone to see.

Including Holly Wentworth.

Ten

⌣

Sitting in bed with the crystal ball between them, Mini and Reuben stared at the spinning gold wedding ring in openmouthed shock. They jumped simultaneously when the ring fell over.

Finally Reuben sputtered, "He's such an idiot!"

Mini was speechless. Another moment more and they would have missed the ring, for she had been on the verge of putting the ball away so the couple could have their privacy.

"What could he be thinking?" Reuben continued to snarl. He punched at the pillows behind his back, flopped against them, and folded his arms across his chest. His black eyes gleamed with fury. "Of all the *idiot* things to do, he had to go and let her see that blasted ring he wore around his neck!"

Startled anew, Mini looked at him. "You knew about the ring?"

With an arrogant toss of his head, Reuben snorted. "Of course I did. I noticed it the day he came in to be interviewed. I advised him to put it away and put the past behind him."

"What did he say?"

"He said he'd know when it was time." Letting out a

steamed, explosive breath, Reuben leaped from the bed and began to pace the room. "That's the last time I feel sorry for him!"

"You . . . you felt sorry for him?" Bewildered, Mini watched her husband pace the room. "Why would you feel sorry for Lance?"

"Well, because he lost his wife." Reuben's lip curled with derision. "Apparently my sympathy was wasted on an *idiot*."

"I think 'idiot' is a rather strong word," Mini chided, secretly delighted by his confession. It revealed a sensitivity she sometimes feared he lacked. "And your sympathy wasn't wasted, darling. He *did* lose his wife, and I'm sure it's not easy letting go of someone you love."

Her words of wisdom seemed to calm Reuben. His pacing slowed, but the stubborn angle of his jaw remained. "But he should have listened to me! Now look at the mess he's made. Holly will never believe he's getting over his wife after this."

Unfortunately Mini had to agree. "You saw how nervous he was about going out with Holly. I'm sure he forgot about the ring."

Reuben dragged his hair from his face before he pivoted and marched back to the bed. He flopped down. The movement nearly sent the crystal ball tumbling from her lap.

"Where was that damned cat when we needed her? She could have zapped that ring before Holly had a chance to see it, made herself useful for a change. Instead, she's out catting around, picking up strays."

"That *cat*," Mini interrupted, "was giving us a little much-needed privacy." Her voice dropped to a sultry murmur. "I don't remember you complaining earlier."

Slightly mollified, Reuben sighed. "Well, she could have gone to spy on those mortals instead of roaming the neighborhood."

Mini placed the crystal ball on the nightstand and snuggled close to him. "I'll talk to her, okay? Ask her to keep a better eye on Holly and Lance if we're otherwise . . . occupied." She drew a path on his chest with her nail, smiling as his nipples peaked with awareness. "Meanwhile, we've got a little time left. . . ."

"Hmm. You have a good point, dear. I'll get the lights."

"Yes, get the lights. Tomorrow's another day, and there's nothing we can do tonight to help the mortals."

"Another good point."

"Oh, I've got *plenty* of good points to make, darling."

He growled and pulled her into his arms.

"It's nearly midnight, Lance. I've got emergency room duty tomorrow, and *you* have to work as well."

Lance ignored Casey and aimed the cue stick. He hit the number three ball with more force than necessary. The ball jumped the pool table and bounced onto the carpet.

With a sigh, Casey chased it down and returned it to the table. "Are you at least going to tell me what happened, since I'm here?"

"You're welcome to leave," Lance said curtly, aiming again. It wasn't his turn, but Casey didn't seem to notice. This time the ball rolled neatly into the pocket. Wonder of wonders, Lance noticed, he failed to experience even a smidgen of his usual satisfaction.

"*You* invited me, remember? The least you can do—"

"I can't sleep."

Casey snorted. "Tell me something I *don't* know. Like what happened with Holly tonight. Did she ditch you like that Terri woman did?"

"No, she didn't *ditch* me. She just politely asked me to take her home."

"And this is the reason you can't sleep?" When Lance remained stubbornly silent, Casey drew in a sharp, incredulous breath. "Wait—surely you weren't expecting to score on the first date? I mean, I know this is a new century, man, but there are still a lot of women out there who take sex seriously."

Lance missed the ball and let out a frustrated oath. He couldn't blame his friend for having drawn the wrong conclusion. If Casey didn't get answers, Casey invented them. Lance had always known that about his friend. "No, I didn't expect Holly to sleep with me." *Wanted,* yes. *Expected,* no. Make that *desperately* wanted—for the first time since Mona. In fact, he could honestly say he'd lost his head. He ground his teeth, remembering that Holly had, too. They'd both been mindless, which was the beauty of it. He'd hardly thought about Mona the entire time he and Holly were together.

Then he'd dropped that damned ring. How could he have been so stupid?

"If you don't tell me," Casey warned, "I'm going to leave."

"Fine!" Lance snapped, throwing the cue stick onto the table and scattering the balls in every direction. "Let's go get a drink. A *real* drink." He headed in the direction of the pool and the bar hoping Casey would take the hint and get off his butt.

"Lance . . . you're not going to start drinking again, are you? Your heart—"

Lance whipped around, stopping Casey in his tracks. "My heart is fine, and I drank for *two* weeks after Mona died. That doesn't make me an alcoholic, Case. You're a medical doctor, you should know that."

Casey's mouth opened, then closed. His eyes narrowed. "You drank for two weeks nonstop, which might not make you an alcoholic, but it nearly killed you."

"People are allowed to grieve. It's part of the natural healing process." God knew he'd done his share. He continued on to the pool, hoping Casey would take the hint and get off his butt. Without looking to see if Casey had followed, he reached for the vodka and orange juice. He mixed one for himself, and then, seeing his friend, poured Casey a straight orange juice.

In silence, they sipped their drinks and stared out onto the patio at the beautiful pool Lance's father had spent a fortune designing and building—where he and Holly had laughed and frolicked only a few hours ago. Mona had been more of a lounger. In fact, he could only remember her getting into the water a few times.

Finally Lance knew he'd run out of time; Casey was waiting, and he wasn't known for his patience. Keeping his eyes on his drink, Lance began in a voice harsh with self-disgust, "It seems I forgot more than my pants tonight, ole buddy."

Casey raised his hand, then halted it in midair, for once in his life keeping quiet.

"I also forgot to take the ring off my chain."

"You—" Casey stopped and took a hefty swig of his drink as if it *did* contain fortifying alcohol. He swallowed hard. "You're talking about the wedding ring. You had your wedding ring on the chain around your neck, and Holly saw it."

Lance nodded, staring morosely into his drink. "I forgot about it. I meant to take the ring off earlier, but it wasn't until we were changing into our swimsuits that I remembered."

"That's when she saw it?"

"No. I took it off then and put it in my shirt pocket. She saw it later, while we were in the gazebo. It fell out of my pocket."

"How did—"

"Don't ask," Lance growled. "Let's just say that I was one big idiot and leave it at that."

Casey whistled. "I'll say. Did you try to explain to her that you meant to take it off?"

"She wouldn't have listened. I could see it in her eyes." Lance shrugged as if it didn't matter, when in fact it did. A lot. More than he would have thought.

"So she thinks you're still hung up on your . . . on Mona?"

"I'd say there's a pretty good chance she thinks that, yes."

"You know what this means, don't you?"

Lance blinked. "No, I don't."

"*She's* hung up on *you.*"

"Dream on." His heart skipped a beat, although he didn't believe Casey for a second.

"Seriously. Why else would it bother her that you still honor your wife's memory?" Warming to his theory, Casey turned and refilled his glass. After a slight hesitation and a sheepish grin, he added a teensy bit of vodka. "Think about it, Lance. If she were serious about just going out with you to see what you were doing wrong, then why would she care about a wedding ring? Did she tell you that you'd made a major blunder? Correct your mistake like she was supposed to do?"

"No. She just told me to take her home in a voice that dripped icicles," Lance said dryly, frowning at the unpleasant memory.

"Well, then, there you have it." Casey's smile was smug. He raised his glass in a triumphant toast. "She cares."

"Lot of good that observation will do me now—*if* your theory is right and she's convinced she has competition."

"You'll just have to convince her that she doesn't."

"And how exactly will I do that if she won't go out with me again?" If Casey had a plan, he was all ears. He shook his head, wondering if he'd gone off the deep end. Casey was notorious for coming up with harebrained schemes that usually backfired.

"You should go out with other women."

Lance closed his eyes. It was just as he suspected. "It's past your bedtime, Casey. You're not making any sense."

"I am, if you'll just hear me out. If you date other women and have the time of your life, it will prove that you're over Mona. Since Holly owns the agency, she'll be monitoring your dates, won't she? She'll see with her own eyes. She might even be jealous."

He was either drunk or sleepwalking, Lance decided, because Casey was actually making sense. It was a scary thought. Then, remembering the resolute look on her face when she'd realized it was his wedding band spinning on the floor of the gazebo, Lance drawled, "I'd have to be pretty damned convincing, I'm afraid. She's a sharp lady." And beautiful, fun to be with, caring . . . Damn.

Casey gave him a jovial clap on the back, nearly spilling Lance's drink. "You can do it!" he enthused. "Remember our college days? We used to party hearty!"

Lance rolled his eyes. "Casey, that was you and Skip. *I* was the serious student."

Unperturbed, Casey shrugged. "Whatever. This just means you've got some making up to do."

But it wouldn't be with Holly. Not surprisingly, Lance discovered the idea of "partying hearty" with anyone but Holly held little appeal.

It was no use. She wasn't going to get to sleep until she hashed it to death.

With a restless sigh, Holly turned over and reached out in the darkness, her fingers combing through Nike's silky hair. "You asleep?" she whispered.

Her father would have howled the house down to hear her talking to her dog as if he understood, but Holly wasn't a fool; she knew that although Nike *didn't* understand, he cared. That's all that mattered to her.

The soft snores she'd been hearing only seconds before stopped. Nike lifted his head and whined. His tail thumped on the bed—not as enthusiastically as she would have liked, but the most she could expect at midnight.

Nike, after all, liked his sleep.

Her hand found his ear. She began to scratch him in his favorite spot. It was the least she could do after rousing him from his sleep. "I'm just not good at relationships. Either I get too serious too fast—with the wrong man— or I don't like them at all. Maybe I'm destined to become an old maid, Nike." She sighed and stretched her arm over her head, thinking about Lance and his sexy, bedroom eyes. And his laugh . . . It was like an aphrodisiac.

Regret flowed like bitter wine through her veins. She had a sad feeling she would never meet another man like Lance. "Don't get me wrong—he's a wonderful man, and someday he might get over his late wife and love someone else. In the meantime, I'm afraid he's got some growing to do." She'd just be a stepping-stone as he made his way across the healing path to the one woman who could make him want to put his wedding ring away forever—and maybe even replace it.

Nike's soft snores reached her again. She smiled faintly, not blaming him one little bit. She was about to put *herself* to sleep with her boring recital. "I'm not mad at him," she whispered into the night. "I actually admire him for being faithful to the woman he loved." She turned over and snuggled into her pillow, grateful that sleep finally seemed within her reach. "But I'm selfish. I want him all to myself or not at all."

Tomorrow, she thought as she drifted off to sleep. Tomorrow she would help Lance by finding him one of those stepping-stones. The woman Holly picked would need to be someone who didn't fall easily, or foolishly. Someone who would be better at resisting Lance's powerful charms than she, yet someone strong enough to help him recover from his devastating loss. A companion, one who wasn't interested in happily-ever-afters.

Someone who would *know* that the magic Lance created wasn't real, and wouldn't be silly enough to let herself believe it *could* be.

Safely out of sight beneath Holly's bed, Xonia wiped a tear from her eye with her paw and blinked her golden eyes. She sniffed, disagreeing with Holly about being selfish. If and when *she* fell in love, she would want it all, too, and she most definitely wouldn't want to walk in the shadow of another woman.

She wanted it all, the way Mini and Reuben had it all.

The thought was there before Xonia could stubbornly reject it. Reluctantly, she had to admit that she envied Mini and her wonderful marriage to Reuben. Her snide remarks and insulting observations about Reuben were mostly designed to cover her shameful jealousy. She and Reuben were more alike than she cared to admit—both proud and arrogant, sometimes to the point where judgment became sadly clouded.

In these past few weeks, she'd realized that she'd been unjustifiably hard on the reformed warlock from the day he'd married Mini. She also realized that envy and jealousy could blind the soul as effectively as revenge and greed. Perhaps—just *perhaps* she'd think about mending her ways, giving him a chance. After all, as long as he made Mini happy, *she* should be happy.

As for Holly . . . Xonia's cat eyes glowed bright yellow with determination. She silently emerged from beneath the bed and padded to the kitchen, where she'd left a window open. She could have zapped herself back to the apartment, but she rather liked the outdoors, and she needed the exercise. Too many meals and too much sleep were making her fat and lazy.

Hopping onto the sink, she turned to peer back at the shadowy hallway leading to Holly's room. She easily visualized Holly fast asleep with that lazy hound crowding more than his share of the bed.

Xonia made a vow then and there—a witch's sacred promise—that she would do everything within her considerable power to help Holly get her man. And Lance was her man, of that Xonia had no doubt. She'd been there tonight, unseen and watching from a tree up above the pool as the couple frolicked in the water like carefree teenagers. She would have been there later as well, in the gazebo, if that wicked cat next door hadn't spotted her and thought to frighten her into leaving.

She would have relished a good old mortal catfight if she hadn't been working. Instead she had quickly transformed herself into a cat-eating Rottweiler, shamelessly anticipating the cat's fright.

Only she had forgotten that dogs can't climb trees.

The fall hadn't hurt much, but it had knocked her silly for a few moments. By the time she'd gathered her wits, that coward of a cat had vanished, and Holly and Lance were leaving. From her hiding place in the bushes she had seen their faces and knew something momentous had happened. She had also sensed that it hadn't been pleasant. But it wasn't until she reached the apartment and watched a replay in the crystal ball that she found out about the ring.

Because of that blasted cat, she had not been there to zap the damning evidence out of the gazebo before Holly saw it. She had failed in her duties.

Poor Holly. With a sympathetic meow, Xonia twitched her tail and conjured a vase of fresh yellow roses to grace the small kitchen table. That should gladden Holly's heart in the morning, she thought. Of course, their mysterious appearance would probably drive Holly insane, but the distraction would be helpful.

It was just the beginning.

By Allhallows Eve, Holly Wentworth would believe in happily-ever-afters . . . and magic, or Xonia wasn't a witch.

A deeply growled meow snapped Xonia out of her daydream. She stuck her head through the open window behind her and glanced down at the big seal-point Himalayan waiting below. He watched her with huge, adoring blue eyes, his powerless tail twitching to and fro. Although she knew him to be a mortal cat, she sometimes imagined him as a man. He'd be big and husky, with a hard, square jaw and crystal blue eyes. One of those brawny sex machines who didn't need brains to make a woman feel like a woman. Just a body that made her mouth water.

Xonia began to purr. She licked her lips with anticipation and whispered, "I'm coming, handsome. Just hold your—whatever it is that you hold. And this time, can you not make so much noise?" Of course, he didn't understand her, being an ordinary mortal cat.

That was the beauty of it.

Eleven

The office was eerily quiet; Mini and Reuben had gone out to lunch.

Holly sat at her desk, chewing on her knuckle and contemplating the single yellow rose in front of her. She'd found it and eleven others this morning, sitting in a vase just as pretty as you please on her kitchen table.

After her initial shock, she and Nike had searched every crack and crevice in the apartment for a clue or even a card, looking in closets, behind the shower curtain, and in the small cubbyhole that housed her washer and dryer.

There had been those few terrifying moments when Nike stayed inordinately long under her bed, but he finally emerged with an apologetic whine, and she'd been forced to conclude that if someone had been in her apartment, he or she was gone now.

But the roses had *not* appeared out of thin air, just as the vase hadn't.

Calling the police would have been ludicrous. There was no sign of forced entry, nothing missing or out of place—just a mysterious set of muddy paw prints in the kitchen sink, which Holly hadn't noticed until she rinsed her empty coffee cup under the faucet.

Cat paws. Even if by some miracle Nike could have

gotten up on the counter, the prints were too small to belong to the retriever. Holly didn't own a cat, and she never allowed a stray into her apartment because she feared Nike's reaction. Since she lived two stories up, a cat slipping into the apartment through a window was also out of the question.

As if a cat would have anything to do with the roses, anyway.

Holly gave her head a bewildered shake, remembering her short conversation with her landlady. Mrs. Teasedale had assured her she'd locked the main door downstairs nice and tight last night after Holly came home, just as she always did. Holly believed her.

The one and only logical answer was that someone had taken her apartment key from her key ring and had a duplicate made. The possibility caused a riot of goose bumps to spring along her arms, especially when she considered her suspects. Mini and Reuben, of course, would have plenty of opportunities to get her key, make a copy, and replace it during the course of the day without her being the wiser.

But she knew they wouldn't. She didn't know *how* she knew, she just knew. Besides, why would they do something like that, then leave roses on the table? Yes, they were a little odd—maybe even eccentric—but they were honest and harmless; she'd bet her next mortgage payment on that. If they wanted to send her roses, they would have them delivered.

Then there was Mrs. Teasedale, whom Holly dismissed right away. It just wouldn't be something the sweet little old lady would do. And if she for some reason did, Holly couldn't imagine Mrs. Teasedale lying about it afterward.

Which left her father and Lance. Her father was in Washington attending a convention, and she couldn't imagine when Lance would have had unseen access to her purse. She had carried it into the ladies' room at the bar and into the changing closet with her right before they went swimming.

Yet, since she had systematically eliminated any other suspects, she reasoned that Lance had to be the one. He would have had the motive, considering how the dreamlike night had ended, and romantic yellow roses would be his style.

Holly took a deep breath into her lungs and closed her eyes. The problem with *that* scenario was that there wasn't a florist in Lovit, California, who kept yellow roses in stock. She knew, because she had wasted the better part of the morning going down the listing for florists in the Yellow Pages and calling each one.

The ringing phone made Holly jump. She reached out and plucked the receiver from its hook. "Romance Connection. Holly Wentworth speaking."

"Good afternoon."

This time Holly was able to get a handle on her emotions *before* the inevitable meltdown that normally accompanied the sound of Lance's voice. She gripped the phone, her eyes on the rose in front of her. "Lance. How are you?"

"Good. And you?"

He was talking as if nothing had happened, Holly realized. She wavered between anger and relief. "A little tired." Especially after lying awake half the night thinking about him!

His husky chuckle speared a thrill into her belly. She steadfastly ignored it. He could pretend nothing had happened, but she hadn't forgotten.

"Swimming will do that to you," he drawled, his voice warm and flirty.

For the first time, Holly considered that perhaps Lance Wilder used that same flirty tone with all women. The possibility made her wince at her gullibility. "Was there something *else* I could help you with?" There. Surely he would notice her emphasis on the word "else"? She had agreed to tutor him in the art of dating, and she'd kept her end of the bargain. The fact that she'd gotten *more* than she bargained for was her own fault.

"Yes, there is. First I want to thank you for a memorable evening and apologize for the awkward ending."

Holly scraped her bottom lip with her teeth. "I haven't given it another thought," she managed to say evenly. It was the biggest lie she'd ever told. She braced herself to hear a long and awkward explanation about why he still kept his wife's wedding ring close to his heart. Maybe she could pretend a client walked in—

"Secondly, I wanted to talk to you about my next date."

She had to lift the phone away from her mouth so that he wouldn't hear her startled gasp. "Of course. What was it that you wanted to know?" He was either cruel or just plain dumb, she thought, aching inside. Another date. After last night, all he could think about was another date. One who wouldn't mind, perhaps, that a ghost shadowed their every step.

"Have you found her yet?" he asked.

His words echoed and reechoed in her mind. It was a moment before she could speak around the painful knot in her throat. "Not yet, but I intend to start trying as soon as I hang up the phone."

"Good. I'm looking forward to it. Let me know something when you find out. Good-bye, Holly, and thanks again for helping me out."

"Thanks again for helping me out." Holly wanted to crash the phone down, but she tempered her wild anger in the nick of time, landing the phone in the cradle with a brittle little snap. Jaw set, heart bleeding, she swung her chair around to face her computer screen. Hitting the keys so hard she broke a nail, she typed in her secret password, then Lance's last name at the prompt.

When the screen brought his file into view, Holly resolutely began the search.

She ignored the silent tear that tracked a path down her cheek, and the painful reluctance in her heart.

Mini knew something was wrong the second she and Reuben entered the office. Holly's face was red and blotchy, and she had a strange, resigned look in her eyes that stirred Mini's maternal instincts.

Something or someone had hurt Holly, and she didn't have to wonder who that someone was—Lance Wilder.

Holly didn't fool Mini with her false, bright smile when she announced she'd be off to the bank now that they had returned from lunch. Glancing at Reuben, Mini realized by his sympathetic expression that Holly hadn't fooled him, either. Yes, something was wrong, very wrong.

When Holly had gone, Xonia, who had been pretending to sleep while Reuben and Mini were out, pranced from their office. She hopped onto the chair by the computer Holly had vacated and twitched her tail.

A name appeared on the screen in big black letters.

Mini and Reuben crowded close. "Debbie Mosely," Mini read out loud. She frowned at Xonia. "Does this name have some significance?"

Xonia nodded, then twitched her tail again at the screen. The hard drive on the computer began to click. Finally a file appeared on the screen under Debbie Mosely's name. Mini began to read aloud.

"Former 1990 Miss Georgia, age thirty. Widowed, no children, but would like one or two. Measurements: thirty-six, twenty-seven, thirty six. Weight: one hundred and five pounds. Height: five feet three inches. Occupation, divorce lawyer. Hobbies: basketball, baseball, football, tennis, reading, horseback riding, gourmet cooking, art, swimming, and interior design. Long blond hair and blue eyes."

Mini finished and sat down hard in the computer chair, realizing the significance of the file. She felt faint. "She isn't real, is she?" she asked, looking from one to the other.

Reuben cleared his throat. Xonia gazed steadily at her with glittering gold eyes.

"Okay," Mini conceded, returning her gaze to the screen. "Maybe she is, but she's got to have *some* flaw somewhere." She continued to read, her heart sinking with

every word she spoke out loud. "Not interested in marriage . . . looking for companionship with a man who
knows how to have a good time." Mini gasped, her eyes
bugging out of her head as she came to the sex-preference
section. Her voice lowered to an embarrassed whisper.
" 'I'm extremely open-minded and willing to try anything
new, providing it doesn't involve drugs, guns, or pain.' "

Reuben coughed to cover a laugh.

Mini glanced sharply at him. "This isn't funny! Do you
realize this is every man's dream right here on this screen?
Unless she's got a wart on her nose, or her front teeth are
missing, we've got a serious problem!" This wasn't someone she'd screened, so that meant Debbie Mosely was a
longtime client. With those incredible assets, she could
have her pick of men!

Xonia twitched her tail, and the screen went blank. She
fixed her golden eyes on Mini, and, curling the end of her
tail like a finger, pointed it in the direction of the bathroom.

Jumping to her feet, Mini shot Reuben a warning look
and followed Xonia to the tiny rest room. She shut and
locked the door before turning to the cat, who had jumped
onto the commode seat. "Are you *certain* this is the
woman Holly picked for Lance? I can't imagine her—"

"It is," Xonia interrupted gravely, whispering in case a
certain nosy warlock was lingering outside the door listening. "But it's Lance's fault. He called asking about his
next date."

Mini gasped. "No!"

" 'Fraid so. I don't know what he's up to, but I do know
that he cares about Holly."

"Then why—?"

Xonia shrugged. "Beats me. We should do a replay on
the crystal ball and find out what we missed. I've got a
hunch this silly idea wasn't Lance's."

"Casey?" Mini chewed her nail.

"Possibly. That mortal is about as smart as the cat I
met last night. It should be illegal for him to think."

"He's a doctor, Xonia. He can't be that dumb."

"There's a difference between intelligence and common sense, as I've learned since taking up residence in this mortal world."

Mini felt like wringing her hands. "What are we going to do? Oh, I wish I had my powers!"

"If you did, what would you do?"

"I'd—I'd—" Mini stuttered to a stop, an idea forming in her mind. Her emerald-green eyes began to gleam. "I'd make sure that Lance didn't enjoy this date."

"Like the one with Terri?"

"Even *less* than the one with Terri. In fact, by the time I finished with him, he'd be *afraid* to go on another date."

Xonia arched her back and carelessly dug her claws into the soft, padded commode seat. "You got it, girlfriend," she stated, winking at Mini.

A banging on the door startled them. Reuben's miffed, embarrassed voice drifted through. "I hate to interrupt, but a mortal urge has overcome me. . . ."

"Be right out, husband," Mini called sweetly, smothering a girlish giggle. In a whisper, she said to Xonia, "Reuben will never get used to mortal ways, I fear. Having to go to the bathroom is at the top of his list."

Xonia lifted her paw and scratched earnestly behind her ear. "Don't go into shock, but I'm afraid I'll have to agree with him on this one," she grumbled. "These fleas multiply like rabbits. The moment I zap one into outer space, another is born to take its place!"

Mini doubled over with laughter.

Twelve

By Thursday Holly had a firm hold on her emotions. She was ready to meet Debbie Mosely, woman extraordinare. After all, she was a businesswoman, and she couldn't let her little crush stand in the way of doing her job, and her job was to *connect* people. Lance deserved the best—and he was going to get it.

But when the former Miss Georgia walked into Romance Connection at two o'clock sharp and took a seat in front of Holly's desk, Holly could barely manage to hide her acute dismay.

Debbie Mosely was every man's fantasy and *then* some.

She wasn't just blond and blue-eyed; she was a natural light blonde, with lighter, whiter blond streaks that Holly would bet her next cappuccino did not come from a bottle. No, the sun had given her those, along with a gorgeous tan on every inch of exposed skin.

There was a lot of exposed skin, too, yet Holly had to admit the woman looked elegant instead of sleazy. She wore a simple, sleeveless navy dress that clung to and shaped every curve. Matching heels and a plain gold watch completed her outfit. No jewelry and very little, if any, makeup. Holly squinted and leaned forward, trying not to appear too obvious as she tried to see if the woman was at least wearing a coat of mascara to darken her lashes.

"I hope I'm not too early," Debbie said in a soft, feathery voice that made Holly want to cry. "It's just that I'm eager to hear all about Mr. Wilder." She folded one slim, tanned leg effortlessly over the other. Her narrow foot began to swing in a gentle rhythm.

Holly swallowed a ball of envy and tapped her pencil against her teeth, sharply enough to remind herself of her manners. "No, you're right on time, Ms. Mosely. I'm sorry I had to call you back in, but it's been so long since our last interview, I wanted to make sure you were—that I remembered you correctly."

A perfect blond brow rose in question, but the expression in her blue eyes remained friendly and slightly amused. "And did you?"

"Um, yes, I did." Holly's lips felt frozen as she forced a smile. "You're *exactly* as I remember you." Pretty, perfect, and petite. She wondered if the woman would think her insane if she told her she had a pair of pantyhose to give away. Just her size, too.

Debbie leaned forward, supporting her youthful-looking chin with a perfectly manicured hand. "So tell me about my date. Is he handsome?"

"Very."

"On a scale of one to ten?"

Holly felt a small ripple of nausea as she said, "Oh, about a seven, I'd say." Closer to ten and a half, but she wasn't *that* conscientious.

Looking pleased, Debbie settled back in her chair. "How about funny? I like a man who appreciates humor."

Holly thought about Lance's quick, crooked grin and bone-melting chuckle. She cleared her throat. "I think he might suit you in that department, as well."

Now Debbie's blue eyes gleamed with a different light, one that made Holly want to stick her fingers in her ears.

She was absolutely one hundred percent certain she didn't want to hear the woman's next question.

"What about . . . the other department?" Debbie hesitated, her cheeks tinged with a becoming peach blush. "Do you think he'll be good in bed?"

Wondering how horrified Debbie would be if she emptied her lunch in the wastebasket, Holly said, "I can't know for sure, but judging by his . . . qualifications, it definitely sounds promising." Another few moments in the gazebo and *she* might have known firsthand, Holly thought.

Debbie clasped her hands together and nibbled her full bottom lip. She fairly quivered with anticipation. "He's not bashful, is he? I mean, I don't want to waste a lot of time going out before we . . . that is—"

"I think I get your meaning," Holly managed to croak out. Her nails left impressions in the wooden pencil. Not for the first time, she realized that interviewing Debbie Mosely again was a big, big mistake. She should have left well enough alone. She could have set up the entire date without coming face-to-face with either of them again.

And she damned well *should* have, if the queasy feeling in her stomach was any indication.

Throwing the pencil aside before she did something she would regret, Holly said, "No, he doesn't have a bashful bone in his body." She saw her mistake the moment Debbie's eyes narrowed.

"You sound as if you know him personally."

Holly's hackles rose at the faint challenge in the other woman's eyes. It was almost as if Debbie already thought of Lance as her property and sensed that Holly had encroached. Stiffly Holly informed the former Miss Georgia, "At Romance Connection, we pride ourselves on conducting thorough interviews of our clients—for *your* protection."

Debbie relaxed visibly, laughing in a husky way that prompted a choked snarl from Holly. If the interview didn't end soon, Holly was very afraid she might do something unprofessional. The woman was pretty and perfect and petite, but it was becoming clear to Holly that she was also the possessive type. Lance didn't strike her as the kind of man who would be flattered by a possessive woman. He'd more likely feel put off, maybe even irritated.

The thought put a smile on Holly's face; Debbie's next statement quickly eliminated it.

"I envy your position, you know," the woman drawled with another husky laugh. "It must be heaven to have your pick of men."

"I don't date my clients." The lie nearly stuck in Holly's throat. It wasn't exactly a lie, she reminded herself, because her date with Lance had only been a work assignment. At least, it had begun that way. The ending had been sheer stupidity on her part and a starved libido on Lance's.

Debbie arched her brow in surprise at Holly's defensive retort. "You mean to say you've never been tempted? All those men looking for the right woman . . . ?"

Holly decided it was high time they return to the business at hand. The woman was getting far too personal for comfort. "This interview is about you, Miss Mosely, not about me. Now, if you don't have any further questions—"

"I do," Debbie interjected quickly. "Lots of them. I want to know *everything* there is to know about Lance Wilder before I go out with him."

Clenching her teeth, Holly knew she had no one to blame but herself. "Okay. Ask."

"Does he like children?"

Holly didn't have to glance at the file beneath her elbow to answer. She knew all of the answers by heart, and a few by experience. "Yes."

"Wealthy?"

"Comfortable."

Debbie flung a swath of shimmering hair behind her shoulder. "Has he ever been married?"

"Yes."

"How many times?"

"Once." Oddly enough, Holly felt disloyal answering questions about Lance's personal life, even though she knew it was standard procedure. The woman had a right to know about Lance, just as Lance had a right to know about Debbie Mosely. Those were the rules—rules *she* had devised.

"Divorced, I suppose?"

Holly smiled humorlessly. "Widowed, like yourself."

"Do you think he's over her?"

It was all Holly could do to keep from bursting into hysterical laughter. Instead she countered smoothly, "Does it matter? You stated in the first interview that you weren't necessarily looking for a serious relationship."

A slow smile curved Debbie's lips, revealing perfect white teeth. "I wouldn't force the issue, but I'm not averse to the possibility. I've discovered I miss sex on a regular basis."

An uncontrollable flush heated Holly's face at the woman's bluntness. "Then I'm afraid that's a question you'll have to ask him yourself." She could have offered an opinion, but she didn't think it would be fair to Lance. Debbie Mosely might have had a different reaction had she seen the wedding ring spinning on the floor of the gazebo. The sight of the ring and its implication might have made a woman like Debbie more determined to win him over.

Perhaps *she* shouldn't have given up so easily, Holly thought.

Looking at the beautiful blonde seated in front of her, Holly had a sinking feeling that it was too late. Everything about Debbie Mosely seemed right for Lance.

When the former beauty queen stood and made for the door, Holly barely stifled a shriek at the sight of Debbie's bare back exposed by the low cut of her elegant dress.

Dimples.

The woman had dimples in her petite little back.

• • •

Lance was in between clients when Holly called to tell him she'd found a match. Pretending an eagerness he didn't feel, he said, "Great! When do I get to meet her?"

The length of silence that followed made Lance grin as he imagined those luscious lips pursed in disapproval over his reaction. It was wishful thinking, of course, but what could it hurt to think that Holly might be a tad jealous?

"Tomorrow night. Is there anything you'd like to know about her first?"

There wasn't, but Holly's cool, businesslike tone scraped across his ego like sandpaper. He quickly put himself in Casey's place and tried to imagine what type of questions his friend would ask. It didn't take him long to make a mental list.

Grinning to himself, he said, "Her measurements. I'd like to know her measurements."

"Thirty-six, twenty-seven, thirty-six."

The devil in Lance prompted him to whistle as if impressed, when he was more impressed—and disappointed—by the fact that Holly's tone hadn't changed in light of his typical sexist question. "How about hair color? Eye color? Anything outstanding?"

He thought he heard her choke, but after a moment he decided he must have imagined it.

"She has blond hair and blue eyes."

"And?" Lance prompted, sensing there was more that she wasn't telling him. "Anything else?" Another pregnant pause followed, this one so long Lance began to think the connection had been broken. Finally, Holly spoke, and the slight reluctance in her voice gave Lance hope.

"She likes just about every sport you can imagine."

"Hmm. Sounds like my kind of woman." He'd meant it as a joke, but Holly didn't laugh.

"She's a lawyer."

"Divorced?"

"No. She's a widow."

"A widow." Lance grunted. "Do you think that's a good idea?"

"I don't think *she* has a problem," Holly said sharply.

Lance moved the mouthpiece away so that she wouldn't hear him chuckle. There was no mistaking her meaning, but he chose to ignore it. "Good. My idea of a good time doesn't include reminiscing about the past."

"Yes, well, your idea of a good time is your business." Holly had recovered her brisk, businesslike tone, but there was an underlying layer of frost in her voice that Lance heard loud and clear. "If you're finished asking—"

"Oh, but I'm *not* through asking questions." Lance smiled smugly at the tangible drop in temperature. "I want to know all of the juicy details." There was a snapping sound, followed by a muffled curse. "Holly? Are you all right?"

"I'm just fine. Ask away."

She didn't sound just fine, Lance thought, smothering another chuckle. Maybe for once in his life Casey was right about something. He just hoped their little plan didn't backfire.

"Tell me, Holly, what questions did my date ask about *me*?"

The silence stretched into a few seconds, then a few more before she answered.

"She asked if you were handsome."

"And you said?"

"Yes."

"Do you think so?"

"This isn't about—"

"Do you?"

"Yes! Yes, I do." The words were clearly said through clenched teeth. "Now, is your ego satisfied?"

Lance chuckled out loud. "I didn't mean to make you mad."

"I'm not mad!"

But she sounded mad. Pissed, in fact. "What else did she ask you about me?"

"She asked if you were wealthy."

"What else?" While he waited, he glanced at his watch. His next client was due to arrive any moment.

"She . . . she wanted to know if you were bashful."

When he realized she wasn't going to volunteer her answer, he prompted, "And you said?"

"I told her that I didn't think you were."

"Why did she ask?"

"I'm not sure."

Lance sensed that she *did* know, but wasn't telling. He also sensed that wild horses wouldn't pull it out of her, which made him doubly curious. He made a mental note to ask Debbie. "Next question."

"I don't think you want to know—"

"Tell me."

"It's rather personal."

"I'm a big boy. I'm sure I can take it."

Holly's noisy sigh crackled through the phone. "Okay, but I don't think you're going to like it. She asked if I thought you were over your wife."

Every muscle in Lance's body froze. His smile dropped from his mouth like a stone. "And how did you answer?"

Slowly she said, "I told her that she should ask *you* that question."

Lance digested this information in silence, wondering why Holly didn't just ask him herself. Before he could begin to tell her the answer, he heard a sniffle behind him. When he swung around, he found his next appointment standing in the doorway. His frown dissolved beneath an avalanche of concern at the sight of the teenage girl's swollen eyes and blotchy face.

Her name was Bridget Wooten, and she was sixteen years old. Her worried parents believed she was having some sort of breakdown, but by the end of their first session last week, Lance suspected Bridget was suffering her first heartbreak over a boy.

"I think I'm pregnant!" Bridget suddenly wailed, apparently heedless of the fact that Lance was on the phone. She then burst into noisy sobs.

It was worse than Lance thought. Softly he said into the phone, "I've got to go, Holly. I'll call you back later and get Debbie's number."

"Is everything okay?"

The concern in her voice was unmistakable and gratifying. "Nothing I can't handle." He hung up, hoping and praying he was right.

"If you ask me, Lance is going a bit too far with this game he's playing," Mini said to her husband later that evening as she sat cross-legged in front of the television reading from a small, paperback instruction manual. She waved the book in the air for emphasis. "How does *he* know his plan won't backfire? He could wind up making Holly think he's nothing but a skirt-chasing playboy."

Reuben crouched before their brand-new VCR, cursing and punching buttons at random. "This thing doesn't work. I'm taking it back tomorrow, and that thieving mortal *will* return my money." He sat back and glared at the flashing digital lights.

"Perhaps you should let me try," Mini suggested gently. "I've read the manual, and it says—"

"I can do it myself," Reuben growled. "That silly book tells me nothing."

Straight-faced, Mini threw the book aside. "You're right, it doesn't. Why don't you try that button there." She pointed to a button with the tiny letters SET written above. "I'm just guessing, darling. Humor me."

Reuben's brows lowered with suspicion, but he did as she asked. The letters stopped flashing. Reluctantly he looked to her for further assistance.

"Now push the small square button below it."

He did, and the time began to move forward. When it landed on seven, he let go.

"Now push the SET button again."

He continued to follow her instructions until the time and date were correct and the irritating lights had stopped flashing. When he finished he turned around, then sat cross-legged in front of her. "You learned all that from reading the book," he stated rather than asked.

Mini sucked her lips inward and nodded. Solemnly she said, "Mortal men aren't so very different from warlocks."

Reuben cocked his head. "Oh?"

"Yes. They are both stubborn and prideful to a fault. Take the familiar, for instance. She's shown you nothing but kindness recently, yet I haven't heard you utter one single word of acknowledgment."

"That's because I'm waiting for the other shoe to fall," Reuben stated, scowling. "She's up to something. I can feel it deep in my warlock bones."

"Why do you have to question her motives? Why can't you just accept her as she is?"

He shook his head. "Because she stares at me as if she knows something I don't. Just because I've lost my powers doesn't mean I've lost my instincts." He waved an arrogant hand in the air, dismissing the subject. "Let's go over our plans for tomorrow night."

Mini sighed but let the subject drop—for now. "Good idea. We're going to have to be on our toes if we're going to make sure Lance doesn't have *too* much fun with Debbie Mosely."

"Yes, you're right. Even though he seems smitten with Holly, a woman like Debbie could change a man's mind—" Reuben wisely broke off as Mini's eyes narrowed. He hastily reconstructed his statement. "I mean, someone like *Lance* might be bewitched by a woman like Debbie."

With fire in her eyes, Mini demanded, "Meaning *you* wouldn't be tempted?"

Reuben toppled her onto her back with one easy move. Then he slowly lowered his mouth until it hovered over hers. "No, I wouldn't. You're the only witch for me."

"I'm not a witch anymore," she murmured.

"Ex-witch, then. You're the only *ex*-witch for me."

She smoothed a lock of blue-black hair from his brow with a loving hand, scanning his handsome, serious features. "And you're the only *ex*-warlock for me."

Thirteen

They were waiting for her when she and Nike returned from their customary evening walk.

Surprise was Holly's first reaction at finding Lance standing in the foyer talking to Mrs. Teasedale as if they'd known each other for years. Then she noticed the blotchy-faced teenager standing behind Lance, wearing baggy jeans and an oversized black T-shirt that read Y2K SURVIVOR.

Her emotions shifted gears without hesitation.

Holly suspected her sympathy stemmed from her own traumatic teenage years; she'd been caught in the middle of her parents' bitter and endless divorce, tugged to and fro, her emotions pulled and stretched until she felt like a piece of taffy at the county fair.

Whatever the case, her heart went out to the troubled teen.

Lance transferred his gaze from Mrs. Teasedale to Holly, his expression both anxious and bewildered.

"Lance, what are you doing here?" Holly cast a curious glance at the girl hovering behind him. "Is there something I can help you with?"

"I hope so. Can we talk somewhere private?"

"Of course. Mrs. Teasedale, would you mind taking—"

"Sally," Lance supplied.

"Would you mind taking Sally with you for milk and cookies while Mr. Wilder and I talk?"

Mrs. Teasedale beamed. "I'd love to. It's been years since I've had a good long chat with a youngster. And such pretty hair, too. I don't think I've ever seen that shade of red in all of my livelong days." The chatty landlady hooked her arm through the girl's. "Are you wearing those trendy new contacts, dear? Your eyes are such a beautiful amber color! I've thought about getting a pair of those myself. Tell me, are they expensive?"

Before Sally had a chance to protest, Mrs. Teasedale pulled her across the threshold of her apartment. The door slowly closed on Sally's dismayed expression.

Holly led the way upstairs, her mind questioning the wisdom of getting further involved with Lance Wilder in any shape, form, or fashion. Yet she couldn't turn him away. He needed her help, and unlike the last two times he'd needed her help, this one was different.

Once inside the apartment, Holly unclipped Nike from his leash. He immediately bounded into the kitchen for a noisy drink of water. She straightened to find Lance pacing her small living room, running a distracted hand through his hair.

"Trouble?" she guessed. He grimaced at her question, his handsome face tight with nervous tension.

"I'll say. Bridget's one of my patients—"

"Don't you mean Sally?"

He looked startled, then dismayed. "Yes, I meant Sally."

Then, with a flash of that endearingly crooked grin, he added, "Actually I try to remember to call all of my female patients Sally."

Holly returned his smile, her toes curling inside her shoes. "Your secret's safe with me. With all of the things I know about you, it would be silly *not* to trust me at this point, don't you think?"

"Would it?" he queried softly, walking steadily in her direction.

Suddenly nervous, Holly tried to put distance between them by walking backward. The kitchen was behind her. "Yes, it would. Well, except for the secrets I'm duty-bound to share with your dates. Would—would you like something to drink?"

"No, thanks." He stopped and shoved his hands in his pants pockets, as if he'd suddenly remembered he wasn't here for pleasure. "Relax, Holly. I'm not going to pounce on you."

It wasn't disappointment she felt, truly. "I didn't think you were," she lied, tilting her chin. "Are you going to tell me what's going on with Bridget—I mean Sally?"

His earlier frown returned. "She thinks she's pregnant."

The gasp was out before she could stop it. "Oh, no! She's what—fifteen?"

"Sixteen," he corrected with a grave nod of his head.

Holly slid bonelessly into a nearby chair. "Is she certain? How did her parents react to the news?"

"No, she's not sure, and she hasn't told her parents. They're out of town for a few days, and Bridget's been staying by herself. Today she refused to go home. Said she didn't want to be alone. She's terrified of their reaction."

"Of course she is!" Holly couldn't begin to imagine the fear and confusion Bridget was experiencing right now. "What about the father?"

Lance's eyes darkened a shade. "According to Bridget, he's denying any involvement."

"Well," Holly said dryly, "she certainly didn't get pregnant all by herself. . . . What are you going to do?"

He removed a hand from his pocket and threaded his fingers through his hair. "I honestly don't know. I mean, I was trained to handle adolescent problems, but this one's beyond me. Technically I can't break Bridget's confidence, but if I don't . . ."

"If you *don't* tell them and Bridget does something dangerous, they would blame you," Holly finished. "What if she runs away? Or decides to have an abortion?"

Lance shrugged helplessly. "Exactly. I was hoping you might have a suggestion or two."

This was serious, Holly thought, deciding she needed a drink of water. Or whiskey. No, she told herself, better keep her mind clear. She moved to the kitchen and put ice in two glasses. She ran tap water over the ice, then returned to the living room and handed a glass to Lance.

He glanced at the clear liquid, his expression hopeful. "Vodka?"

She smiled and shook her head. "Water. I think we both need a clear head right now. Have a seat. I have trouble thinking with you pacing around like a caged lion." She didn't add that she also had trouble keeping her eyes to herself.

"Make that a helpless lion," Lance corrected. "I feel helpless."

Holly settled into the chair she'd recently vacated, and Lance took a seat on her sofa. "When you decided on this profession, you didn't really think you could solve the world's problems, did you?"

His rueful grin said it all. "I think maybe I did."

She arched a brow. "Don't tell me this is the first time you've run into trouble?"

"No . . . but this is the first case like this one. I can't send her home if she doesn't want to go, not in the state she's in, and I absolutely cannot let her stay with me."

Holly had a feeling she knew where this was leading. "Are you asking what I think you're asking? You want her to stay here with *me*?"

He shot her a pleading look that was as irresistible as his smile. Heaven help her if he ever discovered the power he could wield over her.

"I don't know anyone else to ask."

Her bones liquefied at his low-voiced confession. "What about school tomorrow?" she asked.

"She says she's not going."

"I suppose I could ask Mrs. Teasedale if she can stay with her while I'm at work," Holly mused, nibbling on her lip.

"Or you could take her to work—keep her busy *and* keep an eye on her."

She could, she supposed, knowing instinctively that Mini and Reuben would be a wonderful influence on the troubled girl. "When are her parents expected home?"

"Saturday."

"And what about your date tomorrow night?"

"I'll reschedule, of course."

The words were out before Holly could think them through. "I don't think you should cancel." *Was she out of her mind?* What point was she trying to prove? Lance was offering to cancel, and she was encouraging him to go out with that blond bombshell.

"I can't ask you to do this alone," Lance said quickly— too quickly. "I've been without a social life for four years. I believe I can wait another week."

He doesn't sound too eager to go out with Debbie, Holly realized with a forbidden surge of pleasure. She scolded her unruly heart, reminding herself that Lance was a heartache waiting to happen. Indeed, this seemed to prove it: Apparently he'd gotten cold feet since she'd told him about Debbie on the phone.

It wasn't just Debbie, though, Holly thought, feeling foolish now that she thought about it. It was any woman— including herself. Lance was still hung up on his wife, and if he didn't get out and start meeting people, women in particular, he might never break the invisible tie with her. He would never be *free.*

As much as it pained her, he *needed* this date with Debbie. This date, and many, many more.

Holly gave herself a rueful mental shake over her contrariness. She didn't want him to date other women, but she did. When he indicated excitement over the prospect, she experienced a violent surge of jealousy; if he indicated reluctance, she became worried that he was hanging on to the past.

Nike bounded into the room and placed his head on her lap. Holly absently stroked his ears as she looked at Lance. "I really think you should keep your date with Debbie," she said, pleased to hear herself sounding so firm and neutral. "Bridget and I will catch a movie or rent a few videos. Maybe she'll open up to another woman." When Lance hesitated, Holly deliberately misconstrued his reluctance. "I promise to take good care of her. Meanwhile, you be thinking about a solution."

Lance rose from the sofa and approached her. Nike scrambled out of the way and flopped onto the floor beside her chair. Holly tilted her head to look at Lance, her heart pounding faster as he leaned over her and placed his hands on the chair's arms. They were close, so close she could see the admiration in his eyes and the stubble cropping up along his chin and jaw. Her stomach did a funny little flip-flop and continued to spasm as the low, vibrant sound of his voice washed over her.

"You are an incredible woman," he said, staring into her eyes. "I count myself lucky to have you for a friend."

She didn't want to be his friend. She wanted to be his lover, his life. *His wife.* The silent confession jolted Holly. Her gaze widened as if she feared he could read her mind.

She managed to say lightly, "Surely you have other women friends?"

"Passing acquaintances. Friends of . . . Mona's." He shook his head. "I couldn't have called them—I don't feel comfortable with them the way I do with you."

"Comfortable" was the last word Holly would have used to describe how she felt around Lance. Her knees trembled. Her thighs ached, and her heart thrashed against her rib cage like a banked fish. Deep in the recesses of her mind, she could hear the whispered chant, *He's the one, he's the one.*

Holly knew it, but she was so very afraid that *she* wasn't the one for *him.*

"I probably shouldn't have pulled you into this—"

"I don't mind." *Suck-up.* Holly couldn't argue with the

snide little voice. "I remember what it was like to be a teenager."

"You still look like one."

"Flattery will get you everywhere," Holly teased. Only it came out in a provocative whisper. She saw by the sudden darkening of his eyes that Lance had noticed and was drawing his own conclusions.

He didn't have far to go to reach her parted lips.

The unexpected kiss tempted her to forget about her smart decisions regarding Lance Wilder. For just a few rebellious seconds, she kissed him back, closing her eyes and letting the thrills shimmy down her spine and pool in her belly. She could kiss this man for hours and never grow tired of it, she thought.

But she *would* need air. Gasping, she broke away and turned her head, breathing fast and hard. Avoiding his desire-inducing gaze, she attempted to dispel the dangerous moment by joking, "Do you kiss all of your 'friends' this way?"

"I told you, I don't have any like you."

"Oh." With a shaky laugh, Holly gently pushed him away and stood. Her legs matched her voice. "I think we'd better go see about Bridget, don't you?"

His gaze dropped to her moist mouth. "Yeah, maybe we should. It's getting a little warm in here."

"Warm" was an understatement, Holly thought, watching the movement of his tight butt as she followed him to the door.

Hot was more accurate.

It was late before Lance managed to return to Holly's apartment to look in on Bridget. He checked his watch as he waited for someone to answer the door. Eight o'clock. His stomach gave an embarrassing rumble, reminding him that he hadn't eaten since noon, and then all he'd had was a stale tuna sandwich. Hardly what he'd call lunch, but it was all he'd had time for.

The door opened. Holly stood on the threshold, looking

rumpled and sexy in jeans and a T-shirt. She raked her hair from her eyes and offered him a shy smile, one hand propped on her hip.

Lance wished she'd offer him more than just a smile.

"Sorry I'm late," he said, moving into the apartment when she stepped aside. Bridget was nowhere in sight. "I had an unexpected emergency crop up and had to make a house call."

"You make house calls?"

He smiled faintly at her obvious surprise. "When it's an emergency. Where's Bridget?"

Holly crossed the room, gently opened the closed door, and peered inside. She stood back and indicated that Lance should take a look.

Lance inhaled the faint scent of Holly's perfume as he gazed through the crack in the door. Bridget lay on Holly's bed, one arm flung above her on the pillow, her red hair a wild, confused mass around her face. The golden retriever was stretched out beside her; both dog and girl were snoring softly.

Quietly Lance pulled the door closed and waited until he'd moved away before he spoke again. "How long has she been asleep?"

"About two hours."

"Did she say anything relevant?"

Holly shook her head. " 'Fraid not. I made spaghetti for dinner—she said it was her favorite—but she hardly spoke a word. After she finished eating she announced she was tired and wanted to lie down. I don't think the poor angel's slept a wink since her parents left town."

"Hmm." He'd hoped that Bridget would open up to Holly.

"Lance, have you met her parents? Do they seem like ogres to you?"

"That's the problem: I never met them. Mrs. Wooten called last week and made the appointment, but Bridget came in her own car."

Frowning, Holly moved to a chair and propped her

knee on the seat and her thumbs in her pockets. The innocent pose pulled the T-shirt taut across her breasts, outlining her nipples. Lance felt a kick in his groin at the delectable sight.

"Don't you think it's strange that they would leave her on her own when she's clearly having problems?"

"I questioned Bridget about that, and she said there was a death in the family, so they had no choice but to leave her."

"They could have insisted she go with them."

Lance shook his head. "Bridget cleared that up as well. She told them she had an important test at school that she couldn't miss. She was hoping to get Eric, the father, to talk to her."

"But he wouldn't," Holly mumbled as if to herself. Her frown deepened. "There's just something fishy, something I can't quite put my finger on. If *I* had a troubled child under a doctor's care, I would never think of leaving her alone."

"I feel the same way, and thanks for not calling me a shrink." He would have said more, but his empty stomach chose that moment to complain loudly. Holly's head shot up at the betraying sound.

"You haven't had dinner?"

"How did you guess?" Lance asked with a rueful grin. "I was on the verge of grabbing a sandwich when the phone rang. By the time I convinced Junior that it wasn't his fault his gerbil died, it was already so late—"

"I'll heat up the spaghetti." She disappeared into the kitchen, leaving Lance to follow if he wished.

He did. Holly was a lure that he couldn't ignore—not that he wanted to. He leaned against the doorway, watching her move from the counter to the microwave, then back again as she chopped lettuce and diced tomatoes for a salad. His stomach caught the spicy scent of spaghetti sauce heating and voiced its anticipation in a loud series of embarrassing rumbles, earning a cheeky grin from Holly.

Lance caught his breath at the beauty of her smile. He wondered what she would do if he lifted her onto the counter and proceeded to make wild passionate love to her. Given that option, he was certain his stomach could wait.

Tossing him a glance over her shoulder as she pulled a plate from the rack above the sink, she asked, "Did you want children when you were married?"

Taken aback by her personal question, Lance shrugged. "We'd planned on having one or two. How about yourself?"

"I thought I wanted a half dozen or so, but after tonight . . ." She shuddered. "Poor Bridget. I don't even know her, but I already feel as if I should do something for her. I'd probably go crazy if she were my own."

"Imagine how her mother's going to feel."

"I can, which is why I've changed my mind about the number of kids I'd have." She set the salad on the small dining table and put the plate of microwaved spaghetti next to it. After adding silverware and a glass of milk, she urged him to sit.

Lance did as she instructed, his mouth watering at the sight of the spaghetti. She sat across from him, her chin propped in her hands. Audience or not, he was starving. He wound a forkful of spaghetti around the tines and took a vigorous bite. It was delicious.

He'd made a definite hole in the pile of steaming pasta before she spoke again.

"What happened to your wife?"

He nearly choked at the question. Prudently he chewed, swallowed, then took a drink of his milk. He leveled his gaze on hers, keeping his expression carefully neutral. The pain was still there, but he was both surprised and relieved to note that it had dulled with time. He would always cherish his time with Mona, and he knew the memories would be with him till he died, but she was gone. "Advanced ovarian cancer."

"I'm sorry," she whispered.

Lance stared at the shimmering tears in her eyes for a long moment. He knew then what he'd only suspected before: He was fast falling in love with Holly Wentworth. She was as sweet as honey, yet sexy as hell; compassionate, yet tough where it counted. The fact that she was beautiful was just an added bonus.

He cleared his throat. "Thank you. She—she went quickly." Despite his pleas, and finally his raging, desperate demands, Mona had refused treatment to prolong her terminal illness.

"Well," Holly said with a smile, slapping her hands on the table and effectively dispelling the serious moment. "How about some coffee and dessert? The special today is Rocky Road ice cream with hot fudge sauce."

"Bridget, I presume?" Lance was blinded by that smile and amazed that she could lift his spirits so easily.

"It's her favorite," Holly confirmed. "And she nearly ate the entire carton before I forcibly removed it from her hands. That was *before* dinner." She leaned close to whisper in his ear, her breath tickling his neck, "I probably shouldn't tell you this, but the remedy for a broken heart *isn't* another man."

He turned his head to look at her, feigning shock. "It isn't?"

"Nope." She shook her head, her eyes twinkling. "It's ice cream."

As Lance chuckled, he had to curl his fingers around the table edge to keep from pulling her onto his lap. *She's the one,* his heart chanted. And soon . . . *very* soon, she would know it.

Fourteen

When Holly told the sleepy-eyed Bridget over breakfast that Lance had a date and that she would be staying with her again, she never dreamed the teenager would react so violently.

"He's *what*?" Bridget screeched, shoving back her chair and leaping to her feet. She stared at Holly as if she'd suggested they ride a burro to Chicago.

Calmly Holly said, "He's going on a date. I told him that I didn't mind keeping you company."

"But I thought—I mean, what kind of shrink is he, anyway? I'm having a crisis, and all he can think about is—is—" Bridget sputtered to a halt, her red hair a wild halo around her head. She flopped back into the chair, tears welling in her strangely colored eyes. "I just can't believe it! I thought he was—was *different* from other men!"

A quiver of alarm swept through Holly at Bridget's words. The girl thought Lance had let her down—just as her boyfriend had let her down. "Bridget, Mr. Wilder is a professional and very good at his job." She paused delicately. "How many doctors do you know who would have done what he did? Most would have called your parents immediately."

Bridget narrowed her eyes, her tone belligerent. "He said everything I told him was confidential."

"It is," Holly said hastily, "but he could have just told them to come home. He wouldn't have had to tell them *why.*"

"Then why didn't he?" she demanded. She picked at her toast, shredding the bread onto her plate of half-eaten scrambled eggs. "I can't even count on my own shrink!"

"Is that what you really wanted him to do?" Holly asked, beginning to see the picture. "You wanted Mr. Wilder to go ahead and call your parents?"

Bridget shrugged, her expression both tearful and sullen. It was a pitiful-looking combination. "I guess I did."

Holly stirred artificial sweetener into her second cup of coffee. "Maybe you could call them now," she suggested.

"Maybe I could. It doesn't look like anyone *else* is going to."

"You can use the phone in the bedroom."

"Fine." Shoulders slumping dejectedly, Bridget went into the bedroom. The door slammed shut, causing Holly to jump.

A few moments later, Bridget emerged. She wiped at her streaming eyes and looked at Holly. "They're coming home tonight. I guess I'll have to talk to them."

"It might be a good idea."

"*You* don't know my parents," Bridget grumbled. "They'll hit the roof."

"They'll come around. Just give them a little time." Holly hoped she was right. "Meanwhile, how about coming to the office with me today."

"Oh, great. Just what I need—to be around a bunch of idiots wanting to fall in love! Thanks, but no thanks. It was bad enough having to watch you slobber all over Mr. Wilder."

Holly gasped. "Excuse me?"

A feral smile tilted the corners of Bridget's mouth. Her eyes seemed to gleam. "Did you think I wouldn't notice? You've got a monstrous crush on Mr. Wilder. Admit it."

"I don't have a crush." Even to her own ears, Holly's voice sounded feeble. *Was* it that obvious? "He's—he's an attractive man, I'll agree, but I—"

"Cut the crap, Miss Wentworth. I may be a kid, but I'm not dumb." She shrugged. "But it's your life. If you want to let a hunk like Mr. Wilder slip away, that's your business."

"As I recall, a few moments ago you didn't think he was that great," Holly reminded her.

"Yeah, well, I was mad at him."

"And you're not now?"

Bridget tilted her head as if pondering Holly's question. Finally she said, "Nah, I guess not."

Holly relaxed, glad the subject had changed, and equally as glad Bridget's anger at Lance seemed to have dissolved. "I'll drop you at Dr. Wilder's house on my way to work." When Bridget looked at her blankly, Holly frowned. "That *is* where you left your car, isn't it?"

"Oh, yes!" Bridget laughed. "I forgot. I'll just go wash my face and get dressed." She turned toward the bedroom, stopped, then swung back around. "By the way, you're *much* prettier than Mrs. Wilder."

Startled, Holly sat up straight in the chair. "You mean, the late . . . Mrs. Wilder?"

Bridget rolled her eyes. "Who else?"

"What . . ." Holly bit her tongue. No. She wouldn't stoop to asking a child questions about Lance's dead wife, no matter how tempting. "Never mind."

Giggling, Bridget disappeared into the bedroom.

Holly stared after her, swallowing question after question. How did Bridget know what the former Mrs. Wilder looked like? Did Lance talk about her to his patients? Reminisce about old times, despite his earlier comment to the contrary?

Eventually Holly came to a solemn conclusion: Lance must keep a picture of Mona in his office. It was the only way Bridget could have known, unless she'd known her personally, and Holly didn't think she had.

Her wedding ring close to his heart and her picture in his office. With those constant reminders, what chance did another woman have?

Holly's heart sank at the thought.

It was quarter of eight when the doorbell rang. Lance frowned, caught in the act of brushing his teeth. His first appointment wasn't until nine o'clock. Hell, he was only half-dressed, had yet to shave, and his first cup of coffee was still too hot to drink. Grumbling, he grabbed a shirt from his closet and struggled into it as he made for the front door.

He recognized Holly through the misted glass. Alarm warred with pleasure. Had something happened to Bridget? Why else would Holly Wentworth be at his front door so early in the morning? It was a sure bet she hadn't come to see him for a little morning delight.

Ha! As if he could be so lucky!

When he opened the door, he caught a glimpse of Bridget's Honda Civic speeding away from the house. "Something wrong?" he asked, looking at Holly. She was certainly something to look at, he thought, his gaze traveling along her sleek form. She was dressed in a fashionably long metallic silver skirt, complemented by a heavy silver chain and silver hoop earrings. Her blouse was a soft gray silk, molding to her breasts and giving him a clear idea of their size and shape. It reminded him how close he'd once been to filling his hands with their softness.

"No, nothing's wrong."

Her voice brought him back to earth with a jarring thud. He glanced behind her again. "Wasn't that Bridget?"

"Yes. She called her parents and asked them to come home." Her gaze flicked over him, leaving a tingling awareness in its wake.

Belatedly Lance remembered that he hadn't buttoned his shirt. But, then, he hadn't shaved or combed his hair, either. He probably looked as if he'd pulled an all-nighter. "I, ah, was just getting dressed."

"So I see."

Again Lance felt the heat of her gaze on his bare chest. He opened the door wider. "Can I interest you in a cup of coffee?" *Or something just as hot?* The lewd suggestion nearly spilled from his lips.

"Thanks, but I've had my limit this morning. I brought Bridget to her car and thought I'd better let you know what's going on. She decided to go into school today, so she was in a hurry."

"I appreciate your help." Nice, polite words. Little did she suspect he was uncomfortably hard inside his jeans. "Would you like to come in? You could wait in the office while I finish getting dressed." He'd have rather had her in the bedroom watching him, but he guessed by the sudden wariness that flared in her eyes that this possibility was out of the question.

She checked her watch, frowning. "I need to get to the office. Actually, there isn't much to tell. Bridget confessed that when her meeting with Eric didn't pan out, she was hoping you'd overrule her and call her parents. When you didn't, she decided to do it herself."

Lance leaned against the door frame with a moan of frustration. He gave his forehead a short, vigorous rub, baring his teeth in a grimace. "I'm a psychologist, not a mind reader."

Holly smiled. "I thought mind reading was a requirement for the job."

The ache in his groin intensified at the sight of her white, even teeth and moist, parted lips. "Obviously Bridget thought so." He cleared his throat of the telltale huskiness, then blew his efforts in the next breath. "Are you sure you won't come in? I could read your palm . . . or something."

She looked amused. "It's the *something* that worries me."

"*Don't* worry," Lance urged, dropping his voice and

leaning closer. She smelled good. Damned good. Almost as good as she looked. "Don't you ever just want to let nature take its course? Allow fate to work its will?" He racked his brain for similar clichés.

"Jump in with both feet?" she supplied helpfully.

"Yes, that too."

"No."

His eyes widened at her unexpected answer. "No?"

"No."

"You've never done anything on impulse in your life?"

She hesitated before answering. "Yes. I went out with you."

Lance's hopes plummeted at her somber tone. "And you regret it?"

With a quick shake of her head, she said, "I didn't say that I regretted it. In fact, I had a really great time."

"But?"

"But . . . once was enough."

"For you, maybe. Not for me." Before she could speak, he held up his hand. "No, wait. I have to ask: Will you go out with me again sometime?"

Her teeth raked her bottom lip. "I don't know."

Lance wanted to dance a jig. Instead he nodded. "At least you didn't say no."

"Maybe I just don't want to hurt your feelings."

"But that's not the truth, is it? You want to go out with me. You had fun, but you're afraid of something."

She laughed, the husky sound rippling over him like warm caramel. "You were right: You're not good at reading minds."

His sheepish laughter echoed hers. "No, but I'm good at fantasies." Boldly he reached out and slid the dark curtain of her hair behind her ear. His fingers remained tangled in the silken strands as he cupped the back of her head. Tugging gently, he drew her across the threshold and into his arms. She braced her hands against his bare chest, inhaling sharply. The sound was sweet music to Lance's ears.

Nothing or no one had ever felt so right.

"Want to hear one of my fantasies?" he whispered.

"Some other time, perhaps?" she whispered back. "I'm late for the office."

"Promise?"

She hesitated. "Someday—maybe." Her gaze dropped from his. "Meanwhile, you've got a hot date tonight. You're—you're just starting to get out. You should play the field, meet lots of new women."

His fingers moved persuasively against her scalp. He watched as her eyes began to droop. She jerked them open. "Why, Miss Wentworth, I didn't know you had a degree in psychology."

Pulling away, she flashed him a mysterious smile. "There's a *lot* you don't know about me, Wilder."

As she turned and began to walk away, Lance called after her, "I intend to find out!"

She looked at him over her shoulder, but kept walking. "Good luck." With a wave and another faint smile, she got into her car and closed the door.

Lance watched until she was out of sight. Finally, with a wistful sigh, he shut the door, intending to head to the bathroom and remove the stubble from his jaw.

His bare toes bumped against something on the floor. Startled, he glanced down at the large yellow envelope at his feet.

He was certain it hadn't been there moments ago.

Intrigued, he scooped the envelope up and opened it. Inside was a neat stack of papers held together by a gold paper clip. His eyes quickly scanned the contents on the first page, recognizing the same questions he'd answered during his interview at Romance Connection.

It *was* an interview packet, and the name at the top had him whistling under his breath.

The interview packet was Holly's own personal file.

Debbie Mosely had the kind of voice that shouted sex appeal. It was low and sweet with just a hint of Demi

Moore–style huskiness. Lance imagined that just talking to Debbie left men fantasizing about the body that went with the mouth. So naturally he was a little nonplussed when he realized that Debbie's 900-number voice did absolutely nothing for his libido.

After talking to her to confirm the pickup time, he found that his heart was still beating at the same, steady pace and that not one single fantasy popped into his mind.

He couldn't even summon up a smidgen of curiosity about her.

Lance turned out the lights and closed his office door. It was time to get ready for his date. He firmly pushed the worries of the day aside and concentrated instead on the file that had so mysteriously appeared.

Inside the file had been a man's most fervent dream: details about exactly what pleased the woman he was attempting to woo.

Inside that file, he'd discovered Holly Wentworth's favorite color, what she liked most in a man, her ambitions in life, her credentials, her pantyhose size, her ring size, and Lance's favorite part—her secret sexual fantasies. There was more, lots more, but for some strange reason, he couldn't recall much past the sexual fantasy section.

He grinned as he twisted the knob on the shower and started to undress, remembering another interesting fact he'd learned from the file: Holly Wentworth had majored in psychology for the first two years of college, but had decided it wasn't for her. Still, he supposed the knowledge came in handy in the business of connecting couples. Hell, Lance figured it was why she was so successful.

Stepping beneath the hot spray, Lance began to sing in a lusty voice while his thoughts continued to roam. When he'd fed her the shrimp at the sports bar and grill, he'd had no idea it was one of Holly's secret fantasies. If he *had* known, he would have kissed her after each bite, just as she'd described the fantasy in her file.

Next time he'd be prepared. In the meantime, he was

going to concentrate on the little things she'd mentioned. By the time she agreed to go out with him again, she would be so overwhelmed by how suited they were that she wouldn't have time for doubts or suspicions. Of course, he'd have to be careful not to do and be *exactly* what she was looking for, lest she find out the truth.

All hell would break loose if she did, Lance had no doubt.

An hour later, he pushed the doorbell of the modest single-story house at 106 Masterson Street and waited for Debbie to answer the door. His collar felt too tight. Of course, it might have had something to do with the white picket fence surrounding the neatly mowed front lawn, or the cute little mailbox in the shape of a rabbit. Everything he viewed screamed *family*.

Not that he was averse to having a wife and a family. True, after Mona died and before he met Holly, that sort of thing had seemed far in the future. Now, however, he found himself thinking about it a lot.

But not with Debbie Mosely.

"It's just a date, Wilder," he muttered. "Not a marriage proposal."

The door opened. His startled gaze flew to the woman standing before him. A lump the size of a goose egg seemed to lodge in his throat. He couldn't speak—could barely breathe. She was beautiful, just as Holly described. Blond, blue-eyed, petite.

And she looked like Mona.

"You must be Lance."

He automatically took her proffered hand, his gaze glued to those cherished features. But, no, this wasn't Mona. She resembled Mona, yes, but she *wasn't* Mona. And Holly couldn't have known . . . could she? Holly was a professional. She would never be so cruel as to pair him with a woman who resembled his late wife.

Would she?

"You do talk, don't you?"

Her husky, teasing little laugh jolted Lance. At least

she didn't *sound* like Mona, he thought, relieved beyond measure. Mona's laugh had been loud and vibrant, her smile quick and without guile.

Debbie's smile was slow and sexy; it complemented the hungry look in her eyes. Lance recognized that look. Hell, he hadn't gotten this far in life without having seen that look.

But he felt no urge to respond in kind.

He swallowed and removed his hand from hers. "Sorry. You . . . you reminded me of someone, and for a moment there I guess I was startled."

A perfectly shaped brow rose in question. The hungry look receded. "Someone nice, I hope."

Lance hesitated. He could blow it off and get through the night as painlessly as possible, or he could be honest with her. Staring into her direct blue eyes, Lance decided to come clean. No need to waste her time and his own, and no way could he "party hearty" with the spitting image of Mona. "My late wife."

Her laughter stunned Lance. Outrage and anger he expected—but not humor!

"I take it Miss Wentworth's never seen her picture?" She chuckled, wiping at her eyes.

With a rueful smile, Lance shook his head. "My guess would be no."

"Gads, I'm glad *you* don't look like *my* dearly departed!" Her comment sent her into fresh laughter. When it subsided, she said, "We'd probably both check ourselves into the nearest mental facility."

Lance was surprised to find himself grinning. Her laughter was infectious, her humor much more welcome than the anger he'd expected. Maybe the night wasn't wasted after all. On impulse, he said, "If you like Italian food, maybe we could have dinner anyway? I have reservations at Goolies."

She waved him inside. "Why not? I guess it's pretty obvious we won't be having anything else, right?" When he blushed, she laughed and swatted his arm as if they were old high school friends. "I have to confess, I'm disappointed. You are truly the hunk Miss Wentworth said you were."

"She said that?" Lance thought his heart might have stopped beating.

Debbie's eyes crinkled. "So, it goes both ways, eh?"

"I'm not following you."

"I got the impression Miss Wentworth was having a difficult time handing you over to me."

"You did?"

"Yes, I did. She mangled the pencil she was holding beyond recognition, and a time or two I swear I saw murder in her eyes." Debbie's grin was pure naughtiness as she looked him up and down. "Can't say I blame her, Lance. Are you *sure* I look like your late wife? It's been, what, four years? Maybe you're mistaken."

She looked so hopeful, Lance had to laugh, which in turn relaxed him even more. Debbie Mosely's quirky personality was contagious. Instinctively he knew she would be a fun date. The cards were on the table; they both realized they could never be anything more than friends.

But Holly didn't have to know the truth, did she?

The thought thrust into his mind and took root, sparking an idea. Did he dare let Debbie in on his secret? Could he trust her?

"So," Debbie said, hooking a friendly arm through his as they walked to his car. "If you two are hot for each other, what's the holdup?"

Bingo.

Lance smiled.

Fifteen

After an extensive search of the apartment, Mini faced the truth: The crystal ball was lost!

She flung herself on the bed and sobbed into the pillow. Since she was thirteen, she'd never gone a day without her crystal ball within reach. It was her friend, her comfort, her legacy.

It was also the last link she had to a way of life she'd lived for several centuries.

Xonia tried her best to console her friend. She patted Mini's head with the end of her tail. "Don't worry, Mini. It's got to be here somewhere. We'll find it."

Her voice muffled, Mini cried, "But where could it be? It didn't just get up and walk away!"

"Maybe . . . Never mind."

Mini lifted her head and stared at Xonia through a blur of tears. "What? What is it? Do you know something?"

"You'll get mad, so just forget I mentioned it."

"Mentioned what, Xonia? If you know something about the crystal ball, you have to tell me." The more Xonia avoided answering, the more alarmed Mini became. "Xonia?"

Finally Xonia sighed. "I was just going to suggest that

maybe Reuben misplaced it." After a short hesitation, she added in a near whisper, "On purpose."

Frowning, Mini sat up. "Why would Reuben have my crystal ball in the first place? I don't think—"

"I was right, you're getting mad." Xonia sounded smug and aggrieved at the same time. "It's beyond your comprehension to think your husband might be less than perfect."

Mini had never been so confused in her life. "Xonia, I don't know what you're talking about."

"What I'm saying, dear friend, is that Reuben might be protecting his privacy by hiding the crystal ball. He doesn't want you to know what he's doing, and he's afraid you'll be tempted to take a look for yourself."

"I don't believe you." Mini made the denial, but it wasn't a strong one. A germ of doubt had begun to grow. What if Xonia was right? What if Reuben didn't trust her? She'd promised him a long time ago she would never use the ball to spy on him, but what if he didn't believe her? Wasn't it true that she'd been tempted? Maybe he'd sensed it.

Close on the heels of these questions came a more disturbing one. What was Reuben hiding? He claimed he was meeting a few of his male friends when he left in the evening, but if it was as innocent as that, why would he hide her crystal ball? Tonight he'd made the same excuse, promising to meet them later at the Italian restaurant where Lance and Debbie planned to dine.

For over two hundred years—two hundred and twenty-five this Allhallows Eve—Mini had never had reason to doubt Reuben's faithfulness.

Should she now? Why *would* she now? He'd asked her to trust him. Was she a fool to trust him? Pinning her bright green eyes on her best friend, she demanded, "Just answer me one question, Xonia. Is Reuben cheating on me?"

Xonia hesitated a heartbeat, but it was enough to launch Mini's heart into arrest.

"Well, no, not exactly. He's—"

The rest of her words were muffled and thankfully indistinguishable because of the pillow over Xonia's head. When Mini was certain she'd gotten the hint, she slowly lifted the pillow. Xonia's scruffy fur looked even scruffier.

Her golden eyes glittered with anger. She arched her back and hissed at Mini. "I'm getting tired of your bullying, Mini. I never knew you were so stubborn! You're losing sleep wondering where your husband's getting himself off to, yet you won't even let me tell you that he's—"

Mini lifted the pillow high in the air, clearly warning Xonia.

Xonia snapped her mouth shut. Her eyes narrowed to slits; her whiskers fairly quivered with outrage. "I can't believe you're treating me this way." She sniffed. "Me, your best friend in the whole world! Why, if I hadn't volunteered to come along as your protector, you might have gotten some horrid, spinster witch who didn't give a fig about you or your arrogant, lying husband!"

"You mean, you care about Reuben?" Mini asked, holding hopefully on to the thought and forgetting the rest. She knew Xonia was angry and that like any normal hot-tempered witch, she said things in anger that she didn't really mean. It was so common, grudges among witches were few and far between.

Of course, Reuben and Xonia had been the rare exception.

"Well, I wouldn't go *that* far, but I do confess he *might* not be the nasty warlock I thought him to be." Grudgingly she added, "I've discovered over the past few weeks that he has a few acceptable traits."

Suddenly she glanced past Mini's shoulder and let out a hair-raising yowl that made Mini jump. "Heavens, look at the time! We've got to get going! Lance and that man-eating ex–beauty queen are probably already there."

Mini followed her friend's line of vision to the digital alarm clock on the nightstand. She let out a shriek that rivaled Xonia's yowl. "If only I had my crystal ball! We don't even know how the *meeting* went."

"I doubt they had time for a quickie," Xonia muttered dryly. "Even Chaos isn't *that* fast."

"Chaos?" Mini stared at Xonia in bewilderment.

Xonia ducked her head and pretended to sharpen her claws on the mattress. "He's a cat I met a few days ago."

"A cat? A *real* cat?"

The feline continued to avoid eye contact. A hint of defensiveness entered her voice. "Yes, he's a real cat, but he's also a real sweetheart. I'll have to introduce you sometime." With a graceful leap, she jumped to the floor. "Now, we'd better get ready."

"Don't forget to change my eye color this time. I don't want Lance to get suspicious."

Xonia rolled her eyes. "I won't forget. I just hope Reuben doesn't let us down. If we're going to be convincing, his presence is imperative."

"He'll be there," Mini stated with far more conviction than she felt.

The atmosphere at Goolies was noisy and relaxing, the air redolent of oregano, basil, garlic, and freshly baked bread. Waiters shouted and cursed one another in a mixture of Italian and English, and everywhere families and couples talked and laughed as they ate. It was a happy place to be, Lance decided, letting the last trace of tension flow from his body. He was with a friend, not a date; the pressure was off.

He ordered the chicken primavera, and Debbie finally decided on Goolies' famous spaghetti served with fat Italian sausages and crusty French bread. When the waitress took their order and removed their menus, Debbie leaned back in her chair with a sigh.

"I'll have to diet for a week after this meal." She patted her firm stomach. "Normally when I come in here, I order pasta with oil-free tomato sauce and no bread."

Lance eyed her trim figure, mentally and shamelessly

comparing it with Holly's fuller figure. "Looks like you could stand to gain a few pounds," he said diplomatically. She couldn't know that he preferred Holly's curved figure to hers. In his opinion, women these days were overly obsessed with staying thin—or *becoming* thin. Teens seemed especially vulnerable, and he'd certainly seen his share of anorexic young women. It was a sad, frustrating condition. Thank God Holly didn't seem to mind a little flesh on her bones!

"You're thinking about Holly," Debbie announced, smiling when he flashed her a guilty look. She waved her hand in a dismissive gesture. "Oh, don't worry. Believe me when I say I know when to fight and when to give in gracefully. This is definitely one of those times when I need to give in gracefully. Far be it from me to stand in Cupid's way."

Contrarily, Lance felt a little offended by her easy acceptance. "You don't have to sound so damned *happy* about it," he grumbled. He wasn't surprised when she laughed.

Finally, when she'd caught the eye of every appreciative male in the restaurant, she sobered. "Are you going to tell me why you two aren't together?"

"You won't think I'm insensitive?"

"For talking about another woman while you're with me?" Debbie shook her head. "Regret is a waste of time. I'm a lawyer, remember? Tough as nails. We have to be able to withstand those corny, degrading lawyer jokes. The fact that I'm a *blond* lawyer—well, need I say more?"

It was Lance's turn to chuckle. "I promise—no lawyer jokes. Although I do know a few blond—" A sharp kick to his shin quickly changed the direction of his thoughts. He told her about Casey, going to the Romance Connection for an interview, and meeting Holly for the first time. "I haven't been able to get her out of mind since then," he said. "But when I finally got her to go out with me, I blew it."

All ears, Debbie leaned forward. "How did you blow it?"

Lance told her. He could tell by the horrified expression on her face that he truly *had* blown it. "That bad, huh?"

"Hmm. I'd say so. If it were me, I'd probably mark you off as a lost cause. If I'm crazy about a guy, I want his full attention, and if I can't get it, I don't want to be with him. Unless, of course, he's just a friend."

"Sounds like you're speaking from experience," Lance said, watching the play of emotions on her face. Hurt had definitely been one of them, however brief.

"My late husband was a good father, but I don't think I ever filled *her* shoes."

"He was a widow?"

She shook her head. "No. He was divorced, but I don't think he ever stopped loving his first wife." She toyed with her water glass, her pensive gaze fixed on the tablecloth. It was clear her memories were painful, and Lance's heart went out to her. "One Sunday morning I woke up early and decided to surprise him with fresh doughnuts from the bakery. We lived in this condo on Clever Street, and the bakery was right around the corner. Anyway, they didn't accept checks, and I didn't have any cash. He was still asleep . . . so I got the money from his wallet."

Lance tensed, sensing her deepening pain.

"I found a picture in his wallet of *her*."

"I'm sorry." His hand found hers across the table. On second thought, it didn't seem enough. He scooted his chair closer to hers and slipped his arm around her shoulders. He gave her back a brotherly pat. "He must have been blind, deaf, and plain ole dumb not to realize what he had in you."

Her tremulous smile broke his heart. "Listen to you. You dumped me the moment you saw me."

"No," Lance corrected gravely, "I dumped you long before I met you."

His deadpan expression earned the desired results. Although tears shimmered in her eyes, Debbie grinned. Finally the laughter bubbled from her throat. He joined her, clapping his hand on his knee and roaring his mirth.

"You used to laugh with *me* that way!" an accusing voice shouted, rising above their laughter.

Blissfully unaware that the voice was directed at him, Lance glanced around to see who was so intent on making a scene.

A woman stood glaring at him from across their table. He did a double take. Glaring at *him*!

His astonished gaze dropped to her protruding, pregnant belly, then rose once again to her softly rounded face. She looked to be in her late twenties or early thirties. She might have looked younger, Lance thought, if her face hadn't been pinched with anger and her gray eyes hadn't looked so . . . so *old* and tired.

He was certain he'd never seen her before.

"Is *this* your next victim?" the woman demanded, transferring her worn-out glare to Debbie, who didn't so much as flinch.

The obvious misconception had gone on long enough. Lance gently but firmly said, "I'm sorry, ma'am, but you've got the wrong person."

Tears welled in the woman's eyes. Her bottom lip began to shake and shimmy. "Please, Lance. Don't do this to me!" She pressed a protective hand to her belly, her voice rising to a piercing wail. "Think about our baby!"

"I don't know you," Lance said evenly, relying on his years of training as a psychologist to keep himself calm. "And I'm certainly not the father of your baby. You've got me confused with someone else." The woman was suffering a breakdown, he thought. It was the only explanation. But it didn't explain how she knew his—

"If you don't know her, how does she know your name?" Debbie, long since over her laughing spell, plucked the question from his mind. She sat still and watchful, glancing at the woman with burgeoning pity, and at Lance with growing suspicion.

"Of course I know his name!" the woman huffed. "I'm

not a slut, you know. He said we were going to get married before the baby got here." The tears threatened again, and this time they managed to fall onto the woman's plump cheeks. She made no effort to wipe them away.

Lance rose from his chair, searching the woman's eyes for signs of dementia. He knew what to look for, and it wasn't there. This was a nightmare much worse than the one he'd suffered when he went out with—

Wait a moment. Casey. It had to be Casey and his sick idea of a joke. Casey knew what had happened the last time. Lance had even made a comment about being cursed.

Casey. Dear old, *dead* Casey. Or at least he would be when Lance reached him. Forcing a laugh—although he was far from being amused—Lance shook his head. "Okay, the joke's over. I know who put you up to—"

Crack! The slap effectively shut him up and echoed around the noisy restaurant like a startling, unexpected clap of thunder. Lance even fancied he heard the sound of a cat meow at the point of contact. The woman must have knocked him senseless!

Dazed by the blow—and obviously delirious—Lance needed a few moments to recover enough to realize the restaurant wasn't noisy any longer.

They had a captive audience of about fifty men, women, and children. Even the staff had paused in their harried duties to watch the scene.

But at the moment Lance wouldn't have cared if the CIA were watching. He was looking at something much more mesmerizing. The woman claiming to know him—claiming she carried their unborn child—wore a charm bracelet on her wrist. Dangling from the bracelet was a charm in the shape of a cat.

He remembered the bracelet from the sports bar, but it wasn't the same woman. The bracelet was quite unusual—surely it was too coincidental that within the same week, two different women he had come into contact with owned the identical unique bracelet? But as hard as he tried, his mind could not come up with a logical explanation.

What *was* becoming frighteningly clear was the fact that he'd been wrong: Casey wasn't involved.

The woman trembled; the tears fell faster. Her chest heaved as she glared at Lance with all the fury of a woman scorned. "You deserved that, you—you *pig*! I don't know what I ever saw in you!"

His jaw throbbing from her mighty blow, Lance regarded the hysterical woman. His gaze dipped briefly to her rounded belly. *Pregnant* woman, he silently reminded himself. In his profession, he dealt with hysterical people on a daily basis. He'd honed his skills over the years.

He had a sinking feeling this would be the mother of all tests.

Flicking Debbie a meaningful glance, Lance gestured to the empty chair opposite his own. In a voice carefully cultivated to inspire trust, he said to the woman, "Why don't you have a seat so that we can talk about this."

Debbie had been amazingly quiet; now she leaped to her feet and grabbed her purse from the chair beside her. "I'll just leave you two alone so that you can talk in private."

It wasn't exactly what Lance had in mind. In fact, her leaving was the *last* thing he wanted to happen. He'd hoped to use her unfamiliar presence to keep the woman grounded in reality. When Debbie left, he feared she could be taking that last lingering bit of reality with her.

He grabbed Debbie's arm and squeezed gently, meaningfully, forcing her to look him in the eyes. "Please don't leave." For a hopeful moment, her gaze softened at his plea.

"Oh, sure," the strange woman opposite him snapped, "by all means stay. He thinks I won't make a scene if you're here. He pulled this stunt last week with some bimbo named Terri."

Lance was astounded by her words. *Not make a scene?*

He hoped he never saw the woman in full action if she didn't consider screeching at the top of her lungs and slapping him a scene!

With a jerk, Debbie pulled her arm free. Her gaze frosted over. "I *liked* you," she stated sadly. "I guess I'm slipping."

Then she was gone, weaving through the tables and disappearing through the exit.

It was the woman's last remark that had done him in, Lance realized, sensing the beginnings of a panic attack. On the way to the restaurant, he and Debbie had exchanged amusing anecdotes of dates from hell. He'd told her about Terri and the credit cards. She had told him about dating a guy who believed his dog was an alien.

Lance forced himself to breathe deeply and evenly. He knew the symptoms—he was on the verge of hyperventilating. This couldn't be happening. It was not only a nightmare, but the most *bizarre* nightmare he'd ever experienced.

The worst, most frightening part was that he knew he wasn't dreaming. This was happening, and no matter how much Casey scoffed at the idea, Lance was fully convinced now that he was cursed.

Three dates. The first with Terri. She'd stomped from the restaurant believing him to be a sorry bum after the credit card companies canceled *two* of his cards.

The second date was with Holly, a very cherished, memorable evening—if one could forget the appalling ending when his wedding ring had fallen out of his pocket.

And now this one. Lance couldn't say it was the worst, because he and Debbie had decided within a few moments of meeting that it would be a "friends only" kind of date. She was stunned, disgusted, and disillusioned, but he didn't think she was hurt.

Not like Holly would have been.

Lance shuddered and turned to face the woman across from him.

He blinked, his heart stuttering to a stop.

The chair was empty; the woman was gone.

Sixteen

Mini and Xonia sat in a booth at Midnight Espresso nursing decaffeinated cappuccinos and deliberating on where Reuben could be. He hadn't shown at Goolies, and Xonia had been forced to zap them out while Lance wasn't looking. It had been a risky but necessary move.

A quick return to the apartment had been fruitless; Reuben wasn't to be found.

Sipping morosely on her French Vanilla cappuccino, Mini tapped her fingers restlessly against the cup. She was beginning to become very, very worried. Reuben had understood the importance of the meeting at Goolies. It wasn't like him to act so irresponsibly.

Fortunately Xonia had managed to improvise for him. Mini cringed to think of how many mortals might have witnessed their vanishing act. The witches' council would be furious if it found out.

If Reuben had shown, the vanishing act wouldn't have been necessary, Mini fumed uselessly. The moment Debbie left the restaurant, Reuben should have appeared—in the guise of a concerned father and incognito—to explain his daughter's mental state and apologize for the disruption. He would have led her away and out of the restaurant as if they were ordinary mortals, restoring Lance's sanity but perhaps changing his mind about his harebrained scheme to convince Holly he was over his late wife and willing to "party hearty."

Xonia's attempt yesterday to play upon his dedication to his profession had failed hopelessly.

"I'm sure the warlock will have a reasonable explanation," Xonia said, aimlessly stirring her cappuccino. The dollop of extra cream she'd ordered had nearly melted into the milky concoction.

Mini sighed and looked at her friend. Xonia had transformed herself into human form, but not any form that Reuben would recognize. They'd left him a note at the apartment telling him where they would be waiting.

For the umpteenth time, Mini glanced at the watch Reuben had bought her the day he'd brought home the VCR. When she'd asked him where he'd gotten the money, he'd shrugged and mumbled something about Holly having given him a bonus for running errands.

She frowned, remembering the scrap of black silk she'd found in the washer. Reuben had explained that as well, telling her he'd planned to surprise her with the skimpy men's underwear the next time Xonia left them alone. Every explanation was sound and reasonable . . . yet she couldn't shake the feeling that he was keeping something from her. And Xonia didn't help, constantly sighing and shaking her head.

Her friend knew, of course, but Mini was determined to continue trusting her husband. If he had something to tell her he would tell her in his own good time.

"Xonia, do you really think Reuben might have hidden the crystal ball?"

Xonia, caught in the middle of slurping her cappuccino, set the cup aside and reached for a napkin. She grimaced as she wiped the dribbling coffee from her chin. "I've been a cat so long I've forgotten how to drink the normal way."

Mini tapped her nails impatiently against her cup.

"Oh, you were asking if I thought Reuben would hide

the crystal ball." She steepled her fingers and contemplated her answer. "How do I put this? I do think he hid it, but I think I understand why." She seemed startled by her own confession. "I mean, when he finally decides to tell you, I think *you'll* understand as well."

Curiosity might have killed the cat, Mini thought, biting her tongue, but it was also killing *her*!

Slyly Xonia eyed her over the rim of her cup. "Are you ready to know?"

"Are you ready to wear this cappuccino?" Mini shot back.

"You know cats hate to get wet."

Mini wrinkled her nose. "I can tell."

The door chime sounded over the entrance to the coffee shop. Eagerly Mini swung around, fully expecting to see her handsome warlock sauntering in. Her heart leaped in anticipation. After she blasted him for making her worry, she would—

She inhaled sharply at the sight of Holly and Lance standing just inside the doorway.

The couple saw her at the same instant—and Xonia sitting across from her. Mini and Xonia wore identical expressions of surprise and confusion.

"Mini!" Holly exclaimed, looking from one stunned face to the other. "And Bridget! I didn't know that you two knew each other."

Mini half turned toward Xonia and snarled in a fierce whisper, "You can zap yourself out of a crowded restaurant, but you can't zap yourself out of an empty coffee shop?"

Keeping a smile on her face, "Bridget" said between clenched teeth, "They were the *last* people I expected to see! Besides, I didn't have time to worry about myself." She dropped a pointed gaze to Mini's bare wrist. "I thought we could explain my presence far easier than we could explain that charm bracelet you were wearing!"

• • •

"Imagine that," Holly murmured as she watched Mini and "Bridget" make a hasty retreat. Lance had asked if they'd like to join them in their booth, but Mini had quickly informed them she had to get the teenager home to her parents. "I know Lovit's a small town, but I never would have guessed that Bridget was Mini's niece!" She turned to find Lance looking as perplexed as she felt.

"Make that two of us. Bridget claimed she had no other family in town. I would have called Mini instead if I had known."

The waitress approached with a smile and a greeting. Holly ordered a decaffeinated English Toffee, and Lance requested straight espresso. Holly lifted a brow. "Doesn't that stuff keep you awake at night?"

"I don't need much sleep, and after this evening's fiasco, I doubt I'll sleep tonight anyway."

When he'd called her earlier, he'd sounded not only grim, but angry. Apparently his disposition hadn't changed. Holly had to admit she was dying of curiosity. "Are you going to keep me in suspense all night?" she asked.

Lance reached out and snatched her hand, folding it inside his own. His skin felt hot and rough. Beneath the table, Holly crossed her legs. Just one touch was all it took. One touch of his hand, one look from his piercing blue eyes and she was instant mush. *Remember the wedding ring,* she told herself.

"If it means you'll sit here with me all night, then I just might."

Somehow she mustered the willpower to reach for her purse with her free hand.

He relented. "Okay, you win—this time." He didn't let go of her hand as he warned, "But you're going to think I'm crazy."

"I already think that," she quipped tartly, glad to see a faint smile break the gloom of his mouth.

"Then you're going to think I'm even crazier."

"Try me."   •

The waitress arrived with their drinks. Lance reluctantly let go of her hand, but the moment the waitress left, he navigated the steaming cups and grabbed it again, threading his fingers through hers.

"I can't seem to be around you without touching you," he confessed.

Holly braced herself against the potency of his voice. Or she tried. Willpower and determination were two of the things that had been lacking most in her life lately.

Since it was becoming apparent that she held no control over her body, she resisted with words instead. "So you asked me to meet you here just to hold my hand?" He smiled, but there wasn't much humor in it, she noted. She supposed she should be insulted by the fact that he'd called her when his date hadn't worked out. Yes, she decided, she should be.

So why wasn't she?

"It wasn't the only reason, but it's a good one." He began to massage her fingers with light, feathery strokes as he announced seriously, "I think I'm cursed."

Holly started to laugh, but one good look at his expression changed her mind. He was serious! "Lance . . . you're not cursed. Whatever happened was just a coincidence, like with the credit cards—"

"I'm going to be a father."

Gulping, Holly could only stare at him in shock. For an insane moment, she thought he was telling her that he and Bridget—that they were— She quickly blotted out the horror of her thoughts.

Lance shook his head and sighed. "At least, that's what the woman who approached our table at Goolies believes. I think she may have convinced my date as well."

Of course he hadn't meant Bridget! Holly's face felt hot as she imagined his reaction if he knew what her thoughts had been. "You're—are you saying a woman—"

"A *strange* woman," Lance corrected, grim-faced and hard-eyed. "I've never met her before in my life. I swear it."

Holly digested this information. She took a sip of her steaming cappuccino, pulling her hand free at the same time. He didn't object. She wrapped her hands around her cup and sat forward. There was only one logical explanation. "Lance, you're a trained psychologist. Wasn't it obvious the woman was . . . ill? If you didn't know her—"

"I didn't," he grated as if he feared she wouldn't believe him.

She fell back against the booth. "Well, then, what are you worried about? You didn't know her, so obviously you aren't the father of her baby. It's that simple. The woman was either deranged, or it was an elaborate joke."

"She didn't look ill, and I'm convinced it wasn't a joke."

"Did she make a scene?"

"Did she ever!" He rubbed his cheek. "She even slapped me when I claimed I didn't know her. It was the most bizarre thing that's ever happened to me."

"Maybe you have a twin," Holly suggested. "You know they say everyone—"

"She knew my name."

Holly's jaw dropped. Lance reached out and gently closed it.

"And she knew that I had a date with a woman named Terri."

"You think she's been stalking you?" Holly squeaked, alarm skirting down her spine. "This could be serious, Lance. How did it end?"

Lance took a gulp of his espresso. "Debbie left when I invited the woman to sit down with us. I watched her leave, and when I turned around to confront the woman, she'd gone."

"Gone? Just like that? You didn't see her leave?"

He shook his head, frowning. "It was as if she vanished into thin air." His frown deepened, and Holly saw him hesitate. "There's something else. . . ."

"Fire away." With growing interest, she watched a red flush creep into his face.

"The woman wore a charm bracelet," he finally said, his voice lowering so that she had to lean forward to hear him. "One of the charms was in the shape of a cat, and when she slapped me I *thought* I heard the sound of a cat meowing."

He mistook her silence for disbelief, when in actuality Holly was remembering the yellow roses and the mysterious cat prints in her sink.

"I knew you'd think I was crazy," he added hurriedly, "but there's more. When you and I were in the sports bar, there was a woman sitting behind us. Do you recall seeing her?"

Holly was not about to admit that she'd had eyes only for him. If the First Lady had been sitting *in* the booth with them, she doubted she would have noticed. She'd been totally bewitched by the virile, sexy man sitting with her. In fact, she was having a hard time concentrating on the serious discussion at hand right now. She shook her head. " 'Fraid not."

"She was wearing a charm bracelet identical to the one the woman wore tonight."

"But you're sure it wasn't the same woman?"

"I'm certain."

"Coincidence?"

"I don't think so." Lance's gaze bore into hers, compelling her to believe him. He found her hand again and clasped it hard. "Either I'm losing my mind, or something *very* strange is going on."

"You look sane to me." Holly swallowed hard, hypnotized by his brilliant blue gaze. She forced herself to concentrate on the conversation. "I guess I should confess as well. Then we can be crazy together."

His brow rose high, disappearing beneath a lock of russet hair. "Don't tell me—*you're* going to be a father, too?"

Her faint smile acknowledged his feeble attempt at a joke. "No, but I do have a strange story involving yellow roses and cat paw prints in the sink." Quickly she told him about finding the roses on her kitchen table. "Nike and I searched the apartment, but the only clue we found was a set of muddy paw prints in the kitchen sink. *Cat* paw prints."

"The window?"

"Locked solid. Besides, I'm on the second floor, remember? As agile as cats are, I don't think one could climb a solid wall that high."

"Strange," Lance mumbled. "Now I'm convinced something is going on."

"While we're debating our sanity, I might as well solve another mystery. Did Bridget know your late wife?"

Lance shook his head.

"Seen a picture of her, maybe?" Holly asked, bracing herself for the answer.

"I don't know how she could have. The only place I keep her picture is . . . Well, she couldn't have."

Holly let it slide. It didn't take a lot of imagination to fill in the blank, but she preferred not to think about it.

"Why do you ask?"

Oh, that she had thought ahead and anticipated the question *her* question would prompt! Hoping he wouldn't probe too deeply, she said, "Bridget implied that we look nothing alike." His gaze roamed slowly over her features. By the time he lifted it to her eyes again, Holly was on fire. The blatantly male appreciation in his eyes didn't help matters.

"You don't. She was your classic blue-eyed blond beauty. Your beauty is more subtle, deeper, with a hint of mystery that can drive a man to distraction." He lifted a lock of her hair and studied it with all the intensity of a scientist peering into a microscope. "Your hair isn't just a vibrant chestnut. It's chocolate, cinnamon, and caramel, and beneath the light the colors shift and change. And your eyes . . . Sometimes they're a storm gray, and sometimes I see a hint of forest green." When she blushed and lowered her gaze, he dropped her hair and leaned away.

Holly bit her lip to keep from blurting out that the highlights he described so poetically came from a bottle. It was safer to forget what he said altogether. She changed the subject. "So do you think Bridget was just guessing?"

"If you're asking if I think Bridget has a connection to all of this, then no, I don't think she does."

A crowd of noisy teenagers came into the coffee shop, shattering the quiet atmosphere. With an impatient look around, Lance said, "Let's go to my house where we can talk in private."

Considering the current temperature of her body and the direction of her thoughts each and every time Lance looked at her with those bedroom eyes or touched her with those skillful hands, Holly didn't think it was a good idea. Being alone with Lance in a coffee shop was risky enough. Her lips formed the rejection, but she wasn't shocked to hear herself say, "My place is closer."

From her perch on the windowsill, Xonia watched Reuben closely as he denied taking Mini's crystal ball. He certainly *sounded* sincere. But if he didn't take it, who did?

"Mini, you know that I would never hide your crystal ball. I know what it means to you." Reuben's pose was defensive as he faced his irate wife across the kitchen table. "You have to believe me."

Mini fell silent as she stared at Reuben for a long, tense moment. What she found must have satisfied her, for she said, "Okay. I believe you. So now we're back to square one. What happened to my crystal ball?"

Oddly enough, Xonia believed him, too. She must be getting soft in her old age, she decided with a little growl of self-disgust. Behind her on the ground outside the window, her lover heard the sound.

The big tom responded by letting out an ear-splitting yowl. It was clearly a mating call, and Xonia knew that if she didn't join him soon he'd simply find another female.

Startled, Mini and Reuben looked in the direction of the sound. Xonia blushed and pretended a sudden interest in her claws. That damned cat was embarrassing sometimes.

This was one of those times.

"Why don't you ask *her*?" Reuben said, pointing a powerless finger her way.

Through narrowed eyes, Xonia contemplated the rug beneath his feet. A little twitch of her powerful tail and she could—

"Don't do it."

Xonia gave a guilty start as Mini issued the warning. She tossed her head and sniffed. Mini had lost the use of her magic, but she hadn't lost her perception. It was a pity, too, because Xonia knew an arrogant warlock who needed an adjustment. She was just the witch to do it, too. *With* pleasure.

"She has nothing to do with it," Mini told her husband with a dismissive wave of her hand. "I've questioned her."

Reuben made a frustrated sound in his throat. "Without the crystal ball, we can't monitor the mortals." He glanced at Xonia again. "Why isn't she watching them instead of staring at me as if I'm her next meal?"

As much as she hated to agree with Reuben, Xonia had to admit he had a point. Lance's next blunder might be irreparable. If that happened and she wasn't there, she'd never forgive herself.

She looked behind her to the alley below. The beautiful Himalayan gazed back at her with hopeful, lust-filled eyes. With a wistful sigh, Xonia twitched her tail and vanished from the windowsill.

Seventeen

~

As Holly fit her key into the lock, she thought of a half-dozen chores she would have done if she'd known she was going to have company.

She'd left a pile of clean laundry on her bed, intending to fold it later.

There was a dirty plate, a fork, and a saucer in the sink, and a pair of pantyhose, a bra, and panties hanging on the shower rod. Hopefully the panties were silk, and not the plain old comfortable cotton that represented half her underwear collection.

The door swung open just as she was trying to recall the last time she'd cleaned the underside of the commode lid—a cleaning chore a single female was hardly expected to remember.

And the fridge was empty. She normally did her weekly shopping on Saturday, so there would be nothing to feed a hungry man who had skipped dinner, unless he was partial to fruit-flavored yogurt or Just-Like-Real-Bacon doggie snacks.

Dust. There would be dust everywhere, for she had skipped her usual Wednesday dusting in favor of an old movie on television. She stifled a groan as she also remembered that on Saturday she usually changed the sheets and fluffed the pillows on her bed. That wouldn't be until tomorrow, which meant her sheets were a week old.

Nike slept in the bed, and she was fairly certain she sometimes drooled on her pillow.

Holly froze in the act of flipping on the light switch, intensely aware of Lance's being right behind her; she could hear him breathing. Surely to heaven she wasn't worried about the *sheets* on her bed? Lance would never see her sheets.

"I was expecting to be licked to death by Nike," Lance said, making her jump.

"I—I left him with Mrs. Teasedale while I was out. She's been spooked since I told her about the roses, and Nike hates staying by himself." Moistening her lips, Holly flipped the switch and waited for Lance to clear the door before she closed it. She automatically engaged the lock. Hopefully Lance wouldn't take it as a signal.

Or maybe she *really* hoped that he would.

Her treacherous heart began to pound at the thought.

To cover her sudden attack of nerves, Holly said with her back still to him, "You missed dinner. Maybe we should order a pizza or something." *Talk, Holly. He said you and he were going to talk. So talk.*

She didn't have time to turn around.

Lance pressed against her from behind, pinning her body to the door. The husky sound of his voice next to her ear sapped the strength right out of her legs.

"You said the magic words," he whispered into her ear.

She gasped as his teeth nipped her earlobe, then moved onto her neck. He swept her hair to one side and continued to savage her with hungry, searching lips. She could feel every hard inch of him pressing into her, could feel his urgency seep into her pores until her need matched his own.

So very glad for the cool wood beneath her hot cheek, Holly whispered shakily, "What—what are the magic words?"

" 'Or something,' " he growled. "Right now pizza is the last thing on my mind."

No need to ask what *was* on his mind, Holly thought, flattening her hands against the door as he continued to make her mindless with need. Not that she had any room to talk. She wouldn't be surprised, she reflected, to find indentations in the door later from the thrust of her hard nipples against the wood.

"Lance . . ." It was all the feeble protest her laboring lungs could manage as he lifted her shirt and pressed his lips to the sensitive spot between her shoulder blades. His scalding tongue licked a path from point to point, then drifted down to the small of her back.

Holly closed her eyes, a tiny, illicit moan escaping from her lips. She clutched the door to keep from sliding down. How did he know? How could Lance possibly know where she was the most sensitive? She'd never told anyone. The one lover she'd had—in college, briefly—hadn't even known.

The room went dark. Holly blinked, realizing that Lance had switched off the light. Just as she mustered another lame protest, he rose against her again. His big, strong hands gripped her hips as he slowly, erotically pressed his arousal into her back. She'd barely gotten her breath from that stunning move before he moved his hands upward, raking her shirt along and sweeping it over her head. Her bra quickly followed.

"Lance?" This time it was nothing more than a breathy question, thick with need and tight with sexual tension. At this rate, they'd never make it all the way before she exploded. As for the bed? Too far away, in her opinion.

Apparently Lance *could* read minds.

"Don't worry, baby, I want this first time for us to be perfect. I'll carry you to the bed."

He did. Just lifted her into his arms and strode to her bedroom as if he had memorized the layout of her apartment. How else could he have navigated the area so skillfully in the dark?

Maybe, anticipating this occasion, he the layout. Holly discovered she didn't c a split second of panic when she rememb clothes she'd left on the bed. The panic shameless second.

Wrinkled clothing she could handle.

Not having him inside her was something sh *ouldn't* handle and refused to consider. Earthquake, flood—nothing would stop her from this moment. Especially not the commonsense side of her brain when it reminded her of the shiny gold wedding ring that had fallen from his pocket the last time.

She quickly and effectively pushed the painful memory from her mind. Why would she deprive herself of this wonderful feeling for a memory she could barely grasp right now?

To her surprise, she didn't land on a pile of clothing when Lance placed her on the bed. She also didn't have time to ponder the mystery of the missing laundry. Lance was there, one arm beneath her, holding her bare breasts tight against him—and one hand quickly working at the snap and zipper of her jeans. Holly moaned impatiently as she fumbled with the buttons on his shirt. She was bare; she wanted *him* bare, too. Finally she got through the buttons and pushed his shirt aside.

They met flesh to flesh. The bristly hair on his chest scraped against her supersensitive nipples each time she moved. She swallowed a moan. He would think her shameless, a hussy, if she continued to groan and moan and whimper, she told herself. The low, throbbing voice in her ear told her otherwise.

"Let it out, baby. Don't hold back." With his lips working slowly along her jaw to her mouth, his fingers traced the elastic of her panty briefs, teasing, daring. He had unsnapped and unzipped her jeans, but there he had stopped.

It was Holly's fantasy come true, to be driven mindless by the man she loved, to be teased until she was withering

...d begging. Somewhere in the deep recesses of her subconscious, an alarm sounded. How could Lance know? How could he possibly know how to please her most? He hardly knew her! *Don't look a gift horse in the mouth, Holly! Just enjoy it!*

Sound advice, she thought, deciding to take it. Ha! As if she could have done otherwise, because Lance had reached her mouth—and his fingers had finally slid beneath the elastic of her panties.

Holly's senses were literally assaulted. His lips brushed hers, but wouldn't settle. She ached for more and strained her mouth toward his. He in turn moved his mouth out of reach, only to sneak back in and start nibbling on the corner of her mouth.

And his fingers. Oh, God, his fingers. She squirmed and arched her lower body in a vain attempt to bring him closer, but he wouldn't budge from the slow, torturous journey of his hand. A moan rose in her throat, and this time she made no attempt to stop it from slipping free.

"That's right, baby," he panted against her mouth, his breath a ragged stream of fire. "Tell me. Do you like this?"

His fingers reached their destination and rested lightly against the part of her that throbbed and ached. Finally, after what seemed like an eternity of anticipation, he moved his fingers in a slow circle.

Holly nearly screamed. "I like it," she strangled out, clutching his shoulders. "I like it . . . just fine." She would like it better if he would continue!

He kissed her fully on the mouth. Their tongues tangled in a feverish dance. When his hand left her, he swallowed her moan of frustration—and her gasp as well when he cupped her breast instead. Breaking free, he plunged his mouth over her breast, then slowly withdrew, scraping his teeth lightly against her skin and finally her pebbled nipple.

Holly held on by burying her fingers in his hair. She squeezed her eyes tightly shut against the incredible ecstasy he was creating with his hot mouth. She thought his hand was talented! It was nothing compared with what his mouth could do—was doing.

Enough was enough. She let go of her anchor and placed her hands on her jeans with every intention of getting rid of them. He stopped her and lifted his head.

"Oh, no, you don't. That's *my* job."

In a rough whisper, she ordered, "Then do it."

His husky, wicked chuckle liquefied her bones.

Staying true to form, he took his time removing her jeans, sliding them down a few inches, then kissing the exposed flesh before moving on. By the time they reached her ankles, Holly was shaking like someone with a chill.

But it wasn't a chill. Oh, no, it was a fever, and this man was the only one who could cure it.

He stood by the bed and removed her shoes, then pulled her jeans the rest of the way off. A faint ray of light from a street lamp outside shone through her bedroom window. Holly caught her breath as he stepped into the light. His face was tight with tension, his eyes black with need as they watched her lying on the bed. He stood with his arms hanging at his sides, his shirt hanging open to reveal his heaving, magnificent chest.

Clearly he was struggling for control.

Holly smiled her understanding, every nerve ending screaming to be loved by this man. But not just yet.

It was payback time.

Before he could guess her move, she reached out and grabbed his shirt, yanking him onto the bed. He lost his balance and fell onto his back. Holly rose above him, straddling his waist and pinning him to the bed. In the faint light, their eyes met and held—his full of wonder and glazed with desire; hers filled with lustful purpose.

She slowly unbuttoned the fly of his jeans, boldly holding his gaze, so very conscious of the power throbbing inches from her hands. She trembled with anticipation to see him, feel him, to stroke this powerful extension of

Lance. She wanted *him* to wither and moan the way he'd made her wither and moan.

He reached up to cup her breasts, but she smiled and gently pushed his hands away. If he touched her at this point, she would be lost. Although she wanted nothing more than to feel him moving inside her, like Lance she wanted their first time to be perfect.

The sound of his zipper sliding down got lost in the sound of their harsh breathing. He was wearing cotton underwear beneath his jeans. Holly gave him tit for tat, running her fingers along the top of the elastic.

The tips of her fingers grazed his hardness. He jumped and hissed between his teeth. Holly caught her breath in surprise to find him *there,* then smiled at the sight of his clenched jaw.

"Holly . . . you are in big trouble," he warned thickly, curling his fingers around her wrists and holding her still.

"I hope so." Heart thundering, she moved her hips forward, then grew still again. Tugging her hand free, she closed her fingers slowly around him.

The air was thick with expectation. The sound of their breathing became louder, more labored with the effort to hold back. Holly tried to remember the last time she'd wanted anything as badly as she wanted Lance right now—and couldn't.

Their gazes locked and held again. Seconds ticked by.

Finally Lance placed his hands on her hips and lifted her up. He rolled her to the side and onto her back, looming over her. "I want you so badly," he whispered.

She stared back at him, her heart in her eyes, there for him to see if he chose. "I want you just as badly." To prove it, she began to tug at his jeans. He helped her, and soon he was back against her, naked and trembling.

Then he was inside her.

Holding back became a distant memory as they began to move together in perfect harmony. When she needed him to increase the pace, he did it without prompting— as if they shared the same soul during this joyful joining.

In the faint light, she watched the moment of release crash upon him before closing her eyes against the intensity of her own release. Afterward, they lay still and shaken, clasped in each other's arms.

When her stunned brain allowed thought to creep in, Holly squeezed a tear from her eye. The perfection of their lovemaking had both frightened and exhilarated her, but a lingering sadness remained.

She didn't have his love, but she had this memory.

Her hand trembled as she brushed her fingers against his damp temple, then followed it with her lips.

It wasn't enough.

Lance jerked awake at the sound of Holly's scream.

In a flash, he was off the bed and running toward the kitchen. His heart threatened to burst through his chest as he slid to a halt on the tiled floor.

Holly stood in front of the refrigerator, wearing his shirt and nothing more. She had her hand clamped to her mouth as if to stifle another scream.

"What is it?" Lance demanded, glancing wildly around. She'd turned the light on over the range top, and in the soft yellow glow her face looked white as a sheet.

As if she'd seen a ghost.

Lance felt the fine hair at the back of his neck stand up. He stepped closer and pulled her into his arms. She was rigid. "Holly? What is it? Did you see someone?"

Her gaze remained fixed on the refrigerator. Slowly she reached out and opened the door, tensing as if she expected something to jump out at her. The light flicked on, illuminating the inside of the box. She pointed a shaky finger at the food inside.

"I have fresh grapes and strawberries," she said.

Bewildered, Lance saw that she did.

"I also have a roasted chicken, a bottle of wine, and assorted cheeses." Gingerly she stretched her hand out and poked at the cheese tray. "It's real," she whispered.

As if she couldn't bear to look any longer, she slammed

the door and whirled around. She pointed at the table. "See those beautiful roses? A delicate, hard-to-find shade of peach. My *second*-favorite color in roses."

Before Lance could do more than glance at the flowers, she grabbed his hand and led him into the living room. She flicked on a lamp. With growing concern, he watched as she ran a finger over the gleaming top of the end table.

"See? No dust. I *know* there was dust there yesterday. And the clothes. There was a pile of clean laundry on my bed."

"There wasn't any laundry, Holly," Lance felt compelled to tell her. He would have remembered if anything had gotten in the way of loving her.

Casting him an enigmatic look, she stomped into the bedroom. Lance followed. He reached her as she flung open her closet door and pointed an accusing finger at the clothes hanging there.

"Those clothes were on my bed when you called me tonight. I did not hang them up."

"Someone did," Lance observed, beginning to understand. Believing was a different story. "Why would someone break in and hang your clothes?"

She turned incredulous eyes on him. "Why would someone leave a mountain of food in my fridge? And roses on the table? Why would they dust my furniture?" Pushing her hair behind her, she pressed her palm against her forehead. "This is getting spooky, Lance. Something is going on, and I'm beginning to think—to *believe* it's something magical."

Lance swallowed hard. He wasn't afraid, but damned if he wasn't getting the creepy-crawlies. She sounded so convinced . . . and who was he to disbelieve? He'd heard a cat meowing from a charm bracelet!

Group hypnosis was a possibility, of course, but Lance knew in his heart it wasn't the answer. He hadn't told her about the personal file he'd found, but he hadn't forgotten the mystery of its appearance. Someone or some*thing* had put it there.

Magical, she'd said. Maybe she was right. It sure beat the hell out of *his* theory—that of his dead wife haunting him. Mona had always been a good sport about things, but he didn't think she'd go to *this* much trouble to help him win Holly over.

"We should give this some thought before we jump to conclusions," he heard himself say.

Holly's agitated gaze moved down his body. Something else had crept in to overshadow her fear by the time she lifted her eyes. "Then maybe you should get dressed. I can't think with you running around naked."

After a few moments of standing outside the back door, Mini wished she had thought to grab a sweater. October in southern California meant warm days and cool nights. Tonight was a little chillier than usual, she thought, shivering as she peered into the alley behind their apartments.

Where could she be? It was late—almost midnight—and Reuben had long since gone to sleep. He was furious with Xonia for keeping them in suspense.

Suddenly Mini was enveloped in an invisible cloud of warmth, heralding Xonia's arrival. Her friend had sensed her discomfort and conjured a warming spell around her.

"Xonia?" Mini whispered, staring into the dark shadows.

"I'm here." Xonia came trotting into view; behind her, Mini saw another cat crouched and waiting. His eyes glowed in the darkness. Despite the warming spell, she shivered.

"Why don't you introduce me to your friend."

Xonia glanced at the big tom. "He doesn't like strangers, but I'm working on him. Sorry I'm late."

"Reuben's angry."

"Reuben's *always* angry," Xonia retorted. "Now maybe he knows what it feels like to wait and wonder."

Mini decided to ignore Xonia's remark, although she had to admit there was definitely some truth in it. "Well? How did it go?"

Xonia preened. "Terrific! Lance and Holly went back to her apartment, and the moment they were through the door—boom!"

"Boom?"

"Boom. Hubba hubba. Maka-luva." When Mini remained silent, Xonia cackled. "You are *so* naive! They did the *wild thing*."

"Oh." Mini felt her face grow warm. "And afterward?" As a woman, she knew that the afterward was sometimes just as important as the act of love itself. She suspected it would be to Holly.

"They're still at the apartment. Something tells me they won't be leaving anytime soon."

"Xonia . . . what did you do?"

"I, uh, left a few conversation pieces."

Mini groaned and covered her face with her hands.

Eighteen

Two hours later—after numerous theories, a feast fit for a king, and several frantic bouts of lovemaking—Holly walked Lance to the front door.

It was a mistake, as it reminded him of where and how things had started.

The man was insatiable.

Catching her breath after a long, lingering kiss, she gave his chest a feeble push. That's how she was around Lance—feeble. Weak. Hopeless. "It's late. We should get to bed."

His teeth flashed in a wicked smile that would have put a pirate to shame. "I agree. Let's go."

Laughing, Holly shook her head. "You know what I mean!"

"Yeah, but I like *my* interpretation better."

So did she, but she wasn't about to encourage him by voicing her agreement out loud. What she'd said earlier was true: She couldn't think with Lance near, clothed or unclothed. And she had a lot of thinking to do.

"I'm afraid."

Holly's laughter died in her throat at his suddenly serious tone. "You? Afraid?" She couldn't imagine in her wildest dreams that Lance was afraid of anything.

"Yes, me. Of walking out that door and discovering this has all been a dream."

Attempting to lighten the conversation, Holly peeked around his shoulder in the direction of the kitchen and the incredible buffet littering the table. "Some of it, I hope, *is* a dream." Sobering, since he seemed determined to remain serious, Holly voiced the one theory she had avoided. "Lance . . . do you think this could have anything to do with Mona?"

He hesitated. "I don't know. She was a generous, loving person, but I don't know if she would go this far."

They were talking about a bona fide ghost as casually as they might discuss the weather, Holly thought with an amazed shake of her head. But then, it wasn't really any more incredible than some of the other theories they'd touched on.

She suddenly felt very exposed. What if Mona was watching them now? How would she feel seeing them wrapped in each other's arms this way? How would *she* feel if she were Mona? Frustrated, sad, and hurt, among other unpleasant emotions.

As if Lance were thinking along the same lines, his arms dropped slowly from her waist. Holly felt a sharp pain in her chest at his withdrawal and at the sudden tension in his face.

"I think I'd feel her presence," he said, but didn't sound convinced.

"You were very close." It wasn't a question; it was a statement.

"I won't lie to you—we *were* close." When her eyes started to close in denial, Lance reached out and cupped her chin. His voice roughened. "We had fifteen good years together. I can't just wipe out fifteen years of memories as if they never happened."

"I know," she whispered. And she did. She *knew* she wasn't being fair in thinking that he could.

"I promised her that I would never forget her."

This time Holly *did* close her eyes. The pain of his words were too much to bear.

"And she got mad."

Holly's eyes flew open. He smiled faintly.

"She said that if I *didn't* find someone else she would come back and haunt me."

"She—she said that?" Holly didn't think she could be so noble—not if it were Lance she was leaving behind. It was a selfish thought, one that made her feel immediately ashamed. Obviously Mona was the better woman; no wonder Lance couldn't forget her.

"I want to keep seeing you," he stated, sliding his knuckle over the outline of her nipple through her pajama top. Like a trained soldier, it stood at attention. "Ghost or no ghost."

Despite her body's vote, Holly said, "I don't know. I need time to think." She was smart enough to know that hot, lusty sex could cloud one's judgment. It was clearly clouding his.

His brows clashed in a frown. "After tonight you have to think? How can you even begin to deny that we have something special?"

"I'm not denying that we have a strong attraction to one another. Obviously I'd be lying." Very, very obviously. After making love in the bed, they'd made love on the kitchen counter, and then on the sofa. Each time was more incredible than the last. She was sore and aching, yet she knew that if Lance didn't leave soon, she'd be tempted again.

"This is more than a sexual attraction, Holly."

He reached for the doorknob. Holly moved aside, curling her fingers into her palms to keep them from reaching out and holding on to him so that he couldn't leave.

"Sooner or later you're going to realize it."

He placed a hard, possessive kiss on her mouth and opened the door. "Lock up tight," he instructed before leaving.

She stared at the closed door, knowing she would never

be able to look at it again without remembering the start of their lovemaking. A deep shudder shook her. Hugging herself against the sudden, bereft feeling that came over her, she turned around and headed for the kitchen to put away the remains of their mystery feast.

As she entered the kitchen, a cool draft of air swept into the room and sent a napkin flying from the table. Holly automatically grabbed it before it could fall to the floor. She froze, her gaze on the napkin. She took a slow, shaky breath, inhaling a lungful of night air.

Night air.

She hadn't left any windows open in the house, and she and Lance had just left the kitchen moments ago. It was possible that Lance had opened the window, but Holly quickly dismissed the idea—she couldn't remember a single instant when she might have taken her eyes from him. Oh, no, he had most certainly held her undivided attention.

Bit by bit, with goose bumps racing along her arm and her scalp prickling, Holly edged her gaze to the window. Finally she looked straight at it.

It *was* open, and there was something sitting on the windowsill. She forced herself to tiptoe closer to get a better look, feeling like a frightened heroine in a tacky horror movie, the kind where the foolish girl was going into the house when she should have been running for her life.

Reaching the sink, Holly stared at the object, rubbing her eyes just in case there was something in her vision causing her to see what she saw. The object was still there when she looked again.

It was round and clear, but on closer inspection, Holly saw little bubbles suspended in the ball. It resembled one of those crystal balls that fortune-tellers used at carnivals and in movies.

Of course, it wasn't real. There was no such thing as a magical crystal ball.

The food, Holly. You shouldn't have eaten the food.

Dry-mouthed, Holly swallowed. The logical, chiding voice inside her head was right. She and Lance shouldn't have touched the food. Obviously it contained some sort of hallucinogenic. How stupid could they be?

She reached out and touched the ball, fully expecting her finger to slide right through it.

Her nail bumped against the glass with a distinct and very real clink.

"Probably just a glass paperweight," she muttered. "Those things are a dime a dozen. I've even got one on my desk at work." But that didn't explain how it came to be sitting on her windowsill—two stories above the ground.

A ghost wouldn't have to worry about heights, she reminded herself. Ghosts could float, fly, and appear anywhere they pleased. She watched enough horror movies to know the rules.

"Okay, you've convinced me. Now you're starting to scare me." Holly turned and pressed her back against the counter, her gaze wandering around the room. "Mona, if you're here, show yourself." She was pleased at the steady sound of her voice. Strange, when her heart wasn't a bit steady. In fact, it was doing some incredible acrobatics right at the moment.

Was she actually trying to communicate with a ghost?

Moments ticked by. Holly felt foolish but determined. There was no one here to witness her insane actions, and if Mona *was* responsible, then she wanted to meet her face-to-face. *And tell her what? That you love her husband? That she should just step aside and let Lance be happy? That you and Lance don't need her help?*

"I just want to talk to you." She took a deep breath. "We have something in common, you and I. Seems we love the same man."

The only sound in the room was the ticking of the kitchen clock on the wall. A sudden breeze blew against her back from the open window, reminding Holly of the crystal ball on the sill. A sign? Shivering, Holly turned to face the ball again.

Maybe this was the answer. Maybe Mona sent it, and this was the only way she could communicate.

Gathering her flagging courage, Holly closed her hand over the ball.

"You should have let me fix the washer," Xonia grumbled from her position on the coin-operated dryer at Johnson's Laundromat.

As the familiar spoke, Mini cast a quick, nervous glance around to make sure they were still relatively alone. A woman and a young girl busied themselves folding clothes at the opposite end of the Laundromat, but Mini decided the country music blaring from the boom box sitting on the folding table between them was an effective cover.

"Or better yet," Xonia continued in a plaintive voice, "let me use a spell to clean the clothes. It pains me to watch you do menial labor. You're a witch."

Mini paused in sorting through the basket of clothes. She placed a hand on her hip and frowned at Xonia. "Why should witches be any different from everyone else?" she demanded.

"Because they are. Witches are special."

Her friend's arrogance grated on Mini's nerves. "Mortals are special, too. Besides, Xonia, I really don't mind. In fact, some things are kind of fun the mortal way. I haven't felt this useful in years!"

Xonia pretended to faint, flopping onto the dryer with an exaggerated moan. "Gads! She's turning into a mortal before my very eyes!"

Unamused by her dramatics, Mini flung the socks into the washer and fished through the basket in search of underwear. "Perhaps if you weren't so free with your spells, we'd still have the crystal ball," she said without thinking.

In a flash, Xonia was on her feet. Her tail swished rapidly back and forth, and her golden eyes narrowed to slits.

"I can't believe you said that! Now you're blaming *me* because *you* lost your precious crystal ball? Oh, girlfriend, you need a reality check."

"I didn't lose the ball," Mini denied flatly. She didn't. She couldn't have. It was unthinkable.

"Oh? If you didn't lose it, what happened to it?"

"If I knew, we wouldn't be having this ridiculous conversation." She dumped a cup of detergent into the ring and slammed the washer lid. Before she could stick quarters into the slot, the washer hummed to life. "See what I mean? You do it without even thinking. The witches' council said—"

"The witches' council *this* and the witches' council *that*," Xonia mimicked sarcastically. "To hell with the witches' council!"

Mini drew in a shocked breath at her slander. "Ssh! If they hear you, they'll zap you onto the next planet!"

"I don't think they've given us another thought since landing us in this place, Mini. Otherwise they wouldn't have let the crystal ball out of their sight. If that ball falls into the hands of a mortal—"

Covering her ears and squeezing her eyes tightly shut, Mini blocked out both the words and the image they conjured. "Please! Don't remind me."

Using her powers to transcend the barrier of Mini's hands, Xonia said, "It's something we need to consider, Mini. We also need to face a few unpleasant facts."

Reluctantly Mini lowered her cowardly hands. "What do you mean?"

Xonia sat on her haunches. "Maybe the crystal ball isn't just lost. Maybe someone took it."

"We *have* considered that fact, Xonia," Mini pointed out impatiently. "Tell me something new."

"I mean, someone like us." She shook her head, her gaze apologetic. "Like *me*, rather. A witch with powers." After a brief hesitation, she added, "Actually it would have to be someone more powerful, because whoever it is, they're able to hide from me."

A ripple of unease thrummed through Mini at her grave words. "But, who? Who would work *against* us? And why?"

"Hmm. I have my suspicions, but I'm not sure. What I *do* know is that it's a mighty big coincidence that the crystal ball disappeared just when we needed it most."

"As if someone knew how important it is to us," Mini murmured. "Why didn't you say something sooner?"

"Because I didn't think you were ready to listen. I'm still not sure."

"Since when did you start reading *my* mind?"

"Since, my dearest friend, you starting wearing your feelings on your sleeves. This thing with Reuben has your defenses down, and that worries me. You may be without powers, but you inherited your natural perception from your grandmother."

Xonia was right—she had been distracted lately. Reuben's suspicious outings with his friends kept her in a constant turmoil. Perhaps if he would introduce her to a few of them, she could relax and stop imagining all sorts of scenarios—not a single one of them pleasant. With a sigh, she said, "I can't help but worry about Reuben, Xonia. When you get married you'll understand."

"You're worried because you know he's hiding something from you."

Her remark rattled Mini's protective instincts. "Your constant nagging is the reason I'm not trusting my husband."

The familiar's back arched again. "Nagging? I'm trying to relieve your mind so that you can be yourself again! In case you haven't figured it out, Mini, I think we have a nasty warlock in our midst."

"Reuben's not . . ." Her words died away as Xonia's meaning sank in. She put a hand to her throat and swallowed hard. "You mean, *another* warlock?"

"I can't be positive. I can't be positive that it's Jestark, either, but—"

"*Jestark?*" Mini squeaked. "You think it's *Jestark?*"

"Who else?"

"But he's Reuben's *friend*! He wouldn't sabotage our plans to get Holly and Lance together!"

Xonia shook her head as if saddened by Mini's naïveté. "Mini, Mini. Warlocks aren't capable of loyalty. Besides, just as it's a cat's natural instinct to hunt mice, it's a warlock's natural instinct to create havoc. Surely Reuben's talked to you about the good ole days?"

Mini managed a jerky nod. "Yes, but since our marriage, he doesn't do that . . . any longer." Again, her voice died away. Her horrified gaze met Xonia's.

"Jestark didn't make the same vows that Reuben made."

"No, he didn't." Mini slowly closed her eyes as she whispered, "Reuben won't believe us."

"I've given this some thought, and I think I might have a way of convincing him. Meanwhile, don't say anything."

The spinning washer ground to a stop. Mini hardly noticed as Xonia twitched her tail and transferred the clothes into the dryer and turned it on. "What if we're wrong? What if Jestark isn't behind this?"

"Remember the incident at Lance's house when I fell out of the tree and missed seeing the wedding ring?"

"Yes, I remember. The neighbor's cat tried to pick a fight with you, and you turned yourself into a dog or something."

"Yes, well." Xonia cleared her throat. "I don't think it was the neighbor's cat. I wish I had known—"

"Xonia, be careful. He's a powerful warlock."

Xonia sniffed. "Powerful, maybe. But not particularly smart. From what I remember about Jestark, he'll get bored with sneaking around like the coward he is and reveal himself. When he does, I'll be waiting."

A terrifying thought occurred to Mini. "Reuben is powerless. What if Jestark—"

The familiar let out a furious yowl that echoed from the Laundromat walls. "He'd better not touch a hair on

Reuben's head!" she snarled. "Nobody messes with *my* friends."

Mini stared at her in amazement. "Who are you and what did you do with Xonia?"

"Oh, shut up."

Despite her worry, Mini smiled.

Nineteen

~

Monday morning Holly arrived at the office before the doughnut shop opened four doors down. She was gritty-eyed from lack of sleep and irritable from too much caffeine, but she had some serious surfing to do. She refused to spend another night thinking about that damned crystal ball hidden away in her underwear drawer.

Logging onto the Internet, she typed in the words *crystal ball* and sat back to wait while the search engine did its job.

Her eyes widened when the search ended with over a thousand links. Blowing out an impatient sigh, she tried to be more specific.

Magical crystal ball, she typed in, then hit the ENTER key.

This time, over fifty listings popped up.

Most of them ended or began with the word "witchcraft."

Holly hovered with her fingers above the keyboard, chanting the word in her head: "witchcraft, witchcraft." Not ghosts, but witches. She gave her forehead a sarcastic mental slap. Of course! What was she thinking? She wasn't dealing with the *other* side—she was dealing with the dark side!

A half hour later Holly had lost her sarcastic humor. According to the Web sites she'd visited, true witchcraft had nothing to do with the dark side. Most witches were good witches and kept to themselves.

True witchcraft.

This time Holly didn't laugh. She supposed other people might laugh *at* her for not laughing, but they hadn't experienced the reality of magic as she had. Although she and Lance had certainly generated a lot of magic on their own, there had definitely been some *real* witchcraft magic going on as well.

The final proof had hit her late last night while she lay wide awake in bed. She'd thrown the covers aside and raced to the bathroom, where she'd lifted the lid on the commode, somehow knowing what she would find.

A pristine white surface.

Proof. Nobody but nobody had known about her silly little worry that Lance would notice if the underside of the commode lid wasn't pristine and that he'd think her a slob. In fact, no one could have known about each and every concern that had flown through her mind as she unlocked her apartment door Friday night with Lance on her heels.

Longing for another cup of bracing coffee, Holly suddenly remembered something else: She'd found four packages of pantyhose in her underwear drawer.

Just her size—and her favorite shade, nude with seamless toes.

So who was it? *What* was it? A ghost or a witch? A witchy ghost? A witch wanna-be ghost? Somehow, she didn't think Lance would appreciate her referring to his late wife as a witch, even a wanna-be one. Holly brushed her hair from her eyes, wondering if an overdose of caffeine might be responsible for her loony thoughts. She sighed and settled into her chair, closing her eyes and forcing herself to think.

Okay. So what if there was a ghostly witch in her apartment? Obviously it meant no harm. On the contrary, she could grow used to not having to shop or dust or worry about buying the wrong pantyhose. But what about the crystal ball? What was its significance?

Since she'd put it away in the drawer, she hadn't gathered the nerve to touch it again. Not exactly a good way to find out its meaning.

Holly turned the computer off, grabbed her sweater from the back of the chair, and checked her watch. It was six o'clock. She had two hours to work up the nerve she so obviously lacked. If she didn't get it over with, she would never be able to concentrate when she returned at eight.

Some twenty minutes later, armed with a hot cappuccino and a fresh bagel smeared with cream cheese, Holly entered her apartment. Nike greeted her with his usual exuberance—as if she'd been gone for weeks instead of an hour. She shared her bagel and slowly sipped her cappuccino. Finally she ran out of excuses.

With great care, Holly lifted the crystal ball from the drawer and carried it to the kitchen table. Nike stood on his hind legs and gave it a curious sniff. With a whine and a bark, he ran from the kitchen.

"Coward," she muttered shakily. "It can't bite you."

But it *could* burn, Holly discovered when she placed her hands over it. Jerking them away, she watched in horrified fascination as the crystal ball began to glow and pulse with a faint pink light.

Her heart lodged in her throat. Around the lump, she croaked, "Mona, if that's you, I think you should know that I am seriously freaked."

As she watched, transfixed by the pulsing light, an image appeared in the center of the ball. With a gasp, Holly leaned in for a closer look. The image was that of a young woman, and she was laughing. Her blond hair was swept up in an artful French twist, and she wore a delicate ring of flowers in her hair. She held a bouquet of matching flowers in her cupped hands.

A wedding. She was watching a wedding. Was this

Mona? Holly blinked. The woman looked oddly familiar, but Holly knew she'd never seen Mona before, in real life or in a photograph.

"If you're Mona, then where's Lance?" she wondered out loud.

And then she saw him. It was a younger, leaner version, but it was definitely her man.

Mona's man. *Their* wedding. He was standing beside the bride wearing a black tuxedo and smiling into her happy face, his expression that of a deeply devoted man.

Holly pressed a hand to her fluttering stomach. Was this little show a message from Mona? If it was, it wasn't necessary. Holly didn't need to see the evidence of their love to know that it had been real. "But you're dead now," she whispered. "Surely you don't want him to be alone forever?"

The image abruptly changed. Holly covered her mouth to stifle another gasp at the sight of a coffin being lowered into the ground. A close-up of Lance standing by the gravesite clearly showed his ravaged face and red-rimmed eyes. Holly's own eyes brimmed at the proof of his grief.

Through her fingers, Holly defiantly whispered, "But he's better now. He's getting on with his life, as he should."

Again the image changed, this time to show Lance sitting on the edge of his bed. He was older, but even more handsome, she saw, then gave a start of surprise as she realized that she must be looking at Lance in the present. He was holding something in his hand. On closer inspection, she saw that it was a photograph . . . of Mona.

"Mona again."

And there she was, her smiling face expanding inside the ball.

Catching on, Holly quickly murmured, "Lance."

Lance came back into view almost instantly. Holly couldn't believe it was so simple. Who would have thought she'd be commanding a crystal ball? Her giggle sounded a little on the hysterical side. She sobered quickly at what she saw next.

Lance brought the photo he'd been holding to his mouth and placed a tender kiss against the picture frame.

"Well, that's enough for me." And she meant it.

The crystal ball went blank. The pulsing light slowly faded. Holly stared at it a full ten minutes before looking away. She focused instead on the vase of roses.

Tears fell fast and furious, but she ignored them.

Of course he loved his late wife: She was beautiful, and vibrant, and they'd been together a lot of years. She only wished Mona had presented the enlightening crystal ball *before* she'd made love with Lance; then Holly's heartache wouldn't have been so profound. The way Mona had waited seemed almost cruel. No, it *was* cruel.

Holly felt the breeze against her neck seconds before she heard the voice behind her.

"You weren't meant to see that, you know. At least that last part. No—don't turn around yet. Just listen. I don't want you fainting on me."

Holly should have been shocked, or at least afraid, but she wasn't. After a weekend of miracles and a crystal ball that showed the past and present, she didn't think she *could* be shocked. Instead, she found herself stifling a giggle with her hand.

"Don't get hysterical on me, either."

"I'm not getting hysterical, *Mona*." Holly felt smug as silence followed her statement. Ha! Surely the woman didn't think she was stupid?

"No, I don't think you're stupid, but you *are* wrong. I'm not Mona. In fact, Mona has nothing to do with this. As far as I know, she has no idea you've been doing the wild thing with her husband. I don't think they let them watch X-rated movies where *she's* at."

Holly sucked in a harsh gasp. She was wrong—she *could* still be shocked. The room tilted. She gripped the table and closed her eyes. "If you're not Mona, then who are you?"

"My name is Xonia. Are you holding on to that table good?"

"Y—yes."

"Well, keep holding on to it. I'm a witch—a *good* witch. Okay, so not everyone would agree with my assessment, but basically I'm considered a good witch. Just a little more selfish than most."

"And honest," Holly squeaked out, amazed she still had a voice at all. The crystal ball had been a wild experience, but this topped the cake. If it wasn't a hoax.

Very, very slowly, she began to turn her head. Just a peek, she thought.

"Don't do it. I really don't think you're ready yet."

Holly froze. Far be it for her to argue with a witch. A *good* witch, that is. Another giggle bubbled up. She wisely swallowed it. Reaching out her hand very slowly, she curled her fingers around the cup of cappuccino and began to drag it toward her. If she couldn't look, then she had to do *something*.

"You don't need any more caffeine, Holly. The last time you had that much caffeine, you didn't sleep for two days, remember? You vowed to limit yourself."

Unnerved, Holly let go of the cup. "How do you know so much about me?"

"I told you, I'm a witch. Oh, very well," she added in an aggrieved tone. "I got bored one day and did some nosing around in your past on the crystal ball."

At her admission, something snapped inside Holly. Her fear began to recede. "Ever heard of invasion of privacy?"

"A mortal law that doesn't apply to me," the witch replied arrogantly. "And *you've* got a lot of room to talk. I believe that's exactly what *you* were doing when I came through the window."

Holly flushed. "I wasn't aware of what I was doing. Can you say the same?"

"Oh, I think by the time you got to Lance holding the photo on the bed, you knew *exactly* what you were doing."

She was arguing with a witch. Holly gave her head a disbelieving shake. "Why can't I look at you?"

"Do you think that you're ready?"

"Would I ask otherwise?" Holly retorted flippantly.

The witch cackled. "That's what I like about you, Holly. You've got backbone. Too bad you're a coward when it comes to love."

Enough was enough. If she was going to be insulted, she was going to see who was doing the insulting. Holly twisted around in her chair. Her jaw dropped as she stared at the fluffy orange cat perched on her windowsill. It was Sheba Haggetha, Mini and Reuben's cat. Did they know their cat was a witch?

A memory surfaced of that first day they'd brought the cat to the office. Holly remembered having the silly feeling that Mini had understood the cat.

Well, at least the mystery of the cat paw prints was solved, she thought, closing her mouth.

Which meant . . . "You left the roses? And the food, and did the dusting—"

Xonia waved a dismissive paw in the air. "Yeah, yeah. It was nothing. I was getting lazy anyway. Mini insists on doing everything the mortal way."

"Are you saying—" Holly licked her dry lips. "Are you saying that Mini and Reuben are witches, too?"

"They were. It's a long story."

"And the crystal ball? It's yours?" This was fantastic, Holly thought, still more than a little dazed.

The cat hesitated. "It belongs to Mini. She's been looking for it everywhere."

"How did it get *here*?"

"Well, that's another long story. Got any cheese left?"

When Holly nodded, the cat leaped onto the floor and hopped into a chair. She twitched her tail, and the cheese tray Holly had put away earlier materialized before her.

As the feline witch nibbled on the cheese, she began to relate the most amazing story of love and loyalty that Holly had ever heard.

She listened in silence.

Lance stared at Mona's image in the photograph. He had caught her at an unguarded moment, laughing into the camera at something he'd said. This time when the sorrow hit him, he let it wash over him in waves that not only hurt, but healed as well.

He didn't love her any less because she was dead, but he knew now that it had become a different kind of love. It was a past love—and it belonged in the past.

Holly was the future. He knew in his heart that Mona would understand and approve. Now if he could just convince Holly that she wouldn't be second best. This new love that was growing inside him in leaps and bounds was just as precious and everlasting as the love he'd felt for Mona when she was alive.

But how was he going to prove this to Holly? He'd sensed her lingering reservations despite their newfound intimacy. He wanted those reservations out of the way once and for all. But how? What would it take to convince her?

Lance rose from the bed and went to the closet. He removed a plastic storage box from the shelf and put the picture to rest.

It was the last of them. Over the past four years he had gradually eliminated her things. Some he'd given to charity, and some he'd packed away. Casey had been urging him to finish the job sooner, but Lance had ignored him. Casey hadn't understood his pain and loss, and how hard it was to let go of his memories.

Now Lance forced himself to consider that maybe Casey *had* understood. Maybe he had known that as long as Lance kept the memories fresh and Mona's picture visible, it would delay the healing process.

He turned from the closet and surveyed the room he

and Mona had shared for fifteen years. Holly would never make love in this room—in that bed he and Mona had slept in—and he understood why.

There were six other bedrooms in the house, a few even bigger than this one. Why hadn't he changed bedrooms long ago? Laziness? Reluctance to let go of the past? With a rueful grin, Lance decided it was both, but a lot more of the latter.

Well, now was the time for change. In fact, the entire house needed a change. Everywhere he looked he saw Mona's touch. How could he expect another woman to feel comfortable here? He needed some advice about what to do to erase Mona's lingering presence. Not from Holly, though. He wanted Holly to see the results *after* the fact.

Mona's friends were out of the question. They were perfectly happy believing he would grieve forever. He heard it in their voices when he talked to them on occasion and saw it in their faces when he happened to run into them.

Debbie—she would have been helpful, he mused. She was smart, savvy, and practical. He had enjoyed her all-too-brief friendship and regretted losing it the way he had. If only he could convince her that the incident in the restaurant had been a farce, he'd bet she would be willing to help him.

Lance froze as an idea came to him. Casey was his best friend, and very persuasive when he needed to be. Casey knew everything that happened in his life, right down to the intimate details—or most of them. If Lance could get the two of them together, maybe Debbie would listen to Casey.

With hope in his heart and a new spring to his step, Lance picked up the phone.

At a quarter of eight, at Xonia's prompting, Holly called Mini and Reuben and told them she would be late. When she returned to the table she found a fresh cup of coffee and a small glass of orange juice waiting for her.

Xonia said, "Don't worry: It's unleaded. And drink the juice." Her whiskers twitched. "I've got a feeling you're going to need all of your strength to keep up with that lusty man of yours."

Holly stared into her coffee, unamused. Xonia didn't get it, she thought, fighting the pain that threatened to overwhelm her. "He's not *my* lusty man. After what I witnessed, I don't think he's going to be anyone's lusty man for a while."

"So you saw him kissing a picture of his late wife!" Xonia scoffed. "In case you haven't noticed, she's dead. She can't make him laugh or cry. She can't have his babies, and she damned sure can't make his—"

Holly held up a stalling hand. "That's enough. I get the picture." The sigh came wrenching out of her. "You don't understand how I feel."

"Then explain it to me."

"I can't."

"Try." Xonia twitched her tail. The juice glass rose in the air and began to wobble. "If you don't take it, I'm going to let it fall."

With a snarl, Holly retrieved it. She tilted it up and drank it down, then slammed the empty glass onto the table. "Bully." Seeing a cat smile was a first for Holly. But then, she'd seen a lot of firsts this weekend. "Tell me, why don't you want Mini and Reuben to know that I know about them?"

"First of all, I'm aware of the fact that you're deliberately changing the subject. Secondly, I don't want to hear their boring lectures on the hazards of revealing ourselves to mortals any sooner than I have to. Besides, right now Mini needs the distraction of playing Cupid. Reuben's evening escapades are keeping her tied in knots."

"Oh." Holly digested this in silence. The story of Mini and Reuben's plight tugged at her heartstrings. She wanted to help them as they had tried to help her. "You never did tell me what he's really doing."

"You'll find out tomorrow night when you go with me to talk to him. When this business with Jestark is straightened out, then we're going to focus on *your* insecurities."

Softly Holly said, "Xonia, you can't make Lance forget his wife."

"Wanna bet?"

Holly looked at her sharply. "That wouldn't be fair. If you used witchcraft, then it wouldn't be the same. I'd know, and I'd always wonder."

"All right, all right. I won't use witchcraft." She sounded smug. "I won't have to, anyway. Lance *is* over Mona. You're just too stubborn to see that. Or too scared."

"I'm not scared." But it was a lie. She *was*. Terrified, in fact. "I just don't want him confusing lust with love, then waking up one morning realizing he's made a mistake." It was what her father had done with her mother, and they had ended up divorced and disillusioned.

Her voice thick with sarcasm, Xonia said, "Oh, yeah. I see what you mean. That's probably what happened when he met Mona. He confused lust with love for fifteen years. In fact, he was so confused, he kept right on confusing it for four years after he stopped having sex with her."

"That's different."

"Is it?" Xonia's golden eyes hardened with purpose. "Tell me, what did you think of Debbie Mosely?"

"She was perfect for him." She hoped the sassy witch didn't know how hard it was for her to say those words.

"If she was so perfect, then why didn't he jump *her* bones the way he did yours?"

"Because he didn't get the opportunity," Holly pointed out with an exasperated sigh. The witch should have studied law, she thought; she'd have been able to badger witnesses to tears in a matter of seconds. "Obviously you two must have believed there was a possibility, or you wouldn't have gone to such lengths to interfere."

"It wasn't *Lance* we were worried about," Xonia protested. "It was that blond bombshell he was with. *You* know what I'm talking about, so don't pretend that you don't."

Unfortunately Holly did.

Twenty

Get It On was the hottest spot in town, and on ladies' night, the crowd swelled to twice the normal size. Getting a seat might have posed a problem—if you weren't accompanied by a clever witch.

Holly studied the sign on the door, hanging back as a crowd of restless senior citizens waited in line behind her. She looked at the older woman standing beside her. Xonia, I can't go with you in there! This is 'Over Sixty' night!"

Xonia cackled. "You didn't look in the rearview mirror before you got out of the car, did you? Really, Holly, you should pay more attention to your appearance. You've let yourself go."

Startled, Holly looked at her hands. They weren't the same. She felt her face; it felt softer, laxer. And her hair! It was thinner, and when she pulled a strand in front of her eyes, she let out a yelp. It was streaked liberally with silver.

"What did you do?" she demanded, glaring at Xonia, who had transformed herself earlier into an older woman. Holly had just assumed Xonia truly *was* older in witch form.

"You age well, if I may say so myself."

Frantically Holly dug around in her purse until she found her compact. An elderly woman behind her nudged her in the back. "Come on, lady. We don't want to miss the show!"

Ignoring her, Holly flipped the compact open and stared at the unfamiliar—yet familiar—face in the mirror. "Is this truly what I'll look like when I get older?"

"Not bad, huh?"

It was a shock to see herself twenty-five or thirty years older, but Holly had to agree. Other than the wrinkles and the gray hair, she didn't look half bad.

"If you're not going in, will you at least get out of the line, missy?"

Xonia swung around with a hiss.

Holly quickly grabbed the witch's hand before she could work her magic. "Don't, Xonia. You'll cause a scene, and I thought you didn't want Reuben to know we were here until *after* the show." She was relieved to feel the tension seep out of Xonia's arm. "Come on. She's right, anyway. I'm holding up the line."

They stepped inside the door. A heavy young man with a thick mustache and bloodshot eyes took their money, grabbed each of their right hands, and stamped them with red ink. He barely glanced at their faces as he said, "Remember, ladies: Look but don't touch."

Mulling over his mysterious statement, Holly followed Xonia. About fifty tables were crammed into the dimly lit room. She and Xonia squeezed between the tables until they came to a small table for two against the wall. The place was swiftly filling up with women of every shape and size.

All looked sixty or older, and a few looked downright ancient. Apparently the minimum age was strictly enforced.

"They must have a good band here," Holly said, raising her voice to be heard above the babbling of a hundred women.

"Not a band." Xonia's smile was crafty. "This is a male strip joint, darling."

Before Holly had a chance to react, a waitress appeared at her elbow. "What'll you have, ladies?"

"Thanks, but we've got our drinks," Xonia told her.

Surprised, Holly glanced down to find a frosty drink sitting in front of her. When the waitress shrugged and left, she asked suspiciously, "What is it?"

"A frozen banana daiquiri. Your favorite, isn't it?"

"Xonia, I'm driving, remember?"

"Oh, all right already." She flicked her hand at the drink. "A *virgin* daiquiri." She added beneath her breath, "Weenie."

"I heard that."

"Well, hear this—" The sound of a drumroll interrupted Xonia. She broke off and twisted around in the chair, looking in the direction of the stage. "It's show time."

Holly had a direct view of the stage. What she saw made her jaw drop.

"They call him The Warlock," Xonia said, sounding amused. "Imagine that."

"Majestic" was the word that came to mind as Holly watched Reuben stride onto the stage wearing a top hat and a red and black cape. The cape billowed out behind him, and he swung an ivory cane to and fro as he walked. His long black hair gleamed beneath the spotlight that followed his movements.

Aside from tiny black bikini underwear, he was naked beneath the cape.

When Holly gasped, Xonia cackled, but the sound got lost in the roaring of the crowd. The women were on their feet and going wild at the sight of Reuben prancing on the stage wearing less than Tarzan. A few were whistling sharply, others were clapping and cheering. To Holly's ongoing amazement, an upper plate of teeth whizzed by her head and landed on the floor beside their table.

The red-faced woman who retrieved them was plump and gray-haired. She looked like someone's grandmother!

But then, they could all be grandmothers, Holly reminded herself. *She* was the only impostor!

Imagining Reuben's embarrassment if he knew that his boss was watching his performance, Holly leaned across the table and shouted in Xonia's ear, "You are a very wicked witch!" She meant it, too.

Xonia whipped her head around, her golden eyes alight with laughter. "Yes, I am," she agreed. "But I'm not as bad as you think. I could have brought Mini instead of *you.*"

Her face burning, Holly reluctantly watched the show. She felt like a voyeur in her disguise. Why was Reuben doing this? Did he need the money that badly? What would Mini think? Even as she watched and wondered, a woman darted to the edge of the stage, money clutched in her upraised fist as she urged him over. Reuben obliged, his hips swinging to the sultry tune, "Black Velvet." He was smiling as if he was fully enjoying himself!

When he thrust his hips forward, Holly covered her eyes. All around her, the older generation of women screamed and clapped, calling out lewd suggestions that scandalized even Holly, who thought she'd heard it all. Something rapped sharply on her ankle. When she risked a peek through her fingers, she saw a woman reaching for her fallen cane.

A cane. *Good grief!*

"He's good, isn't he?" Xonia tugged at her hands, but Holly refused to budge. She couldn't watch! "He doesn't take anything off, Holly, so relax. That's why he's so popular with the ladies—because he leaves them wondering what's under that little black scrap—"

"Enough!" Holly shouted through her fingers. Her face heated several more degrees. "Just tell me when it's over." As far as Holly was concerned, it couldn't be soon enough. If Mini found out she'd been here, Holly would just die!

The music finally died away. There was another mo-

ment of ear-splitting applause before Xonia said dryly,
"You can look now."

Slowly Holly parted her fingers. She let out a relieved
sigh to find the stage empty.

"Now, this next part is a little tricky, so you might want
to close your eyes again."

Holly didn't argue. She quickly squeezed them shut.

When she opened them again, the room was spinning.
She realized they were no longer in the club, but sitting
on a lumpy sofa. The only other furniture in the room was
a mirrored dresser littered with makeup pots and brushes.

"You'll have to adjust quickly, so I'm going to tell you
where we are. We're in a small changing room backstage.
See the costumes? Any minute now that cocky warlock
is going to come prancing through that door—there he is
now!" Xonia leaned close to whisper, "Remember, if ob-
jects start flying, just duck."

Deciding then and there that she wouldn't shed a tear
if she never met another witch, Holly braced herself for
the storm Xonia predicted.

Xonia wasn't wrong.

Reuben saw them immediately. He jerked to a halt, his
black cape settling around him and thankfully covering a
good portion of his bare body. His deep voice seemed to
bounce from the walls of the small room. "I'm sorry, but
visitors aren't allowed backstage."

Squeezed against her side on the short sofa, Holly felt
Xonia take a deep breath. The witch is nervous, she realized with a jolt of surprise. She soon discovered, however, that Xonia didn't intend for Reuben to know this
interesting tidbit of information.

"I'm surprised you don't recognize me, Reuben," Xonia
drawled.

Winged black brows—enhanced by cosmetics Holly
had spotted on the dresser—rose in shock. "Xonia?"

"The one and only."

The brows came crashing down in a frown. "Did you
come to see Mini? She's at—"

"I know where she is and what she's doing," Xonia interrupted. "When I left her this evening, she was attempting to bake a batch of *your* favorite cookies in the hopes that you'd stay home tonight."

"She was doing that when *I* left, so you couldn't have been there."

"Oh, but I was." Xonia rose from the sofa. Her hand made a slow circle in the air, ending with a flick of her fingers. In the blink of an eye, she was a cat. She leaped onto the sofa and sat on her haunches. "*Now* do you recognize me?"

Reuben was speechless. Finally he sputtered, "If this is a joke, it isn't funny. Mini would have told me if *you* were the familiar!"

"Like you told *her* what you were doing tonight?" Xonia tsk-tsked. "If I were you, I'd take a good long look in the mirror before I started pointing that witchy finger."

Holly jumped as Reuben swung his glowering black gaze on her. This wasn't the gentle, grumbling, clumsy man she knew and employed; this was a warlock on the rampage!

And now he was looking at *her*.

She tried to swallow softly, but ended up gulping noisily instead. *For heaven's sake,* she chided her cowardly heart, *I helped this man remove a painful hangnail last week!*

He lifted an accusing finger. "And who's *this*? Another meddling witch?" His voice rose to a roar. "Are you from the witches' council?"

"No." Holly said the word—she was sure of it—but no sound emerged. Fear had snatched her voice. She was very glad she *wasn't* who he thought she was, but she didn't think he was going to be much happier to discover the truth.

"I don't think you want to be shouting at her," Xonia said just as calmly as you please. "She might decide to skip you when it comes time for your next pay raise."

This time the silence lasted a lot longer.

Holly groaned inwardly, not for the first time wishing she hadn't agreed to come along with Xonia. She watched in hopeless horror as Reuben's black gaze ran the gauntlet of emotions, beginning at stunned disbelief and ending at one she'd dreaded: acute embarrassment.

"You lie," he croaked, shaking his magnificent head. His hair swished softly against his shoulders. "You always were a joker, Xonia. Only I never found you very funny."

Xonia sighed. "As you wish." With a flick of her fingers, Holly became herself again. "There, see for yourself, warlock."

"How do I know it's not a trick?"

It was time to speak up, Holly decided, praying her voice wouldn't let her down again. "Reuben, it's me. Holly." She cleared her throat. "I'm sorry, so truly sorry—"

"Oh, stop!" Xonia cried. Her tail twitched rapidly in her agitation. Beyond her on the dresser, pots and brushes began to dance in the air. "You're making me ill. Why are *you* apologizing to him? *I* brought you here! But *he's* the one who should be apologizing. If he's so ashamed—"

"I'm not ashamed." Reuben drew himself up to his full five feet eleven inches. Oil gleamed on his chest. His voice lowered and softened. "In another ten years, some of those women will be in retirement homes. That's how all of this began." His pitch-black gaze focused on Holly, his pride evident. "One of your clients works part-time as a dancer—he mostly freelances for birthdays and bachelorette parties—and he asked me to fill in for him since his date coincided with a job. The job was at a retirement home for a woman's eighty-fifth birthday. I needed a second job, so I agreed."

Xonia, who had been listening in silence for a change, piped up, "If you didn't see any harm, then why didn't you tell Mini?"

Reuben's gaze hardened to rock again. "That's none of your business, witch. Mini doesn't have a clue, so—"

"Um, I think she does."

Uh-oh. Holly sensed another storm brewing.

"What do you mean?" Reuben suddenly bellowed.

Holly winced; Xonia arched her back and hissed.

"She wouldn't let me tell her, but she knows you're not getting together with your friends!" Xonia shouted back. "Unlike *some* people I know, *I* don't lie to her!"

"Why, you meddling, wart-nosed witch!"

"You arrogant, hip-swaying Elvis wanna-be!"

A makeup pot came flying through the air in their direction. Holly ducked just as Xonia instructed. Another followed seconds after the first. Soon they were being peppered by harmless brushes and tissue boxes. With her arms protecting her face, Holly shouted, "Stop it! Xonia, stop throwing things!"

"I'm not! *He* must be doing it!"

Her revelation stunned them all.

The boxes and brushes clattered to the floor.

For a solid moment, there was absolute silence in the room.

Xonia spoke first, her voice sounding unnaturally fearful. "Reuben, that was you, wasn't it?"

With a bewildered shake of his head, Reuben gazed at the littered floor, "I—I think it was!"

A heartfelt sigh exploded from Xonia. "Thank God! You're getting your powers back."

"He is?" Holly squeaked, looking from feline to warlock. "But didn't you say—"

"Yes, yes," Xonia said impatiently. "Apparently Reuben's caught the council's eye." She shook her head. "Although I can't imagine why. I guess they approve of his stripping in front of a bunch of old, dried-up— Meow. Meow, meow." Xonia's mouth moved rapidly, but the only thing that emerged was a fast series of meows ending with a very prominent and plaintive, "Meoooow!"

Alarmed, Holly glanced at Reuben. He stood with his arms folded over his chest, a silly grin splattered across his face. With an arrogant wave of his hand, he released the spell.

Xonia drew in a furious breath. "If you *ever* do that again, I'll—I'll—"

"Hold it!" Holly had had enough of their petty bickering. They were wasting valuable time. "Reuben, please keep your spells to yourself. Xonia, stop calling Reuben names, and let's get down to the *real* reason we're here. Tell him about Jestark."

Reuben responded to the urgency in her tone. "What about Jestark?" he demanded, stepping forward.

Still miffed, Xonia tipped her nose in the air and turned her back to Reuben. "I'm not saying another word until that brute apologizes." She sniffed pitifully. "Picking on a poor, defenseless cat."

One look at Reuben's stony face and Holly knew she was on her own. "Very well, I guess I'll have to tell him. Just don't blame me if I get it wrong."

"Whatever," Xonia said, staring at the back of the sofa.

Taking a deep breath, Holly began. "Jestark—"

"You mean, *Jerk*stark," Xonia mumbled.

Holly clamped her mouth shut and glared at the cat.

After a moment, Xonia whirled around. "Oh, very well! I'll tell the story. At least I know *I'll* get it right."

Thankfully she ignored Reuben's skeptical grunt.

It was makeup, all right. And it wasn't hers.

Mini dropped Reuben's shirt on the floor and sat down hard in the kitchen chair. At first she had refused to believe it, but two batches of burned cookies later, she forced herself to face the truth—the truth Xonia had been trying to tell her for the past week.

The flimsy excuses to get out of the apartment; the tiny scrap of underwear he'd claimed to have bought for her, but had never gotten around to *wearing* for her; and finally the makeup on his shirt, an oil-based brand she couldn't wear because it made unsightly bumps on her face—all of it pointed to one terrible conclusion.

Reuben was fooling around.

Why? How long? With whom?

She caught a painful gasp in her throat and forced it down. It had to be a mortal, because Mini knew that another witch wouldn't dare mess with an ex-warlock in disgrace with the witches' council.

A mortal, then. Reuben had met a mortal woman, perhaps one who could do everything *right* the mortal way. A tearing pain seized her, but Mini stubbornly weathered it without so much as a moan escaping her lips. Perhaps the woman had something they lacked, like mortal money to buy the things Reuben wanted. He was accustomed to getting his way. Before their banishment, he'd been able to simply snap his fingers and conjure whatever his heart desired.

What was she going to do? What *should* she do? To think she had gladly given up her powers to live a mortal's life. To think she had wasted the last two hundred and twenty-five years on a faithless warlock.

Mini let her burning gaze travel around the kitchen. It resembled one of her cooking classes. Bowls, pans, and countless other items littered the small counter space. It was more proof of what a fool she'd been.

To think she'd been laboring over a hot stove, baking his favorite cookies! Now the kitchen was a mess, and the one time she would have welcomed Xonia's help, she wasn't here.

Squeezing her eyes tightly shut against the pain, Mini waved her hand at the mess, mentally sweeping it from her mind. It was a useless gesture, she thought bitterly. Because of her misguided loyalty, she had lost her powers.

When she opened her eyes again, she let out a startled gasp of surprise.

The mess was gone. The counters were sparkling clean. The cookies she'd baked—no longer burned, not a single one—were put away neatly in the cookie jar.

Quickly she searched the kitchen for Xonia, but her friend was nowhere in sight; she would have felt her presence anyway, she reasoned. Her heart began to pound as realization sank in: The witches' council knew what Reuben had done and had released her from her pledge.

Her powers had been restored.

She could visualize them now, a dozen old witches shaking their sad, smug heads. They pitied her, but they would also say they had warned her about marrying a worthless warlock.

The conjured image struck a spark of rebellion inside Mini. Because of the witches' council, they had been sentenced to live as mortals, and because of the witches' council, Reuben may have fallen in love with a mortal. Despite what she knew now, Mini still believed with all her heart and soul that Reuben was innocent of the crime they accused him of. Yes, he had been with Jestark on that night, but he wouldn't have participated had he known what Jestark was about.

He'd been judged and sentenced because of his past history; it was a simple, bald case of discrimination.

Mini reached for the damning shirt and clutched it in her shaking hands. The image blurred as two hundred and twenty-five years of memories played out in her mind.

Was she truly considering giving up without a fight?

Her spine stiffened. Purpose dried her eyes. She let out a shaky breath. No. She would not give up without a fight. Reuben was *her* husband, and no woman—mortal or otherwise—was going to take him from her.

Twenty-one

~

Lance thought it was a good sign when she answered the doorbell after peering through the peephole.

When she waved her arm to indicate he and Casey should come inside, he even felt a small flame of hope flare to life.

But when Debbie Mosely stood with her pretty lips pursed together in a tight line, and her slim arms folded over her chest, he knew he had hopelessly missed his mark.

"I know what you must think," he said. He nodded in Casey's direction. "This is Casey. He and I are close friends—real close. He knows everything about me."

"I'm happy for you, and you have no idea what I'm thinking."

Lance actually shivered at her freezing tone. "Let me take a stab at it. You think that I'm not only a sleazy kinda guy, you think I'm also a liar and a cheat."

"Go on." Her foot began to tap against the floor. "You're getting warm."

Ignoring the insult, Lance nudged Casey. "Tell her, Case. Tell her that there's not a snowball's chance in hell I knew that woman in the restaurant, so I couldn't be the father of her baby."

But Casey, apparently, had lost the ability to speak. He continued to gawk at Debbie as if he'd never seen a woman before.

"Casey?" Slightly alarmed, Lance waved his hand in front of his face. He snapped his fingers. Casey didn't even blink. "Casey? Remember me, old buddy? Remember why we're here? You were going to help me out, explain to Debbie that it was all a misunderstanding." He leaned in close to add in a whisper, "So that she can give me some advice about Holly and what to do with the house."

Debbie tapped her foot and waited.

Casey continued to stare at Debbie.

Lance felt the floor open up beneath his feet. In a few more minutes, he would cheerfully jump into the yawning hole. "I don't know what's wrong with him. He was fine until you opened the door."

"Maybe he changed his mind about lying for you."

"I'm not lying. Tell her, Casey."

"Yes, tell me, Casey."

At the sound of her saccharine-sweet purr, Casey came to life. His Adam's apple bobbed up and down as he swallowed. Lance looked on with morbid fascination as a line of sweat popped out above Casey's freshly shaven upper lip.

It was Lance's first inkling of what might be wrong with Casey. He'd seen him react this way before when in the vicinity of a pretty woman.

What his friend did next made his suspicion absolute. Casey stumbled in Debbie's direction, grabbed her by the arms, and proceeded to kiss her open mouth.

Lance closed his eyes and groaned. Nine times out of ten when Casey pulled this outrageous stunt, the woman slapped him soundly. Debbie would be no exception— given her tough background—and then she would come after *him*. She would never tolerate such a chauvinistic move.

Within moments he and Casey would be standing on her porch nursing sore jaws.

His chance to explain himself and regain her friendship would be lost. Damn Casey!

But he was wrong again, he discovered when he risked a peek at the couple. Debbie was kissing Casey back as if he were her long-lost lover.

After an uncomfortable moment, Lance cleared his throat.

The couple ignored him—or didn't hear him.

He did it again, louder this time.

Finally their mouths broke apart with a comical sucking sound. Debbie looked downright dazed, and Casey . . . well, Casey didn't look the way he usually looked when he got away with this stunt.

Usually he looked triumphant, cocky, and very smug.

This time, Lance noted, he looked just as dazed as Debbie.

Interesting . . . But it *wasn't* what they were here for.

"Now that you've sucked her brains out, will you tell her the truth?" Lance drawled sarcastically.

It was almost frightening to see a man like Casey blush—a bona fide blush from a man who had been bold, brave, and crazy enough to wear nothing but a diaper to the hospital Halloween party last year. *"Nothing gets to women like the smell of Johnson's baby powder,"* Casey had bragged.

Amazingly, he'd been right. Unable to decide between two nurses he'd been chasing for months, Casey had taken them both home. The stories he'd told Lance later still had the power to make his ears burn.

That same man was standing before him now, blushing and grinning like a fool.

"Who—who *are* you?" Debbie asked in a bewildered, breathless voice that reminded Lance of Dorothy in *The Wizard of Oz.*

Funny, Lance was just about to ask the same question. "That's my friend, Casey," Lance said, determined to regain control of the meeting. "And if you want to know anything else about him, you can ask him later. I'm sure you two will have plenty of time to—"

"Will you go out with me?" Casey asked as if Lance hadn't spoken.

"Yes. When?"

"Wait a damned min—"

"How about now?"

"Great. I'll just get my purse." She paused in midflight, gazing back at Casey as if she feared he'd vanish. "You won't leave?"

Clearly besotted, Casey shook his head. "I'll wait right here."

"Casey!"

Casey jumped, reluctantly pulling his adoring eyes from Debbie to stare at Lance. His gaze widened as if he were surprised to see him. In a rush, he said, "Oh, Lance. Yeah, uh, Debbie, Lance didn't know that woman. There was some kind of mix-up. He's really an okay guy to have as a *friend,* and he needs advice on redecorating. Will you help him? I won't let him take up too much of your time," he added with a meaningful glance in Lance's direction.

Without hesitation, Debbie nodded.

Lance didn't know whether to laugh or cry. "Thanks. I think. Tomorrow night?"

"We'll be there," Casey said quickly. The moment Debbie's back was turned, he gestured wildly toward the door. "Go!" he whispered. "I'll catch you later."

Bemused by the mad turn of events, Lance started to leave.

"Oh, and I owe you one, you sly dog you."

Lance made it all the way to his car before he gave in to a fit of laughter that nearly buckled his knees. Finally, wiping his streaming eyes, he managed to get the car door open. He fell into the driver's seat and started the engine before another bout of laughter overcame him.

What a trip! And who would have thought it? He'd have bet a bundle that Debbie and Casey never came *close* to matching at the Romance Connection. Holly would be amazed when she found out, Lance thought, sobering. Thinking of Holly reminded him that it was high time his *own* love life took a turn for the better. Not that Friday night hadn't been one of the best times of his life, but he wanted more than just fantastic sex.

Okay, *awesome* sex. The best.

He let the car idle for a moment as he closed his eyes and remembered Holly's smile, her eyes, and her lips. The way she moved her lips when she talked turned him on. Hell, everything about her turned him on. He loved listening to the sound of her voice, too, especially when she whispered naughty things in his ear.

Just thinking about it made him realize how much he missed her. It had been five days since he'd last seen her. Each time he'd called she'd had some excuse ready and waiting, which hadn't surprised Lance. Cautious Holly would never enter into a serious relationship without thinking things through. While it pained him, he admired that about her and he understood.

It was one of the reasons he hadn't pushed her.

Practicing what he preached to his own patients, Lance had mentally stepped into Holly's shoes. What if she was widowed? What if she had been married to someone for fifteen years, someone he knew she had loved? Wouldn't he worry that she might compare him and find him lacking? Or constantly wonder if she were thinking of her late husband when she was with *him*?

Lance had brought himself out of his self-imposed trance to find that just a few moments of jealousy had left a nasty taste in his mouth. He'd faced a few hard, cold facts, too: He was very, very glad Holly hadn't been married. Thank God they had only *one* ghost to deal with—although this ghost was in Holly's mind and not in his own.

The other reason he hadn't pushed was because he hoped she'd start missing him and give him a call on her own. Ha! She gave new meaning to the saying, "If the phone doesn't ring, it's me!"

He couldn't wait any longer. He needed to see her, feel her, kiss her, and he didn't think it was wise to give her *too* much time to think. Besides, he had the perfect excuse—they still hadn't solved Friday night's mystery, although Lance had since developed his own theories while lying awake in his big lonely bed wishing Holly was lying beside him.

Obviously someone had been playing a practical joke on Holly. Someone who had known she'd gone to meet him, and had perhaps anticipated that he might return with her to the apartment. The person had taken a big gamble, but Lance figured it was someone who knew both of them pretty well.

Lance put the car in gear and glanced in his rearview mirror before joining the traffic, but his mind wasn't fully on his driving; he was thinking of two people who would know a lot about everything.

He couldn't wait to share his suspicions with Holly.

Fumbling in his pocket for the cell phone he rarely used, Lance divided his attention between driving and dialing Holly's number. When she answered, he said without preamble, "I need to talk to you. I think I know the identity of our little ghost."

Her reaction surprised him. "Lance! I'm glad you called because I need to talk to you, too. In fact, I was just about to call you."

Holly couldn't wait to share her story with Lance. Would he believe her? Would he let her finish before he declared her insane? What if he *didn't* believe her? He was a psychologist. She knew from experience that he could be a hard sell on anything not anchored in scientific facts.

After talking to him on the phone, her nerves began to zing and jump with anticipation, and she knew only half of it was a result of the incredible news she had to share. She took Nike to visit Mrs. Teasedale and returned to the apartment to wait for Lance to arrive.

To say she'd missed him would have been a gross understatement.

She'd missed him *badly*.

If this was true love, she didn't know if her heart could withstand the strain.

True love. Yes, she loved Lance. So much it frightened the hell out of her.

Xonia had assured her a hundred times that Lance was ready to get on with his life. Holly wished she could believe her, wished she could just shove her fears aside and embrace whatever fate decided. She hated being a coward.

Steeped in her thoughts, she nearly jumped out of her skin when the doorbell pealed. She raced to the hall mirror, where she quickly smoothed her hair and pinched her cheeks. For a second she regarded her large, frightened eyes in the mirror.

"Coward," she whispered. She fancied she could hear Xonia's cackling agreement. "You'd better not be watching, witch. You promised that you wouldn't."

"Who were you talking to?" Lance asked the moment she opened the door.

He looked breathtakingly handsome, frown and all. "Um, myself. I was talking to myself." She flashed him a shy smile, then shocked him by saying, "Come on. Let's go to the bedroom."

"Well, I—"

"Don't argue." Holly wound an arm around his neck and pulled him close. He inhaled sharply at her bold move. "I don't want anyone to hear what I have to tell you," she whispered urgently into his ear.

She was thankful he didn't ask any further questions, although she could clearly read them in his eyes.

When they reached her bedroom, Holly put a finger to her lips as she pulled the covers aside and tugged him onto the bed. He let her lead him without argument. She stifled a nervous giggle at his shocked expression. After Friday night, how could he be shocked by *anything* she did?

Her skin grew hot just thinking about it. But she couldn't allow herself to think about it, at least not yet. She had a story to tell.

Finally, when she had pulled the covers over their heads and they lay facing each other, she reached beneath her pillow and pulled out a tiny flashlight. She pressed the button. "Now we can talk, but we should keep our voices low."

He looked disappointed. "We're going to talk? *Now*?"

Apparently he hadn't been listening. Holly forgave him. How could she not, considering how difficult it was for *her* to concentrate? He was so close she could move her head just a few inches and meet his lips with her own.

"Yes, we're going to talk. I've got an incredible story to tell you, and I'm afraid you're not going to believe me."

As she spoke, he reached out and tucked her hair behind her ear. She sucked in a sharp breath. She loved it when he did that. It was one of the many, many things she loved about Lance.

"Why would I not believe you?" he asked softly. "You're the most sane, logical person I know." He made an X across his heart with his finger. "I promise to believe anything you say—on one condition."

Cautiously Holly asked, "What condition would that be?"

"That you *not* mention the word 'ghost.' "

Holly bit her lip to keep from smiling. She decided to pretend she hadn't seen his hand move. She also chose to pretend to ignore—for her own selfish gain—the feel of his finger rubbing against her nipple through her shirt. But she'd seen and she felt. Oh, did she feel. "Okay, it's a deal. Now, you've made it pretty clear how you feel about ghosts. How do you feel about witches?"

By nightfall, Reuben's bewilderment had reached an all-time high. Several times throughout the day as they went about their jobs at Romance Connection, he'd sensed Mini wanted to tell him something, but each time she had simply stared at him with this heart-wrenching look and then resumed whatever task she'd been about.

Perhaps she hadn't agreed with his and Xonia's plan to draw Jestark into the open by pretending nothing had changed. But *if* she didn't agree, why didn't she just say so? It wasn't like Mini to go along with anything she didn't believe in wholeheartedly, and *he* couldn't believe that Mini would consider leaving Holly, Lance, and the entire town of Lovit at Jestark's mercy. She knew as well as he did the kind of havoc and destruction his friend could create among mortals.

Reuben sighed and punched his pillow, wishing he had the energy just to conjure a bigger, fluffier one while he waited for his wife to emerge from the bathroom.

But Jestark could be anywhere, watching and waiting, as Xonia had reminded him a dozen times. When he got his hands on his errant friend, he was going to make him very sorry.

Amazing. Xonia had actually made sense when she'd presented her plan. He had to admire her insight as well in guessing that Jestark would show himself on Allhallows Eve night. Reuben almost chuckled until he remembered that he was mad at his friend, although he didn't believe Jestark would do any *real* harm to anyone Reuben knew.

But Xonia was right: Jestark would not be able to resist scaring the daylights out of a crowd of mortals, especially if he believed there were a few helpless witches mixed in. He wouldn't consider it malice, just good ole merry warlock fun.

His warlock friend—his soon-to-be *ex*-friend—was in for a very unpleasant surprise if everything went as planned. Reuben's eyes drifted shut, only to snap open again as he heard the creak of the bathroom door open and close.

Mini stood in the dim light clad in the costume she had insisted on making herself. Reuben's mouth watered at the intriguing sight she presented. Layers upon layers of transparent veils covered her body, from her delectable ankles to her pert little nose.

But the light shot through each and every layer of the harem costume, revealing a hint of her supple body beneath, leaving the rest to mystery. With a little imagination, he could see the faint shadow of her nipples, and the V between her thighs, could visualize every curve and angle, every hollow and plane of her body. He knew it well.

Above the veil covering her face, her emerald-green eyes gleamed and sparkled with a come-hither look that sent his heart crashing against his rib cage.

His mouth went dry. "Come here, woman," he tried to say in a commanding voice. It came out more like a plea.

She bowed low, but her sexy eyes never wavered from his face. "As you wish, master."

Twenty-two

"... Then Xonia saw me with the crystal ball and realized that nasty warlock Jestark must be lurking around. She told me everything. Together we went to a bar that features male strippers—it was senior citizens' night, so Xonia aged us accordingly—to convince Reuben that his friend was in town. Reuben got very angry and started throwing things. That's when we knew that his powers had been restored. Just in time, too. The plan is—"

Lance very gently reached out and pressed his hand against her mouth. "Holly, we need to get you to a doctor. Right away. I'll call Casey. He'll know who we should see."

She snatched his hand down. "Friday night you were willing to believe that the ghost of your dead wife might be haunting us. Now you won't even consider that I'm telling the truth?"

It was her eyes, so clear and direct, that made Lance hesitate before saying, "Holly, the story you just told me is beyond the impossible. There are no such things as witches and warlocks, or magic, or crystal balls." His tone gentled further. "It sounds like Mini and Reuben could be trying to scam you. Did you do a thorough background check on those two?"

Just as gently, Holly ignored his last question as she pointed out, "But what about the talking cat? I *saw* her talking! I also saw her turn into an old lady, then back into a cat to prove to Reuben she was Xonia. Those weren't ordinary tricks, Lance."

"There are lots of new, dangerous drugs on the market—"

"It wasn't drugs!"

"And there's also the possibility—*probability*—of hypnosis." Actually he believed she was having some type of breakdown, or that possibly her hallucinations were a result of a brain tumor. Both scenarios scared the hell out of Lance. Surely God wouldn't be so cruel as to deprive him of this second chance at love so soon?

"I can't be hypnotized." She threw back the covers and rested her head on the pillow, staring at the ceiling. "I told Xonia you wouldn't believe me."

Go along with her, he thought. Just until he could get her to the hospital. "And how did this Xonia person respond?"

Holly turned her head to look at him. She looked so serious it sent a chill straight into his heart.

"She said to tell you that you're not a half-bad shrink, but that you really let her down by going on that date. I explained that it wasn't your fault, really, that I pushed you into it."

"I'm afraid I'm not following you." He hadn't been following her all along, but until now she'd made a twisted kind of sense.

"Remember Bridget?"

"How could I forget?"

"That was Xonia. She was hoping to keep you from going out with Debbie by taking advantage of your incredible dedication to your profession."

"Too bad it didn't work," Lance said, wondering if he should call 911 or take her to the hospital himself.

"Oh, she's sorry about that, too. She was there with Mini. Mini was playing the part of the pregnant woman."

And Lance thought it couldn't get more bizarre. "If she was there, why didn't I see her?"

"You may not have seen her, but you definitely heard her when Mini slapped you. Mini forgot Xonia was on her bracelet. Remember the meow you heard? That was Xonia."

Lance was shocked into silence for a moment—until he realized that Holly must have related his tale to Mini and Reuben, and that they must have conveniently incorporated it into their plans. Perhaps they had known all along that Holly was becoming ill.

His concern escalated into panic. He'd lost one woman he loved; he didn't know if he could bear to lose another. "Holly, we should go now."

Her calm expression unnerved him. "Go where?"

"To the hospital."

With an exasperated sigh, Holly rose from the bed. "We were all hoping to convince you quietly. Guess we'll just have to take a chance on the possibility of Jestark's finding out." She gestured for him to follow.

Fearing she would collapse any moment, Lance jumped from the bed and followed Holly into the kitchen. He watched her closely, his heart aching as she moved to the window above the sink.

"This is the signal for Xonia. I'm to open the window if I can't convince you." Grunting, she lifted the window and peered out, then glanced at him over her shoulder. "Is your heart okay?"

"What?"

"Your heart. Is it okay? Are you healthy? Any history of heart attacks or strokes in your family?"

Dazed, he shook his head. "What about you? Any history of aneurysm, strokes, or brain tumors? How about mental health? Anyone crazy? Prone to depression? Schizophrenic? Bonkers?"

She smiled. "No. Nothing like that. I don't have a brain tumor, Lance, so stop looking so devastated." The doorbell rang. "That will be Mini and Reuben," she announced.

The words were out before he could stop them: "Why didn't they just pop in?"

Holly put a finger to her lips. "Ssh. Remember that Jestark could be listening."

"Of course," Lance murmured. "The warlock. How could I forget?"

"Wait here."

His worried gaze followed her as she left the kitchen. The moment she was out of sight, he fumbled for his cell phone. Casey, he thought. Casey would know what to do.

He punched the power button, and the phone vanished from his hand.

"It wouldn't work anyway," a cranky-sounding voice said.

Lance jerked his astonished gaze from his empty hand to the window. An orange cat perched on the rim of the sink, her yellow-gold eyes regarding him with mild exasperation.

"I've put a spell around the house in case *he's* watching, so there won't be any signals going out or coming in."

His mouth worked, but no sound emerged. He blinked, then rubbed his eyes, but when he looked again, the cat was still there.

Holly appeared at his side, her gentle fingers grasping his elbow. "Are you okay? Any pain in your chest?"

Her concerned voice released Lance from his paralysis. "There's nothing wrong with my *heart*!" he snapped. "But I've obviously lost my mind." Beyond Holly, Mini and Reuben came into view. They looked like an ordinary couple, he thought. But he, for one, knew that it was an illusion. They were con artists—

"He's still not with us," Xonia drawled, as if she believed *he* was the one with a problem. "He thinks you guys are con artists."

"You'd better sit down." Holly led him to a chair and urged him to sit.

Lance was glad, because his knees felt curiously weak, and his head felt light as a feather. The cat had known what he was thinking . . . or was it an educated guess? If they *were* con artists, then it stood to reason that—

"Oh, get a life!" Xonia exclaimed. "Why is it so difficult for you mortals to believe in magic? It's all around you."

Mini beckoned Xonia to her. "Xonia, stand in front of him and change into yourself."

"But, Mini," Xonia whined, "I like being a cat better!" When Mini arched a threatening brow at her, she relented, grumbling as she leaped from the sink and padded over to Lance.

Shaking his head, Lance stared at the cat sitting at his feet and said, "You're a robot. I know what kind of technology they use these days."

Xonia cackled as she tilted her head to look up at him. "Is that so? Well, how about *this*."

Before Lance could blink, Xonia became a homely looking witch, complete with a long nose and wild orange hair.

The golden eyes were the same.

"Some technology, huh?" And with that, she threw back her head and cackled, looking and sounding very much like a *real* witch.

Lance closed his eyes and rubbed the bridge of his nose. He sucked in a deep breath, searching for a logical, scientific explanation for what he'd just witnessed. If he accepted at face value what his eyes had seen, he would have to consider that he had completely lost it.

"Lance . . . you look pale."

It was Holly, sounding worried.

"Maybe we miscalculated," Mini said, sounding just as worried as Holly. "Perhaps his mortal mind isn't strong enough."

Xonia had stopped cackling. "I could cast the Spell of Forgetfulness," she suggested.

Reuben shouldered Xonia aside and folded his arms. "So could I."

"And do a better job, I suppose?" Xonia's eyes narrowed.

"Of course."

"Ha!"

"Ha, yourself."

Mini stepped between the two bristling witches. "Stop squabbling. We've got to decide."

All three of them turned to Holly.

Lance looked on, dazed and amazed and fairly certain now that this wasn't a nightmare or a figment of his crumbling mind.

"What do you think, Holly? You know him better than we do. Will he come around, or do we need to reverse the damage before it has a chance to become permanent?"

Holly licked her lips, studying him until he felt like a germ under a microscope. "Well, we could have used his help, but I don't want to take any chances on—"

"I'm fine," Lance heard himself saying. His voice was faint, and a trifle shaky, but at least it was there.

Holly had said she needed him. How could he resist? And if it meant that he had to accept this incredible fantasy, then he could do it. Reality without Holly held no appeal.

Stronger now, he repeated, "I'm fine. I believe you."

She gave a happy cry and wound her arms around his neck. Her pert little bottom sank against his groin as she snuggled onto his lap. Her mouth covered his in a kiss filled with heat and unrestrained hunger. Too bad they had an audience, Lance thought, kissing her right back.

When he cautiously opened one eye and looked around, he found the room empty.

The three witches were gone.

• • •

"You're giving me a *week* to redecorate?" Debbie's question ended on a squeaky note of disbelief. She looked to Casey for support. When he merely shrugged, she threw her hands in the air. "What you're asking is impossible!"

Lance decided that what Debbie needed was a little challenge. "That will leave us three days to decorate for the Halloween party I'm hosting. You said yourself that you needed a break from your work."

Debbie stared at him as if he'd lost his mind.

If only she knew.

"What about Holly? Why doesn't *she* help you?"

"She offered to help with the party, but I wouldn't let her. The rest she doesn't know about—I want to surprise her." He was hoping she would finally believe that he had put Mona's ghost to rest when she saw the changes.

Seeing Debbie hesitate, Lance went ruthlessly for the proverbial throat. In this case, it was Debbie's pride. "If you don't think you can handle it, I can try to find someone else. It's certainly not your responsibility," he added, smiling to let her know there would be no hard feelings.

"*I* can handle it, Wilder, if you've got the dough. It won't be cheap."

She *would* have to remind him of his flagging finances, Lance thought. But fortunately he'd anticipated the problem. "Casey, are you still interested in buying Dad's '79 Mercedes Roadster?"

Casey's jaw went slack. His eyes began to glisten. "The one you told me never to ask about again?" He paused, staring suspiciously at Lance. "It's not nice to tease your best friend, you know."

"I'm not teasing. It's yours if you still want it."

"I'll talk to the bank tomorrow. Is that soon enough?"

Lance nodded, surprised to discover he no longer felt a reluctance to sell the Mercedes. What good was it to him? He had never felt comfortable driving it, and it was ridiculous to keep something of that value when he needed the money. Casey would cherish the car far more than he ever had, could, or would.

Holly . . . Holly had brought about these changes in him, Lance mused. Beside her, everything else paled in comparison.

"I have a few friends who might be interested in the paintings," Debbie said.

"Sell them if you can." Mona had loved those paintings, but they wouldn't have been Holly's choice. "I want a whole new look."

Debbie frowned. "What if Holly doesn't like my style?"

"Then we'll sell the house and buy a new one."

"Then why—" She broke off with an understanding smile. "Oh, I get it. You're trying to prove a point."

"Exactly."

Monday started out badly for Holly, with a call from a very angry client complaining about her services.

It was the first of many, and by four o'clock, Holly was ready and willing to pull out her hair.

"Yes, Miss Weaver. I know, but—" Holly propped her elbow on her desk and leaned her forehead into her hand as the voice on the other end of the line went into another relentless tirade.

Fifteen tiresome minutes later, Holly hung up. She faced Mini and Reuben. Xonia had disappeared, mumbling something about popping in at Lance's house to see how the party preparations were going.

"That's the eighth call today, ladies and gents. I'd say that's just a little bit too coincidental."

"What was *her* story?" Reuben asked, his dark brows furrowed.

Holly knew his menacing tone had nothing to do with her, or she might have been frightened. Strange how she'd never thought of Reuben as dangerous before. "Seems her date has canine qualities. He not only embarrassed her by lapping his soup with his tongue in front of a restaurantful of people, but he also watered her bushes when he took her home. Once there, he frightened her poodle into a seizure and chased her cat up a tree. She's sending me the vet bill."

Mini winced. "That's almost as bad as the woman who took her clothes off in the park and jumped naked into the fountain. Mr. Lake wasn't impressed."

"He's a retired pastor," Holly added with a frustrated sigh. "He specifically asked for a nice, God-fearing woman." She glanced at Reuben's stony face. "Jestark?"

His jerky nod seemed to be all he could manage.

"At this rate, I won't have a business to return to after Halloween!"

"I'm going after him," Reuben announced, exploding into action. He headed for the door.

Mini clutched his arm. "You know it won't do any good. You won't find him until he's *ready* to be found."

"Why is he doing this to me?" Holly demanded. "What did I do to him?"

"He's not doing anything out of anger," Mini explained, still holding on to her husband's tensed arm. "Warlocks live to create havoc. They *thrive* on it. To him, Romance Connection is just a playground full of wonderful toys."

Holly groaned. "Will he get bored . . . eventually?" She hated to think about the damage he could do before he got to that point.

Mini shrugged. "Maybe, but probably not. He knows we're here. I think this is his way of trying to get Reuben to come out and play."

"Thank God Reuben's different!" Holly said with a heartfelt sigh. "I don't think I could survive *two* playful warlocks."

"Amen," Mini said.

Lance was concluding his last session of the day when Debbie burst into his office. She looked very, very angry.

"Lance, if that wise-mouth criticizes me one more time, I'm going to—"

"Casey?"

"No! That—that wild-haired teenage friend of yours, Bridget! She's trying to tell me how to decorate, as if *she* knows anything!" She took a deep, angry breath. "She claims that she knows Holly—"

"Just a moment," Lance interrupted. He turned an apologetic smile on the sulky teenager slumped on the couch. "See you next Monday, same time?"

The teenager took his time rising from the sofa. He collected his backpack and boom box, then headed for the door. "Yeah, sure, man."

When he'd gone, Debbie tried to apologize. "I'm sorry, Lance, I didn't think before I barged in."

"No harm done. Where's Bridget now?"

Debbie heated up again at his reminder. "She's in the family room poring over carpet samples. I swear, if you don't do something—"

"I'll talk to her."

The wily witch was indeed sitting in the family room looking at carpet samples. It might have been a shock to see her as Bridget if Holly hadn't warned him ahead of time.

Lance grabbed her by the arm and pulled her up. "Come with me."

She went willingly enough—until they were out of sight and out of earshot. Then she tried to struggle out of his grasp.

Lance held on tight.

"You don't want to piss me off, mortal," Xonia snapped. "You could be the first frog to live in a mansion."

"You wouldn't."

"Why wouldn't I?"

Pulling her closer, Lance said, "Because if you do, I'll make sure Holly finds out about a certain little package you delivered to me." He was counting on Holly's not knowing about the interview package.

"You wouldn't!" Xonia gasped.

Lance smiled, enjoying himself. "Why wouldn't I?"

"Oooh, you rat!"

"Witch," Lance returned smoothly and without fear. He'd already sensed that beneath her crackly exterior, there beat a soft heart of gold. "Now that we've gotten the insults out of the way, just why are you here?"

Xonia sniffed. "I came to help out, but obviously I'm not wanted."

"You can help me."

"I can?"

Lance smiled at her hopeful tone. She wasn't such a bad witch when she got her way. "If you promise to behave. I'm planning on changing bedrooms. Maybe you can give me some advice on which one Holly might prefer."

Beaming, Xonia said, "Consider it done!"

He didn't realize she'd meant it literally until he reached his bedroom and found it empty.

Of everything.

"Close your eyes."

Figuring he had no choice in the matter, Lance obeyed. He had to admit to more than a little curiosity about what the witch was up to.

"Okay, you can open them now."

They were in another bedroom, but not one Lance immediately recognized. Heavy drapes of teal green hung at the windows; a matching comforter and shams graced a huge Queen Anne–style bed. The gleaming hardwood floor was bare with the exception of a few rugs scattered about.

Lance turned in a full circle, admiring the open, airy feel of the room. The white walls tipped the scales, he decided, his gaze lingering on the few paintings on the wall. They appeared to be by the same artist, the nineteenth-century costumes worn by the people lending a homey touch.

One painting was of a couple having a picnic by a sparkling stream, and another depicted a woman sitting in a rocking chair by the fire, a sewing basket in her lap and two bright-eyed children sprawled at her feet playing with a bag of marbles.

But Lance liked the third painting best. It was of a couple sitting in a gazebo, their hands entwined, their lips nearly touching as they anticipated a kiss. It reminded Lance of his first date with Holly.

He was about to drag his gaze away when something in the picture caught his eye, something he hadn't noticed at first glance.

At the couple's feet lounged an orange, scruffy-looking cat with golden eyes.

When Lance lifted a speculative brow, Xonia blushed and ducked her head. Her uncharacteristic action moved him.

"I couldn't resist. When I found these at a flea market—"

"You *bought* these? You actually browsed a flea market and bought the paintings?"

"Well, no. Witch's don't *buy* things, Lance. We duplicate them. Anyway, as I was saying, I know these are Holly's favorites, so I've been saving them for her."

"Lance!"

At the sound of Debbie's aggrieved tone, Xonia rolled her eyes. "I don't know how you put up with that woman."

"Be quiet."

"Lance, I'll have to take these samples back," Debbie announced as she came into the room. She stopped short at the sight of Xonia standing beside him. Her pretty face settled into a familiar frown. "I don't know what they're drinking these days at the carpet place, but every one of these samples are the same exact color!"

"Let me guess. Teal green?"

She looked so surprised that Lance couldn't resist laughing.

"Exactly! But how did you—" She broke off, glancing slowly around the room. Her eyes grew larger with each second. "Where—how—*who* did this? I was just in this room yesterday, and it didn't look *anything* like this!"

"Do you like it?" Lance asked, holding his breath—for Xonia's sake.

"I couldn't have done it better myself!" she exclaimed, walking into the room to get a closer look. "And the paintings, they're darling!"

"Debbie, meet your new partner."

Xonia tugged at his sleeve, shaking her head wildly and mouthing the word *"No!"*

Lance ignored her. "Bridget did this room, and since you like it, I'm sure you won't mind her helping you. She's planning to major in, uh, interior design."

Debbie looked at Xonia as if seeing her for the first time. "Really? Well, you've certainly got talent!"

From the corner of his mouth, Lance whispered to Xonia, "Now *that's* how you make friends."

Twenty-three

~~

Thursday at Romance Connection was a nightmarish repeat of Monday, Tuesday, and Wednesday. Holly stayed long after closing time, poring over the account books and praying for a miracle.

She hadn't gotten very far before she began to steam all over again.

In just one week, that nasty warlock Jestark had darn near put her in the red! Client after client had called to complain and cancel their subscription to Romance Connection, and almost no one had called to take their place.

While Holly, Mini, Reuben, and Xonia knew what Jestark was doing to infuriate her established clients—they found out loud and clear from the clients themselves—they had no idea what he was doing to discourage new ones.

But it was obvious he was doing *something*!

Holly nearly snapped her pencil in two. Maybe *she'd* get a shot at him tomorrow night. Oh, she'd love that, really, truly *love* it. "Miserable, havoc-rending warlock," she muttered.

To top off her week, she'd gotten one measly phone call from Lance on Tuesday, and nothing since. In that one brief call he'd explained that he had an unusually large workload and a few things to do around the house, and that she shouldn't think he had deserted her if she didn't hear from him.

"Probably too busy kissing his wife's picture," Holly muttered out loud. She regretted her snide comment the moment she said it. With a tired sigh, she closed her gritty eyes and rubbed them lightly with her fingers.

She needed a break, plain and simple.

And she needed to see Lance. She *missed* him. Several times she thought about making some excuse to go to his house, but then she remembered the image of him sitting on the side of the bed kissing Mona's picture.

She could never go in that room and frankly didn't much care to be in the house again. It was entirely—well, almost entirely—different when Lance came to her apartment. There she could relax without wondering if everything he saw reminded him of his late wife.

In her apartment she could love him without restraint and almost convince herself that she had his undivided attention.

Almost.

It was that "almost" that got to her every time.

She'd once confessed to Mini that when she loved a man, she wanted it all. She hadn't been lying, and she wasn't about to change now, no matter how tempting it was to take what she could with Lance and pretend the rest didn't matter.

Holly still had her eyes closed when she felt something soft press against the back of her head. Her chair flew suddenly backward, and something heavy and hard landed on top of her.

She opened her eyes, then brought up her arms to ward off her attacker and found herself staring into Lance's equally startled face. Someone had turned out the office lights, she thought, baffled, but there was light coming from *somewhere*.

He was lying on top of her . . . naked and wet. Heavy. Wonderfully heavy.

She turned her head to the side and found a pillow mashed against her nose.

"Holly?"

"Lance?"

"Xonia," they both said in resigned unison.

Breathless with the realization that she, too, was naked, Holly tried to laugh. "I'm going to kill her for this! I was in my office working, and the next thing I knew I was falling backward in my chair."

"I was taking a shower and had soap in my eyes. I slipped and tried to catch my balance. The next thing *I* knew I was landing on something soft. . . ." Lance's explanation trailed off, and he chuckled.

The movement sent shock waves coursing through Holly. There was something firm and quivering pressed between her legs. She licked her lips, not daring to move. "She didn't—she didn't—"

"No," Lance said, his voice dropping to a husky, amused whisper. "That, I'm afraid, got there all on its own."

"Thank God!"

He laughed again, and Holly had to bite her lip to keep from moaning her need as the movement brought him even closer. "You don't suppose she's watching, do you?"

"She'd better not be anywhere *close* to where I can reach her."

Holly stiffened at his threatening tone. He didn't sound too happy about his situation. "If you'll just get off me, I can borrow something to wear." Lance seemed to read her mind.

"You misunderstood, baby."

The tender, loving way he said "baby" sucked the moisture from her mouth.

"I'm just put out because *I* wanted to pick the time and place to show you the surprise. Believe me, I'm perfectly happy to be in this position . . . in *any* position, as long as it's with you."

"A surprise? What surprise?" As if she wasn't surprised

right now! She wiggled a little, experimentally. Yes, she *was* completely, absolutely naked. And Lance was fully aroused.

He wasn't alone. Her nipples felt as if they would break off at the slightest movement.

"Be still, or we'll have to finish this conversation another time," he growled.

Holly obeyed, but not as quickly as she should have. Her lips parted, and a moan escaped. She heard Lance curse softly beneath his breath.

"To hell with it. I'll tell you later." He twisted his head to the side and said, "Thanks, Xonia—now get lost!"

The faint sound of Xonia's cackling laughter echoed in the room before fading away completely.

It was much, much later before Holly discovered the surprise—and subsequently found out why Lance had been too busy to see her since last Wednesday night.

Feeling thoroughly relaxed for the first time in a week, Holly allowed Lance to dress her in one of his shirts. She smiled when he took a ridiculous amount of time with the top three buttons.

Finally he finished and slipped into a pair of silk boxers before he turned on the bedside lamp.

Holly blinked and glanced around, realizing at once that this wasn't the bedroom she'd viewed in the crystal ball. This wasn't *Lance's* bedroom.

"What do you think?"

"It's—it's . . ." Holly paused, her gaze widening in shock when she saw the paintings. They were the very ones she'd once seen in a flea market. She'd gone with her dad on a business trip during spring break from school, but hadn't had the money to buy them.

Now they were here. The very same ones.

"Xonia?" she guessed.

Lance nodded. "She said you wanted them. She also said teal green was your favorite color."

"It is." She swallowed a curious lump in her throat,

uncertain what all of this meant. Was he hinting that he wanted her to stay over more? Did he sense that she would never be able to sleep with him in *his* room? "It's all beautiful. Everything."

"There's more. Lots more," Lance said, catching her by the hand. "Come on, let me give you a tour." He led her from the room as he talked. "In a way I'm glad you're here tonight. You can get a better picture of how the house looks before we put up the Halloween decorations."

By the time they finished the tour of the main rooms, Holly was overwhelmed by the changes he'd made. The house was nearly unrecognizable. It looked homey yet chic. "You did all of this yourself?"

"No. Debbie, Casey, and Xonia helped."

"It must have cost you a fortune!" Holly had a sudden, horrible thought. "Lance, tell me you didn't do all of this for me." If he did, the guilt would simply crush her!

"Yes, I did." He sounded completely, one hundred percent sincere. "I hope you like it. If not, we can do something different. I've still got money left from selling Dad's Mercedes and Mona's paintings."

Holly almost wished he'd lied to her. *There's that word again,* she thought. "Almost." Everything with Lance was "almost." "You sold your dad's car?"

"And *Mona's* paintings."

She didn't miss his emphasis on Mona, but she wasn't quite sure of the meaning. Was he trying to make her feel guilty? Because if he was he was doing a damned good job.

"You shouldn't have . . . sold her paintings." Or his dad's car, for that matter.

"Why not?" he asked softly, watching her with those bedroom eyes that muddled her brain. "They were her paintings, things *she* liked, and she's gone now. I don't need the reminder, and neither do you. As for Dad's car, I never liked it, because he spent more time in that car than he did with me. I guess I just hung on to it because I thought I should."

Holly had run out of words. What could she say? He wouldn't understand why she felt guilty, and if she tried to explain, she'd just wind up sounding ungrateful. She didn't exactly understand it herself.

He'd sold his father's car and his late wife's cherished paintings. He had used the proceeds to redecorate a twenty-room mansion. The amount of money it must have taken boggled her mind.

And he claimed he'd done it for her.

What was *wrong* with her? Why would he lie? Why did she think he would lie about his reasons for changing the house?

Suddenly she had her answer, with the return of that hateful image she'd wished she'd never seen. It was the image of Lance kissing his wife's photograph, the one that kept conjuring up that word: "almost."

He was "almost" over her.

She didn't—couldn't—let herself believe that he was completely over her. Changing the house could have been for his own benefit as much as it might have been for hers. She didn't have trouble believing that he was *trying* to forget about Mona, or even that he desperately wanted to.

But he hadn't, not yet. No quite.

Something winked in the light, something shiny and gold.

Holly's gaze dropped to his hand. Her heart expanded in shock, then shriveled and died.

Because if he really had gotten over Mona, he wouldn't be wearing his wedding ring.

Xonia leaped upon the crystal ball, hissing and spitting, clawing at the glass in a frenzy of rage. Mini plucked her off and held her away until her anger was spent. When she'd exhausted herself, Mini gently set her on the carpet.

"Holly's dealt with the results of Jestark's pranks all week long. She's too smart to fall for this."

The familiar lay on the floor, panting from her fit.

"She's not thinking with her head right now. She's thinking with her heart!"

Reuben came into the living room, his hair damp from his shower. They were taking all of the necessary precautions to keep their powers a secret. "What's all the noise about?"

Her expression grave, Mini explained. "Holly just saw a wedding ring on Lance's finger."

"They're together? Right now?"

"Yes. Xonia transported Holly from her office into his bed—his *new* bed." She had advised Xonia against it, but as usual, Xonia hadn't listened.

Her handsome husband glowered at Xonia. "If you had minded your own business, witch, this wouldn't have happened! You knew Jestark might be lurking, waiting for a chance to muddle things for Holly and Lance. Keeping them apart until Allhallows Eve was the only way to keep it from happening."

His criticism was enough to get Xonia on her feet again. She bristled, hair standing on end. "Well, maybe if you didn't spend so much of your free time prancing around half-naked in front of a bunch of sex-starved women—"

Mini stared at her friend in shock. Xonia stared back at her, just as shocked.

"I mean, well, what I mean is—"

"Be quiet!" Reuben roared. He pointed his quivering finger at the kitchen window. "Get out!"

Xonia cowered in the face of his anger, something Mini thought she'd never witness. "Reuben, I really didn't mean to blurt it out that way—"

"Out!"

The familiar didn't bother with the window; she disappeared in a puff of red smoke, leaving behind the acrid scent of burning cat hair.

Reuben stood, breathing hard. He avoided Mini's gaze until she said softly, "I think we need to talk."

"Yes, we do." He let out a frustrated sigh. "I didn't

want you to find out until Allhallows Eve, but after that damned cat let the surprise out of the bag—" He smiled faintly at the mangled cliché. "I'll be right back. Don't move a muscle."

She watched him leave, her heart in her throat, thinking how very much like a mortal he had become in his actions and his words.

He was gone only a few seconds, but it was long enough for Mini to imagine all sorts of horrors. A picture of his mortal girlfriend? A love letter in lieu of an explanation? Maybe—her heart skipped an unsteady beat—it was a mortal divorce paper, ready for her to sign. His mortal girlfriend had probably insisted on it.

He walked up to her and took her hand, pressing a long, flat box onto her palm. Gazing intently into her terror-struck eyes, he said, "Happy anniversary, wife of mine."

They were the same words he'd said each anniversary for the past two hundred and twenty-five years.

With shaking hands, Mini opened the box.

It was a beautiful string of pearls, translucent pink and very elegant.

"That's the real thing, Mini. Not conjured . . . not stolen, but bought with money that *I* earned the mortal way." He sounded proud, so very proud. "That's where I've been going, you see. I've got a second job."

Reuben wasn't seeing another woman; he had another job and he'd gotten the job so that he could buy her pearls for their two hundred and twenty-fifth wedding anniversary.

Mini buried her face against the pearls and burst into tears.

The ring would not come off.

Lance found a bottle of vegetable oil in the cabinet, but after grunting and straining and making a mess, he still couldn't get the damned thing off.

He'd tried soap next, then Vaseline, and finally even motor oil from a can in the trunk of his car. Peanut butter,

butter, margarine, a slimy egg white—these were only a few of the items that he had used and discarded, and that now littered his kitchen countertop.

The ring would not budge from his finger.

With a vicious curse, he flung the open can of motor oil across the garage. It landed with a thunk, the oil gurgling onto the concrete floor.

Unlike Holly, Lance knew how the ring came to be on his finger, had known almost instantly.

Jestark, that mysterious, so-far-invisible warlock.

He knew because he knew that Xonia would never be so cruel, and he knew because he had thrown the ring off the Abernathy Bridge the same day he'd said his final good-byes to Mona.

Lance hoped like hell that Jestark the Jerk showed himself Halloween night, because right at this moment he would risk his life for the opportunity to deck the nasty warlock just one time.

Closing his eyes, he rested against the cool hood of his car, brutally recalling Holly's desolate expression when she'd noticed the ring.

Too bad *he* hadn't noticed before *she* had—he might have chopped off his finger to keep her from seeing it!

"I hope you're happy, you son of a bitch," Lance suddenly shouted into the empty garage.

His words echoed back to him, filled with rage and totally useless.

Twenty-four

~

Lance shocked Casey to his toes by canceling his appointments on Tuesday. He didn't try to explain: Casey would never understand once he mentioned the word "warlock" in connection with the ring that wouldn't come off his finger.

Besides, this was personal.

Rolling up his sleeves, he plunged in with a vengeance to help finish the Halloween decorations for the party, keeping to himself and answering questions in monosyllables as he volunteered to hang the black and orange streamers.

Midway through the day, when Debbie and Xonia nearly came to blows, he tersely ordered the contrary witch to take charge of the spooky elements and leave Debbie to her decorating.

The meaning behind Xonia's gleeful laughter became clearer to Lance an hour later when the sound of Debbie's bloodcurdling scream nearly unbalanced him on the ladder he'd just climbed.

With a string of curses that might have shocked a sailor, he climbed down, following the sound upstairs to the linen closet.

He found Debbie inside the small closet, looking as if

she'd just witnessed a bloody murder. She pointed a shaking finger at an innocent-looking stack of sheets on the shelf. "I know it's Halloween, Lance, but that—that looks *real*!"

Sighing, Lance lifted the stack of sheets and stared at the bloody hand. There was a gold wedding band on one purple, bloody finger.

Xonia had a very twisted sense of humor, he decided, very conscious of the ring on *his* finger.

"It isn't real. Just a fake hand with fake blood." And a fake wedding ring to remind him that he had only a few hours left before the party. If he didn't get the ring off, he might be tempted to add another hand to the Closet of Frights.

Debbie took a deep breath and averted her gaze. "I know, but it freakin' startled me, you know?" Finally her lips twitched in the beginnings of a smile. "I guess that's what it was supposed to do, huh?"

Lance nodded. "If I were you, I would expect a lot more of the same, if I know Xon— I mean, Bridget."

"Right. Well, if you'll just hand me that stack of sheets, I'll get back to work."

When Lance did as she asked, Debbie grabbed the sheets and hurried from the closet as if the hounds of hell were chasing her.

He couldn't resist a grin, which quickly turned into a scowl as Xonia materialized beside him. She looked very pleased with herself.

"Tell me that hand isn't real," he said, trying to look stern.

She tossed her mane of frizzy hair. "Oh, it's real enough. I borrowed it from the morgue. But there wasn't much blood to go with it, so I borrowed *that* from the hospital."

Lance's stomach lurched in reaction. "Send it back and replace it with a *fake* hand and fake blood. Understand?"

Xonia huffed, "You mortals are so finicky."

"Yes, we are," Lance agreed. "And from now on, props

only. Nothing real. Debbie and Casey—and the rest of the guests, with the exception of Holly—are expecting *fake* frights. We want them *laughing* and screaming, not screaming and running for their lives."

"How do you think they're going to react when Jestark shows?"

"Hopefully by then they'll think he's just another prop."

"Do you really think all he'll do is show himself?" Xonia clucked her tongue. "You and Holly are perfectly matched—you're both absurdly naive."

"Better, in my opinion, than being a jaded, cynical, impossible-to-please witch."

"Ouch. The doctor wields his scalpel!"

"Get back to work," he growled. Before she could move, he placed a stalling hand on her shoulder, jerking his head at the bloody hand. "*After* you fix this."

"Oh, all right! By the way, if you don't get that ring off before Holly gets here, I've got an idea for a great disguise that will cover it."

Lance was touched by her offer. "Thanks, I might take you up on that."

The day couldn't end soon enough for Holly and Mini.

She and Mini started watching the office clock at 4:30. Time seemed to drag by as the tension mounted. Reuben had left an hour ago to prepare himself for the confrontation ahead.

The phone rang for the first time all day, making them jump. They stared at it. Finally Holly picked up the receiver.

It was Debbie asking if Holly wouldn't mind picking up a Ouija board at the toy store before it closed. If things got stale at the party, Debbie explained, they could liven it with a scary séance.

Holly told her it wouldn't be a problem, but after hanging up the phone, her eyes met Mini's and they shared a moment of unmistakable premonition.

She shivered, thinking of the horrors that could be lying in wait. "I hope nobody gets hurt," she said, straightening her desk because she needed something to do. "I'd feel responsible, since I talked Lance into having this party."

"He's aware of the risks, Holly. But I trust Reuben, and Reuben doesn't think Jestark will hurt anyone."

"Scaring someone to death is not exactly *helpful*."

"If I know Xonia, she will have a few surprises in store for the guests. By the time Jestark arrives, they'll be used to it."

"Unless he comes early."

"Midnight will be more his style."

"The witching hour?" She'd read the phrase somewhere, she thought, or heard it on some TV show.

Mini nodded. "Holly, I can see that you're frightened, and that's exactly what feeds Jestark's powers."

"As if I have a choice! Believe me, if I did I'd rather be more like Helen of Troy."

"He's already got you on the run. Are you going to let him win?" Mini challenged.

Holly froze. "What do you mean?"

"The ring on Lance's hand. Do you really believe that was Lance's doing?"

"Lance didn't know I was coming." Holly lifted a defensive chin at the faint censure in Mini's bright green gaze. "You don't know for sure it was Jestark who put it there, do you?"

"It sounds like a stunt Jestark would pull. As you mortals put it, I'm about ninety-nine percent certain."

"Like you were so certain Reuben was fooling around?" Holly regretted her words the moment Mini's eyes clouded with pain. "I'm sorry, Mini. I didn't mean that."

"How did you know? I never told Xonia about my suspicions."

Holly rubbed her hands over her suddenly chilled arms. "Because you had that same hopeless look in your eyes that my mother had the day she found out about my father's mistress." She shrugged to show she wasn't looking for pity. "A teenager doesn't forget that sort of thing."

"I'm sorry."

Mini's sincere, quietly spoken words pricked tears in Holly's eyes. She stubbornly blinked them away. "That was a long time ago."

"But you haven't gotten over it," Mini guessed shrewdly. "Instead of dwelling on what happened to your parents, perhaps you should take another look at what you've done here." She gestured to the corkboard above Holly's desk, filled with happy news from couples connected by Romance Connection. "One bad relationship doesn't spoil the whole turnip patch."

Holly found herself smiling. "I think that's 'One bad apple doesn't spoil the whole bushel.' "

"Whatever." Mini smiled back. She glanced at the clock. "We should go. The party starts at eight. You *do* have a costume, don't you?"

"I was thinking about going as a witch."

Mini laughed. "If you need some advice, let me know!"

"I will."

At eight o'clock sharp, Holly parked her car and stepped onto the graveled drive.

The party had apparently started earlier than planned; laughter, punctuated by screams of mock fright—and a few that sounded genuine—drifted through the open front door.

Despite her trepidation over seeing Lance again and her anxiety about what the night might bring with Jestark lurking, Holly smiled at the sounds of revelry as she locked her car and adjusted her costume.

Gravel crunched behind her.

With a gasp she whirled around, then caught her breath again at the sight of the handsome warlock sauntering toward her. He wore a black cape much like the one Reuben had worn for his show, but there the resemblance ended.

It was Lance, looking breathtakingly handsome and

heart-poundingly dangerous. Beneath his cape he wore a black tuxedo with a snowy white shirt. His black satin top hat sat at a jaunty angle, hiding most of his russet hair. In his hand he gripped a beautiful ivory cane.

He reached her, tipping his hat and smiling that slow, sexy smile that made her heart leap into overdrive.

"You look beautiful," he said, his voice low and throbbing.

Holly swallowed hard. "Beautiful" wouldn't have begun to describe how *he* looked to her, but all she said was, "Thank you."

Desperate to break the magical spell that seemed to envelop them and turn her brains to mush, Holly glanced at his hand.

She was relieved to find that he was wearing black gloves, but the fact didn't erase the painful memory of Thursday night, or stop her from wondering if he was still wearing the ring.

"I've been waiting out here for you."

"Really?" Her question, meant to be flippant, came out sounding like a breathless endearment. Damn. She tried again, determined to show him that she wasn't so easily taken in by his charm—however considerable. "It wasn't necessary. I trust Reuben, and he doesn't think Jestark means to harm anyone."

His expression immediately darkened, adding credibility to his costume. "I beg to differ. He's done a lot of harm to me—and to you."

A lump rose in her throat. "You're talking about the ring?" Was she ready to hear his explanation? Ready for him to deny any involvement?

"I'm talking about the ring." He took two long strides to reach her, pressing her against the driver's door with the hard length of his body. His hands closed over her shoulders as if he feared she'd try to run.

As if she could—or would.

"Holly, I threw that ring off the Abernathy Bridge, so it couldn't be the same one that I'm wearing now." When she stiffened at the reminder, he stifled a curse. "You would never believe the hell I went through last night trying to get this damned thing off my finger."

He was right—she wouldn't. But she *almost* did. "Almost." God, she hated that word!

"I don't know what else to do to convince you that I'm ready to go on with my life. The same day I pitched the ring, I said my final good-byes to Mona. I put her picture away—for good."

"Can—can we talk about this later? I think right now we should concentrate on getting through this night with minimal damage." She wondered if he caught her double-edged meaning, and if he had an inkling of the violent struggle going on inside her. *"I put her picture away—for good."* Was that the private scene she'd witnessed in the crystal ball that day, of Lance saying good-bye to Mona?

"Maybe you're right." He gazed into her wide eyes, his own dark with need and heavy with frustration. "But after this is over, you and I are going to have a serious talk."

Together they entered the house. People milled about, talking, laughing, and drinking. Couples strolled upstairs, looking for new frights.

Xonia, who had bravely decided to come as herself, spotted them and came over, dragging a shaggy-haired man along behind her. When the witch smiled, she looked almost pretty.

"Well, if it isn't the witch and warlock wanna-bes," she drawled. "Meet my date, Chaos. He's a little on the shy side."

He was more than just shy, Holly thought, eyebrows lifting as the brawny man began to scratch earnestly at his head. He appeared to be having not only a bad hair day, but a flea problem as well. His eyes, however, were a gorgeous sky blue, like big round marbles, and his hair was a beautiful minx color.

Holly bit back a smile as Xonia yanked his hand away from his head.

"Come on, let's go see if we can find something to eat. Maybe that will take your mind off those fleas."

The mention of food got astounding results. Pressing his shaggy head on Xonia's shoulder, he began to purr and rub against her. Xonia dislodged his head and leaned close to Holly to whisper, "He may not be much of a conversationalist, but he's dynamite in bed!"

Holly laughed and glanced around the room. "Where's Mini and Reuben?"

"Not here yet," Xonia said. "I'm expecting them any moment." Again she fought her clinging date to lean close to whisper, "Reuben's working on a new spell, one that will temporarily suspend Jestark's powers."

"Will it work?"

Xonia shrugged. "Reuben's got the power of love on his side." She flicked a meaningful glance in Lance's direction. "And we all know how powerful *that* can be." An impatient growl snagged her attention. "All right already. I get the hint!"

Cackling, she moved away, her date eagerly trailing behind her.

"Something tells me that man isn't quite human," Lance remarked dryly.

"I think you're right. By the way, you did a great job decorating for the party. The house looks downright spooky."

"You can thank Debbie and Xonia."

"Speaking of Debbie, where is she? Or should I say, *who* is she?"

Lance looked around the foyer, which opened into the big family room where most of the guests were gathered. "She's dressed as Juliet. The last time I saw her, she and her Romeo—which would be Casey—were heading upstairs. I wouldn't be surprised if we didn't see them for a while."

He linked her arm with his, and together they strolled into the main room and began to circulate among the crowd. *Like a couple,* Holly thought, feeling warm and content.

"You know a lot of people," she commented, searching for a familiar face behind clever costumes ranging from goblins to presidents. One particular couple caught her eye and made her smile. The man wore a Bill Clinton mask, and the woman looked remarkably like Monica Lewinsky.

"Mostly Casey's friends from the hospital and Debbie's friends from the law firm," Lance explained. "We thought the more the merrier."

"Safety in numbers?"

"Something like that."

"Are you nervous?"

His hand tightened on her arm.

"I'll admit I was at first. Now I'm just furious."

"Oh." She jumped as she heard a scream, and didn't relax until it was followed by delighted laughter. Xonia strikes again, Holly thought with a faint smile.

They'd reached the buffet table. Holly poured two cups of blood-red punch and handed one to Lance. "Lance, I hope you don't do anything impulsive. Jestark isn't an ordinary man."

His warm gaze settled on her face. "Are you worried about me, Holly?" he asked softly.

What purpose would it serve to lie? "Of course I am."

The lights went out, plunging them into darkness. Hungry lips found hers in a brief, possessive kiss that left her aching for more.

When the lights came back on, Holly blinked into Lance's smug face. "You planned that," she accused without heat. Oh, there was heat all right, but it had nothing to do with anger.

He didn't bother looking repentant. "Desperate times call for desperate measures."

"With a little help from a meddling witch, I suppose."

He shrugged. "She likes to feel needed."

Holly arched a playful brow that nearly disappeared

beneath her pointed hat. Nasty warlocks and wedding rings faded away for the moment. This was here and now, and she was enjoying a spontaneous flirtation with the man she loved.

"Are we talking about the same witch—Xonia?"

"She's not as 'together' as she'd like people to think."

"I'll bet this is the first time you've analyzed a witch," Holly teased.

She turned as someone tugged at the sleeve of her black dress. Holly took one glance at the emerald eyes above the harem girl's veil and said quickly, "Mini! Great costume."

Mini's eyes crinkled as she smiled. "And your costume is, um—"

"Let me guess. It's horrible?" Holly chuckled. "It was the only one left in the store—in the adult section. I think it was called the Working Witch, or something just as raunchy."

"You should have called me."

"I figured you had enough to worry about," Holly said, sobering. "Where's Reuben?"

Mini's smile faded. "He's scouting the guests. He insists that Jestark is already here, that he can sense him."

Holly gave a start, nearly spilling her punch. "He's here?" she squeaked.

With a somber nod, Mini turned to Lance. "Reuben sent me to warn you. He says he might need your help."

Fear grounded Holly to the floor more effectively than gravity. "No!" she burst out, surprising Lance and Mini.

They stared at her in shock.

Lowering her voice, Holly said, "I don't want you to go near that warlock. Please."

Their eyes locked, and something deep and true passed between them. Holly didn't fight it this time. She was frightened for him. Terrified, in fact.

"Why?"

"Because—because—" She stopped abruptly, closing her eyes and praying for the courage to say the words that might keep him from doing something foolish.

"Holly? You were saying?"

"I love you, Lance," she blurted out.

The transformation that came over his face melted her insides—and banished the word "almost" from her vocabulary once and for all.

Tenderly he reached for her face, but his fingers had barely grazed her chin before the angry yowling of a cat froze his actions.

It wasn't an ordinary yowl from an ordinary cat, because Holly knew ordinary cats lacked the power to make the walls shake.

"Xonia!" Mini whispered fearfully.

Holly shook her head, tearing her eyes from Lance. "No, it can't be. Xonia's here as herself. She brought a date—" Her words crashed to a halt. "Her date! He was scratching and rubbing against her like a cat."

But Mini was no longer listening. Her veils flew out behind her as she rushed from the room. Lance quickly set their punch cups on the table and grabbed her hand. They hurriedly followed, pushing people aside with hastily mumbled apologies.

The scene they came upon was something Holly knew she'd never forget.

Reuben was holding Xonia's date, Chaos, by the nape of his scruffy neck as if he were indeed a cat instead of a full-grown man. Dangling in the air, Chaos yowled and hissed, trying to reach his captor with long, wickedly sharp claws.

"Put me down, you weakling witch!" Jestark demanded, kicking his useless feet.

"Not until you agree to behave yourself, you trouble-making warlock!"

Xonia stood watching them, her golden eyes rounded in shock. Her cheeks had turned an alarming shade of red.

Holly felt a pang of sympathy for her newfound friend, who looked humiliated beyond redemption. It was obvious she hadn't known she'd been sleeping with the enemy.

Chaos was . . . Jestark. Who would have thought?

The guests began to gather around to watch this new trick, laughing and clapping, fully believing it was just another entertainment for their benefit.

Out of all the mortals in the room, only Holly and Lance knew the truth.

Holly took her watchful gaze from Xonia for only a second—but it was long enough for Xonia to make the transformation from witch to cat.

Before anyone could anticipate her actions, she leaped onto the helpless warlock with a vengeance, scratching and clawing, spitting and hissing as she worked her way along his dangling body to his face.

"Stop her!" Jestark cried, his marbled blue eyes rolling in genuine fear. "Warlock's honor, I'll behave!"

Reuben plucked Xonia from his body and set her aside. She immediately gathered herself to leap on Jestark again, but one quelling look from Reuben halted her plan.

"You'd better do some damage," Xonia growled, slapping at the air with her paw like a boxer warming up, "or *I* will!"

Lance shoved his cape aside as if he truly *were* a warlock; at that moment, Holly could almost believe he was.

He stepped forward. "I second that motion. If you don't, I will. Jestark and I have a score to settle."

Mini was next. She drew even with Lance, raking her veils aside to reveal her angry, determined face. "Count me in, too."

Holly didn't know where her courage came from, and she didn't care to question it. She reached Lance in two strides. "I'm the one who should get first shot. It's *my* business he's trying to ruin."

Catching on to the game—and totally oblivious—the crowd began to chant: *She's the one, she's the one.*

Ironically it was Xonia who saved Jestark's hide.

With a flick of her tail, she became her true self again.

She grabbed a fistful of wild, tangled hair and jerked his head back so that they were eye to eye. "I'll give you one chance, and one chance only. Do you accept this spell I'm about to cast?"

"Get lost, you ugly excuse for a witch!"

Surprisingly, Xonia smiled at the insult. Trailing her free hand along his chest and down his taut abdomen, she cupped him in her hand. Slowly her fingers began to tighten. "It will be a shame, but—"

Jestark spoke quickly, fearfully. "I do."

As Xonia began to chant, Mini began to laugh. When Reuben joined her, Holly's curiosity got the upper hand. "What is she doing?" she demanded.

"She's casting the Spell of Forgetfulness," Mini answered between gasps of laughter.

"You mean . . . he won't remember *anything*?"

"As mad as Xonia is, I'll be surprised if he remembers his name!"

The crowd watched, enthralled, as Xonia completed her spell. When she finished, Reuben let Jestark go.

The dazed warlock dropped to the floor in a heap.

Silence fell over the crowd as they waited for the outcome.

Finally Jestark stumbled to his feet. He shook his shaggy head and focused on Xonia. His blue, blue eyes narrowed with purpose, but the growling noise that emerged from his throat was far from human.

Grinning smugly, Xonia curled her fingers and said, "Here, kitty, kitty."

The crowd roared with laughter.

Distracted by the scene, Holly gave a startled yelp as arms circled her waist from behind. *Lance,* she realized instantly. He clasped his hands together over her stomach and walked her backward until they were out of the crowd.

She went willingly.

"Did you mean what you said earlier?" he whispered

in her ear as he leaned against the wall and pulled her tightly to his body.

"About getting the first shot?" she teased, covering his gloved hands with her own. "Of course—" The breath left her lungs in a rush as he spun her around to face him. "Yes, I love you. I have for a while now, but I was too frightened to admit it."

"And now you're not?"

Holly tilted her head, getting lost in his mesmerizing eyes. "Should I be?" she whispered.

"Not a bit. Will you marry me?"

She sagged weakly against him, glad, so very glad he was holding her tight. "Aren't you skipping a step?"

He nibbled on her bottom lip, then moved to the corner of her mouth to tease and nip. His breath caressed her lips as he murmured tenderly, "I love you, now and forever. You are number one in my life. If you'll have me, I promise to love and cherish—"

Using her hands to hold his face still, she ended his torturous game by capturing his mouth. Dimly she heard shouts of encouragement from the crowd and a few raunchy whistles.

The sounds grew fainter as Lance took control and deepened the kiss. When the cheering stopped completely, Holly opened one eye.

They were in Lance's room.

Their lips parted long enough to whisper simultaneously, "Xonia."

"She does have her good points," Lance mumbled against her mouth. "Occasionally."

Holly caught her breath as he began to work her dress upward very, very slowly. "Yes!" she moaned. "I mean, yes, she does. Don't you think we should get back to our guests?"

Lance chuckled at her reluctant tone. "I think they've been sufficiently entertained tonight." His hands left her long enough to remove his gloves. He pitched them over his shoulder.

His fingers were bare; the ring was gone.

While his hands began to work the garters holding her black stockings in place, Holly said a little raggedly, "Thank God Reuben's spell worked."

"Hmm."

"Mona was a lucky woman." She gasped as he grabbed her and lifted her high. She braced her hands on his shoulders and gazed down into his loving face.

"*I'm* a lucky man and I'm going to make *you* a happy woman."

Epilogue

It was Xonia's idea to hold Holly's bachelorette party at Get It On.

Secretly Holly would have preferred a private party with just the four of them, listening to oldies, drinking wine, and eating chocolates until they got sick. Or, to be totally truthful, she would have preferred to skip the party and spend the evening with Lance.

But she didn't have the heart to disappoint Xonia; she knew the mischievous witch had planned a little surprise for Mini.

At Xonia's insistence, they arrived early, grabbing one of the coveted tables near the stage. Mini and Debbie watched with growing curiosity as the mob of elderly women began to fill the tables around them. Waitresses moved agilely between the cramped aisles, carrying trays of drinks and taking orders, shouting into hearing aids and sidestepping the canes and walkers littering the aisles.

"Now I understand why you insisted on disguising us," Debbie said, patting the gray bun. "You did a fantastic job, too. Have you ever considered working as a makeup artist?"

When Xonia blushed at her praise, Holly smiled. The witch had confessed to Holly that she had actually *enjoyed* making Debbie over the mortal way, but had immediately insisted Holly swear on her mortal life that she wouldn't share her confession with Mini.

As the guest of honor, Holly was seated to Xonia's left and facing the stage. She adjusted her sagging bosom and winked at Xonia. "I have to confess—in my wildest dreams, I never thought I'd be celebrating my bachelorette party with three little old ladies."

"Sixty isn't old," Mini said, eyeing Xonia's wicked smile with suspicion. "Why, when I was sixty—"

"You mean when you *get* to be sixty," Xonia interrupted with a meaningful glance at Debbie.

But Debbie wasn't listening. She was staring at the drink in front of her. "I'm sure I didn't order this."

"Ha!"

Xonia glowered at Mini's smug smile. "I never said I was perfect." To Debbie, she snapped, "Don't look a gift horse in the mouth. Just drink the damned thing."

They all jumped as a voice suddenly boomed from the speakers placed strategically around the room.

"Ladies, tonight we have a very special program."

The cheers and applause shook the rafters. Amazingly, the voice from the speakers managed to rise above the din.

"Please check your pacemakers, and for your own safety we ask that you remain in your seats tonight. Enjoy the show!"

More clapping and shouting. Xonia cackled with glee, rubbing her hands together eagerly. Mini, who looked regal and haughty with her short cap of gray hair and faded green eyes, remained suspicious.

Holly watched Mini watching Xonia, hoping Xonia's little surprise didn't backfire. Mini knew the nature of Reuben's second job, but she'd never seen him in action.

The music began, a heavy, pulse-pounding rhythm that reminded Holly of jungle drums and dancing natives. The chatter of a hundred women died abruptly. A hushed expectancy filled the air, and all eyes watched the stage.

Holly tensed, her gaze darting from Mini to the stage, then back again.

Smoke began to spiral from the center of the stage, filling the area with a colorful cloud of blue, green, and red. A collective murmur of surprise and delight swept through the crowd.

Finally the smoke began to dissipate, revealing a man standing on the stage, head bowed, arms folded over his broad chest, legs braced wide apart.

He wore a black patch over one eye, tight black pants tucked into hightop boots, and a white full-sleeved shirt open to the waist, but it was the sight of the wicked-looking saber strapped to his side that caused more than a few gasps of alarm.

Holly's heart began to thunder as the handsome pirate slowly lifted his head and stared directly at her.

It was Lance—*not* Reuben, as she had expected.

She sucked in a lungful of stale air. Surely he wasn't going to . . . ?

He was.

The beat rocked on, and Lance rocked with it, undulating his hips in a sexy, seductive way that made Holly's palms sweat and her thighs quiver shamelessly. All the while, his hot, I'm-doing-this-just-for-you gaze never left her face as he danced his leisurely way to their table.

His timing was perfect. The music ended the moment he reached her. Holly's bubbling laughter turned into a startled gasp as he lifted her into his arms. She wound her arms around his neck and pressed her hot face into his chest.

The crowd went wild.

Above the noise, and above the deep, steady throb of Lance's heartbeat, Holly heard the sound of Xonia's cackling laughter.

She smiled.

TIME PASSAGES

SEDUCTION ROMANCE

*Prepare to be seduced...by the sexy
new romance series from Jove!*

**Brand-new, full-length, one-night-stand-alone
novels featuring the most seductive heroes in the
history of love....**

FRIENDS ROMANCE

Can a man come between friends?

□ **A TASTE OF HONEY**
by DeWanna Pace   0-515-12387-0

□ **WHERE THE HEART IS**
by Sheridon Smythe   0-515-12412-5

□ **LONG WAY HOME**
by Wendy Corsi Staub   0-515-12440-0

All books $5.99